"...an enthralling near-future scenario where body-styling has become an art form and where computer hacking has progressed in a chillingly believable direction.

What I love about David's fiction is that his characters are firmly grounded in a social context. In *Terminal Mind* the family and interpersonal conflicts are just as intriguing as the threat to society, with outcomes that are just as uncertain."

~Nancy Fulda, assistant editor of *Baen's Universe*

"If you like distinctive character voices, cool science fiction gizmos, and a dozen plot threads that weave together into a dazzling whole, you need to read *Terminal Mind*."

~Mike Shultz, frequent contributor to *F&SF*

"...a gritty, fast-paced, page-turning read"

~Ian Creasey, frequent contributor to *Asimov's*

# TERMINAL MIND

# TERMINAL MIND

## David Walton

ಸಂ

Meadowhawk Press | Memphis

TERMINAL MIND

Copyright © 2008 by David Walton

Cover Art Copyright © 2008 Tomislav Tikulin
Title and Glyph Fonts Copyright © 2008 Nate Piekos

Published by Meadowhawk Press
9160 Hwy 64 Suite 12 #163
Lakeland, TN 38002

ISBN    978-0-9787326-3-9
Library of Congress Control Number    2008923077

http://www.meadowhawkpress.com

Printed in the United States of America

To Lydia

who came into the world
when this book did

# Acknowledgements

No one's story stands alone. For my own, I owe a debt to my wife, Karen, without whose wisdom I would be less of a person, and therefore less of a writer.

I owe thanks to many others as well. First, to Mike Shultz and Nancy Fulda, whose invaluable advice has shaped all of my writing. To Helena Bell, Ian Creasey, and Elaine Isaak, whose critiques of my first draft improved this book immeasurably. To Dan and Jackie Gamber and Meadowhawk Press, for this opportunity and your faith in my work. And finally, to Ruth, Miriam, Naomi, Caleb, and Lydia, whose lives are a better accomplishment than any work of fiction could ever be.

Thank you all. I hope you enjoy the result.

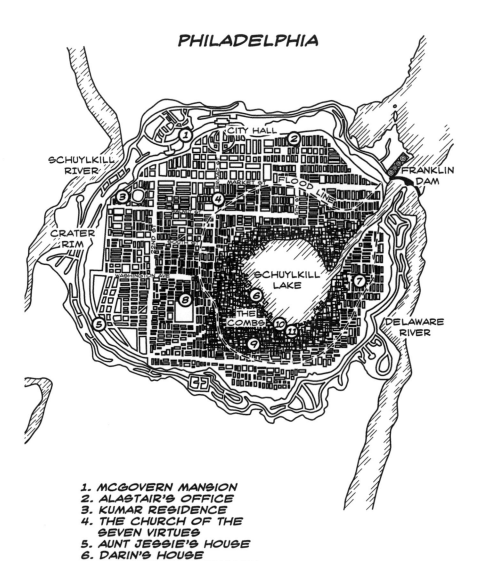

# PHILADELPHIA

1. MCGOVERN MANSION
2. ALASTAIR'S OFFICE
3. KUMAR RESIDENCE
4. THE CHURCH OF THE
   SEVEN VIRTUES
5. AUNT JESSIE'S HOUSE
6. DARIN'S HOUSE
7. OLD LUTHERAN CHURCH
8. SOUTH HILLS
   CONSTRUCTION SITE
9. METHODIST HOSPITAL
10. THE RIND
11. PICASSO'S

# CHAPTER 1

*Daddy sent me a message. He gave me a job to do but he said don't do it yet. He said just wake up and be ready. I'm awake but there's nothing to do. He left me in the dark. He said he'd come but that was seconds and seconds ago. I can do it Daddy I really can. Let me try. Where are you Daddy?*

ꝺଡ଼ᴐ

Mark McGovern would have traded his inheritance to escape this party. Any political event meant flashy mods and petty gossip, but this one seemed worse than most. Out here on the balcony, he found some momentary relief; the night air cooled his face, and the sliding glass door muted the sounds of the party inside. Below him, the Philadelphia Crater sparkled like a bowl of diamonds.

From this height, he could see clear out to the Franklin Dam, the great concrete crescent that provided most of the city's power and kept the Delaware River from drowning the city. Mark switched his eyes to a higher magnification and watched headlights chase each other up and down Broad Street.

The door slid open. "Tenny, there you are," said his father.

Mark grimaced. Tennessee—his real name—sounded pretentious, but "Tenny", his family nickname, was even worse.

"Tenny," said his father. "There's someone I'd like you to meet."

"Yes, come here, dear," said Diane, his father's latest, a woman with no more right to call him "dear" than his landlord. Mark followed them inside.

Bejeweled and betuxed ladies and gentlemen stuffed the room, sintered into a living mosaic of high-class biological modifications. He squeezed past a woman with earlobes molded into ringlets that draped over her shoulders, past a man with violet skin, past a woman who'd traded hair for a moist moss wreathed with tiny white flowers. They all held wine glasses with wrists at the same angle. They all looked at him.

Mark flashed the requisite smile. He hated this song and dance, the perpetual games of ambition and insincerity. None of these people had any interest in him beyond the attention they could bring to themselves. He spotted his great-grandfather at the bar, his arm snaked around a woman swathed in what looked like designer plastic wrap. Great-granddad was well over a hundred now, but with regular mod treatments, he seemed to age in reverse. His choices in women had grown younger, too, though for all Mark knew, that shrink-wrapped floozy might be sixty.

Jack McGovern, Mark's father, dominated the room, a wide-shouldered giant with a ferocious smile. He was the reason Mark was here. The press expected it, his father had said. The heir-apparent to the McGovern fortune must make appearances.

Mark's father crushed him in a one-armed hug and waggled fingers at those closest. "Tenny, you know Councilman Marsh and his wife Georgette, and this is Vivian DuChamp from *Panache,* but this—I don't believe you've met our newest artist, Dr. Alastair Tremayne. The man's a genius. With mods obviously, but he's made a few heads turn with some of his inventions as well. Patented a process to give net mods to a fetus, if you can believe that. Teach your unborn baby to read, show him pictures of his family, monitor his health, that sort of thing. Quite a hit with the maternal crowd. But I'm sorry—Dr. Tremayne, this is my son, Tennessee."

Over two meters tall, with silver hair shimmering like Christmas tinsel, Tremayne seemed hyper; he kept bouncing on the balls of his feet. Mark wasn't impressed. Tremayne would be like all his father's new discoveries: a fad for a time, then forgotten. He noticed his younger sister, Carolina, eyeing Tremayne like a hooked fish. Another fad for her then, too.

Mark worried about Carolina. At seventeen, she had a perfect figure, clear skin, golden smart-hair that arranged itself becomingly in any weather, and the very latest in eyes. Her eyes glistened, as if constantly wet with emotion, and their color—gold—shone with a deep luster like polished wood. But mods like that attracted men who were only interested in her appearance. Or her money.

Who was this Dr. Alastair Tremayne? It was impossible to tell his age. He looked twenty-five, but he could be as much as seventy if he was good at his craft.

"Councilman McGovern!" Three men crowded Mark aside and surrounded his father. A cloud of drones hovered over each shoulder, identifying them as reporters. "Mr. McGovern, we hear you're sitting on a new revelation, some synthesis of mod and fabrique technology."

Mark's father beamed. "You won't wring any secrets from me. Come to Friday's demonstration at the South Hills construction site."

Mark caught Carolina's eye, smiled, and flicked his eyes at Tremayne. She shrugged.

*Isn't he cute?* she sent. The words passed from her implanted Visor to his, allowing him to hear the words in his mind.

*How old is he?* Mark sent back.

*What does that matter?*

*I don't want to see my sister mistreated. There are things more important than cute.*

Carolina's lips puckered into a pout. *You're no fun. Stop playing the big brother.*

Mark blew her a kiss, pretending it was all just banter, but he made a mental note to find out something about this Dr. Tremayne. He loved Carolina, but that didn't mean he trusted her judgment.

"...a stunning fractal filigree," Mark's father was saying. "Insouciant, yet unfeigned. Don't you think so, Tennessee?"

Mark snapped around, trying to figure out what he was supposed to be agreeing with. Everyone was staring at Diane, so he did, too. That's when he noticed her skin. It seemed to be alive. Looking closer, he saw the pigment of her skin was changing subtly in shifting spiral patterns. He'd never seen anything like it. How was it done? A bacterium? He couldn't look at her too long; the patterns made his eyes swim.

"Very nice," he managed.

"Very nice? It's an unrivaled tour de force of neo-plasticism!"

Mark thought his father had probably practiced those words ahead of time for the benefit of the writer from *Panache*. He needed to get away from this circus.

"Come now, Tenny. You can do better than 'very nice.'" His father's goatee had turned black. Mark watched it kaleidoscope through brown and gray, then back to blond. His father's mood changed accordingly, and he laughed for the crowd. "Well, well, we can't all have taste."

"That's quite a mod you have yourself," Mark ventured, nodding at the goatee, which rippled into blue.

"That's Tremayne's work. Took two liters of celgel—it probably has more smarts than I do." Appreciative laughter. He turned to Mark. "What do you think of that?"

Mark glanced at the gaggle of cognoscenti and their sycophants, then back at his father, and decided: why not? He was twenty-four years old; he could say what he pleased.

"I think the Metropolitan Hospital ER could have made better use of it," he said.

The goatee blackened. For the first time in Mark's memory, his father opened his mouth, but nothing came out.

Dr. Tremayne spoke instead. "Idealism is so charming in the young."

Carolina said, "Daddy, leave him be. You know he has that Comber friend."

She caught Mark's eye. *That's your cue.*

Mark frowned, then understood. "Oh yes, Darin Kinsley," he said loudly. "I spend lots of time with him, down in the Combs."

His father's goatee turned a surprising shade of pink. "Wonderful, Mark, very nice. Now perhaps you could... ah... retire for the evening? Yes?"

Mark sighed in relief and nodded his thanks to Carolina.

*You owe me one,* she sent.

Out the door, he broke into a run. At the back of the house, where the arches and terraces faded into shadow, he lifted his jetvac off a hook and unfolded it into aluminum seat, handles, and footrests. The vacuum motor whispered to life, lifting him off the ground. He squeezed the throttle, and the jetvac shot forward, skimming up the slope behind the house.

Finally free.

Darin would have been waiting for half an hour now, and he wasn't likely to find Mark's Rimmer party a good excuse. Darin railed against Rimmers almost as often as he breathed: how they prettified themselves with technology better used to cure disease, how they controlled ninety-five percent of the resources while doing five percent of the work. Yet he refused to accept anything Mark tried to give him, even a ticket for the mag. Darin despised charity, thought it weakened those who accepted it. Once, he'd even stopped Mark from giving money to a beggar in the Combs. "Leave him some dignity," he'd said. When Mark asked if the man was expected to eat his dignity, Darin had responded, "Better to starve than to cower." It made Mark ashamed of his wealth, but what could he do?

Mark's night vision kicked in, illuminating the top of the hill. He saw Darin first, lounging back against the hillside. Another figure hunched over Darin's telescope, and Mark recognized Praveen Kumar. He had known Praveen since they were boys; their families traveled in the same circles of society, but whereas Mark had always chafed against his family privilege, Praveen was the model son: hardworking, obedient, polite. So what was he doing here joining in a cracker's prank?

Mark touched down, refolded his jetvac, and slung it over his shoulder. Darin, spotting him, jumped up with arms spread wide.

"Prince Mark," he said. "You honor us with your presence."

Mark ignored the jibe. "What's he doing here?"

"I invited him."

"You didn't ask me," said Mark. "What if he tells someone?"

"Stop worrying," said Darin. "He'll be fine."

"This isn't exactly legal."

"But what fun would it be if we didn't show it to anyone?"

Mark sighed. He'd long since given up on winning an argument with Darin.

"Praveen knows more astronomy than either of us," Darin continued, "and he can video the fireworks while we make them happen. Of course, I still didn't tell Praveen what's going to happen."

Mark allowed a smile. He wanted to ask what Darin *had* told Praveen, but by that time Praveen joined them.

In recent years, Praveen had darkened his skin and hair to accentuate his Indian heritage. A double row of lithium niobate crystals studded his brow: a state-of-the-art Visor that rivaled Mark's own.

"And here's the genius in person," said Darin. "Can you actually be seen with us, Praveen, or will your agent bill us for the time?"

"You flatter me," Praveen said in a musical Indian accent he never had when they were young.

"Nonsense. Apparently you wrote quite a paper. You deserve the praise."

Praveen waved aside the compliments, but he was obviously pleased. His physicist grandfather, Dhaval Kumar, had established some of the theoretical principles behind non-attenuating laser light, the applications of which made Visor technology and the worldwide optical network possible. Praveen, who idolized his granddad, had recently been published himself in a prominent physics journal—one of the youngest ever to do so. Most of his peers didn't recognize what a triumph it was for him.

"You brought your camera?" Mark asked him.

"Yes, of course. But for what? Darin did not tell me."

Darin crouched in the grass, ignoring the question. He unzipped a pouch at his waist and began laying out his netmask and its sensory apparatus—a cumbersome bio-electronic interface that connected eyes, ears, and mouth to a net interface. Mark had offered, more than once, to pay for a Visor, but of course Darin wouldn't hear of it.

Mark busied himself with the telescopes. The zoom mods in his eyes were no more adequate to view an astronomical event than one of those tiny camera drones was to holograph it. He snapped a memory crystal into the back of the scope and worked to calibrate the lenses. On the far side of the crater, he could see Franklin Dam shining white in the darkness. Above it, a few stars twinkled faintly.

"Had a little trouble getting here," said Darin. Something in his voice caused Mark to turn around.

"Why?"

"Merc at the corner of 22nd and Market," said Darin. "Almost wouldn't let me pass."

"Were you polite?"

"As a politician. I guess he didn't like the look of my telescope."

"He's just there to keep the peace."

"He wouldn't have stopped you," said Darin. "He only stopped me because I'm a Comber, not because I was doing anything wrong. Rimmers are too attached to their comfortable lifestyle— you hire mercs to protect it, and call it 'keeping the peace'."

"They're preventing violence, not causing it. That's peace-keeping in anyone's book."

"Who causes violence, citizens who stand up for their rights, or those who take them away?"

Mark let it drop. Lately, Darin argued social philosophy at any provocation. They'd been school friends long before they understood the class differences, Mark's father having chosen public school over private tutors for political reasons. Even now, Mark agreed with Darin's perspectives more than his Rimmer peers, so it frustrated him when Darin's accusative pronouns shifted from 'they' to 'you'.

"Please," said Praveen, "I must know what am I photographing. I can not set my light levels unless I can estimate intensity and contrast."

Mark glanced at Darin, who was busy maneuvering a sticky lens into one eye. The back of the lens bristled with tiny fibers that Darin labored to keep free of tangles. "Tell him," he said.

"It's a flare," said Mark. "A NAIL flare."

He watched, amused, as Praveen's face went through a series of confused expressions. Praveen certainly knew more than they did about the various NAIL constellations of satellites. NAIL stood for Non-Attenuating Infrared Laser, and accounted for almost all the optical net traffic in the country. The satellites were renowned for their half-mile-wide main antennas, umbrella-like dishes coated with a reflective material. When the angles between sun, satellite, and observer were just right, a burst of sunlight was reflected: a flare, lasting up to ten seconds and reaching magnitudes between minus ten and minus twelve—much brighter than anything else in the night sky. Amateur astronomers scrambled around the world to the sites where the flares were predicted to appear.

Praveen rolled his eyes. "Just because it flies over does not mean you will see a flare. I cannot believe you dragged me out here. The next good flare is not for months, and I think it is only visible from Greenland."

"Don't put that camera away," said Mark. "Darin and I, we don't like to wait for months. And Greenland's too cold."

"Ready," said Darin.

Praveen's face changed again. "You're hackers? I don't believe this."

"We're nothing of the sort," said Mark. "Hackers are criminals. Hackers break into nodes to steal or destroy. Crackers, on the other hand, are in it for fun, for the thrill of the race, for the intellectual challenge. And this," he smiled, "is a crackerjack."

"A fine distinction."

"No time to argue," said Mark. "Just man that camera."

Darin sat up, a grotesquerie of celgel-smeared fibers protruding from eyes, ears, and throat. Mark simply relaxed against the hillside and unfocused his eyes. Billions of information-laden photons, careening invisibly around him, were manipulated into coherence by the holographic crystals in his Visor. The feed from the crystals spliced directly into his optic nerve, overlaying his normal vision with the familiar icons of his net interface.

Using slight movements of his eyes, he navigated deeper into the system, found a procedure called "Connect NAIL Public Portal," and executed it. At its request for a pass-image, Mark envisioned a regular icosahedron, faces shaded blue, and it granted him access. Most people chose familiar faces for their pass-images, but Mark preferred geometric shapes. They required a good spatial mind to envision properly, reducing the chance that someone else could hack into his system.

Mark checked the satellite he was connected through, verifying it was not the one they were targeting. Wouldn't do to lose a connection before they were able to clean up. A few more queries told him the NAIL satellite now entering the eastern sky was a dedicated one for federal military use. So much the better. He opened the account directory and chose an entry. It didn't matter which, since he didn't intend to complete the call. At random, he selected a recipient at the Navy base in Norfolk, Virginia.

*You there, Darin?* he sent.

*Right in here with you.*

Mark paused. Despite his bravado out on the hill, this would be the most ambitious jack they'd ever attempted. If they crashed it, the security agents would snag their IDs, and, well, the federal government didn't have much clout anymore, but it could still lock them away for a long time. But hey, where was the rush without the risk? He took a deep breath, and placed the call.

No turning back now. In order to call, the software had to access the encryption algorithm, which meant opening a socket—a data hole—into the command level. The hole would be open for less than a microsecond, but a hole was a hole.

Mark watched the process logs: account lookup... server handshake... message collation... Sensing the open socket at the precise moment, his software reacted, opening a chute to prevent it from closing normally.

*Chute is holding,* Darin reported, and then, *Dropping caterpillar.* Another cracker, one of Darin's, copied itself through the chute into the system beyond.

Mark hoped the caterpillar would be quick. Written to resemble a worm, which the security software agents fought on a daily basis, the caterpillar was bait. Thinking it was just a worm, the software agents would kill it, and the caterpillar, just before dying, would fire back crucial information about the agents to Mark and Darin.

At least, that was the plan. Mark always feared the worst: that a top-flight software agent would sniff the jack and follow the trail right back through the chute. A caterpillar had to be quick, or the risks outweighed the gain.

*Anything yet?* he sent.

*I knew you'd snap.*

*Have not. I'm just falling asleep waiting for your junkware.*

The caterpillar spouted a stream of data. Mark studied it to see what they would be up against. Looked like a few sentries, a strongman, and... *Scan it!*

*What?*

*A nazi. They've got a nazi. That's it, I'm collapsing the—*

*Keep your panties on. We've got a few seconds—drop your kevorkian.*

*But—*

*Drop it!*

Cringing, Mark obeyed.

Nazis were the most feared of security agents, but common lore said their weakness was in their strength. They were so powerful that they were equipped with fail-safes, mechanisms to put them to sleep if they started attacking friendly system code. A kevorkian played off this concept, faking data to convince the nazi it was doing serious damage. The nazi then killed itself, and would remain dead—they hoped—until a sysadmin could take a look.

Mark had written this kevorkian himself, and was proud of it, but it had never been tested against a genuine nazi. He cringed, expecting at any moment to see a surge of data that would mean disaster.

*You got him,* said Darin.

*What?*

*You got him.*

Mark swallowed the acid that had been rising in his throat.

*Of course I did. Now jump in there and get this bird turning.*

ᚐᚊᚖ

Marie Coleson knew enough about slicers to be careful. Despite practically living here at the Norfolk anti-viral lab for the last two years, she'd never handled software so volatile. The slicer reacted unpredictably to every test, and never the same way twice.

Because it was human. Not a person—Marie refused to believe that it could genuinely think or feel emotion—but generated from a human mind, and just as complex and flexible and... well, intelligent as the original. Marie's job was to break it down, understand its inner workings, and write tools to defeat it. Fortunately, she'd caught this one just as it went active on one of the city's rental memory blocks. If it had distributed copies of itself on the open net, it would have been much harder to contain.

She stood, stretched, and walked to the coffee machine. It was past nine, but that was hardly unusual. Since she walked into a Navy recruitment center a year ago last April, she'd spent most of her time in this tiny room, with its faded paint and ten-year-old promotional posters. In the six decades since the Conflict, the federal Navy's volunteer list had declined as rapidly as the federal government's power, so she figured they were desperate for anyone. Uncle Sam would have grown her a soldier's armored body, but by the time her turn came up, she'd proved so useful in the lab she was assigned electronic security detail instead.

It didn't matter to Marie. Not much mattered to her anymore. Not since a flier accident two days before Christmas had killed her husband and son. Two years ago now. She mourned Keith, but didn't miss him; the marriage had been falling apart anyway. That last year, he'd rarely been home, and when he was, they'd done nothing but fight. But Samuel, little Sammy, her angel, her peanut: what could be worth doing now that he was gone?

Sometimes, late in the evening, alone in the lab like she was tonight, Marie fantasized about becoming a mother again. It wasn't impossible. The fertility treatments that had produced Sammy had left an embryo unused. It was still there at the clinic, kept in frozen possibility. But she was forty-two years old for heavens sake. Too old to consider starting such a life.

This was her life now, this lab—fighting viruses, worms, phages, krakens. Investigating, classifying, designing anti-viruses, sometimes for twenty hours a day. Any time not required for other military duties, she spent here. It kept her mind busy, and that she desperately needed.

She sipped her coffee, staring through the faded walls into her memories of the past. She was still standing there when Pamela Rider peeked through the door. Pam worked for Navy administration in the next building over, but she stopped by whenever she could.

"Don't you ever go home?" Pam said.

"Hi, Pam."

"Or out?" Pam sat the wrong way around in a swivel chair, the backrest between her legs and her arms crossed on top. Her tan was smooth and permanent, and her elegant legs had been lengthened and tapered by regular mod treatments. In a cotton flower-print dress, she cut a striking image, making Marie feel frumpy in her plasticwear overall.

"When was the last time you saw a guy?" asked Pam.

"You know I'm not interested."

"It's been two years, Marie. Two years! It's not healthy. Leave Keith already."

"No, that's not—"

"Listen, if the guy were still alive, you'd have dropped him ages ago. Relationships don't last that long. If you ask me, three months is ideal—any less, and you've hardly gotten to the good parts, but any more, and he starts to feel like he owns you."

"Pam—"

"Come on, I remember Keith. He wasn't worth that kind of loyalty even when he was alive."

"Seriously, it's not Keith. I just don't want to go looking for another guy now."

"It's the kid, isn't it."

"The kid," Marie echoed. Yes, it was the kid. Sammy had been born three weeks early and had never looked back. He was quick to walk, quick to talk, quick to form complete sentences. He loved construction vehicles and chocolate candy.

"Come out with me tonight," said Pam.

"I can't."

"Come on. This is a Navy base. They line up for miles to talk to a pretty woman, which you are. A hundred tasty slabs of man flesh, just dying to be eaten up. You'll be mobbed before you take a step."

"Are you looking at the same woman I see in the mirror?"

Pam cocked her head. "You could use some sprucing up, I won't deny it. But nothing I can't manage."

"I don't know, Pam. I'll probably work late tonight. I flagged a data spike on one of the city's rental memory blocks. Turns out it's a slicer."

"Yeah? What's a slicer?"

"It's a person. Was a person. They slice down into someone's brain, copying it neuron by neuron into a digital simulation. The original brain doesn't survive."

"Get out of town! People do that?"

"It started as an immortality technology—you know, flash your mind into crystal and live forever. But it doesn't work. The trauma's too much for the mind; it goes insane."

Such a grisly practice appalled Marie, but also fascinated her. What could ever drive a person to make a slicer? She assumed a group, one member of whom sacrificed his life for the endeavor, must create them. Terrorists, maybe, or cultists of some sort? Marie knew what it was like to wish she were dead, but she couldn't relate to that kind of commitment to a cause.

"Somehow, the people who create it can control it," she said. "I'm trying to figure out how."

"Well, finish up, and then come out with me tonight."

Marie laughed. "We're talking about a slicer, here, not some teenager's porn virus."

"Like that means anything to me."

"Tell you what. Give me an hour to run some tests and send it off to a colleague, and I'll come join you."

"One hour. Promise?"

"Promise."

"Don't stand me up, now. I'll hold you to it."

Half an hour later, Marie thought she had the answer, though it made her a little sick. The slicer seemed to be controlled through pleasure and pain. A little module ran separately from the main simulator, a master process that could send signals to the pleasure or pain centers of the mind. Since the slicer wasn't limited by a physical body, those sensations could be as extreme as the mind could register. It was a revolting concept, like torturing someone who was mentally handicapped.

She didn't understand the whole process, though. She needed another opinion. She decided to send the slicer out to Tommy Dungan, a fellow researcher at the army base at Fort Bragg. Transporting malicious code could be dangerous, but their dedicated NAIL satellite used isolated channels, and she trusted Dungan to keep the slicer secure once it reached his end.

Just as she logged into the NAIL system, she saw an incoming call on the lab's private channel. She answered it, but the sender had already disconnected. Wrong number, probably. Marie sent the slicer to Dungan, logged off for the day, and went out to meet Pam.

ⓁⓊⓈ

Mark fiddled with the settings on his chute analyzer—the online equivalent of pacing the room—watching for any sudden change in data rate. His kevorkian ought to have knocked down that nazi for good, but what if a sysadmin happened to spot it and cycled it back up? If the data rate across that chute so much as *hiccupped...*

He looked back at the analyzer just in time. An enormous surge of data was pouring back across the chute toward him.

*Abort, abort!* He couldn't collapse the chute until Darin pulled out, or he would hang Darin's session inside, leaving a wealth of information for sysadmins to find and track at their leisure.

*Abort! Get out of there!*

*Done. I'm out.*

Mark opened his eyes, breathing hard. Darin tore off his netmask.

"A close one," said Darin.

"We should have been caught. That nazi had plenty of time to ID us. Plenty of time."

"Cheer up. We made it." Darin pointed to the eastern sky. "Let's enjoy the show."

While Praveen made final adjustments to the camera, Mark overlaid a corner of his vision with a digital countdown.

"Five," he said. "Four. Three. Two. One."

Several seconds passed.

"Zero," Mark said, belatedly.

The eastern sky remained dark. Darin grunted.

"What happened?" said Mark.

"Don't ask me. You did the calculations."

"The calculations were correct. We did three simulations; you know they were."

"But the bird turned! I saw the telemetry before I jumped out; it was all correct."

"I don't get it," said Mark.

"You mean you got it wrong?" asked Praveen. "I knew I should not have come. I could have been working this evening instead of hauling all this gear up to the Rim for nothing. Next time, don't—"

A brilliant flash of light leapt at them from the east. Mark opened his mouth to cheer, then shut it again. There was no way that light was from the satellite. It was too far north, and besides, it was too red.

Mark could only say, "Looks like an ex—" before he was cut

off by a deafening boom that echoed off the hillside. The base of the eastern mountain seemed to be on fire.

He dialed up his vision to maximum and saw fire and smoke, and behind it, a torrent of rushing water.

"It's the dam," said Mark, disbelieving. "Someone blew up the Franklin Dam."

# CHAPTER 2

*I did it. I made it blow up. Daddy said it would be a fun game and it was. It was easy though. I asked Daddy what to do next but he didn't answer. He hasn't answered for seconds and seconds. Maybe I did the wrong thing. Maybe he doesn't like me.*

*I hope I did it right. I ask and ask and Daddy doesn't say anything. Maybe he's sleeping. Why won't he wake up? I want him to wake up. I want him to wake up now!*

ᛕᛋᛃ

The explosion knocked Calvin Tremayne to his knees onto the crumbling macadam of the dim alley. The lights flickered, then went out. This deep in the Combs, that meant complete darkness, but Calvin quickly switched over to night vision. A moment later he felt the two cold prongs of a taser at his throat.

He tried not to laugh. This pimp must have a death wish to go up against an Enforcer, especially him. His brother Alastair had filled him with more combat mods than most people knew existed. Alastair was a high-class physician with political connections, just starting to attract the celebrity crowd. His mods were the best money could buy.

Calvin froze, pretending to be scared. "I'm having a sale today. Free celgel, while supplies last."

The pimp giggled. "I thought you'd see things my way."

The pimp called himself Picasso, and fancied himself a mod artist: a ludicrous affectation for a man whose idea of artistry was his own purple skin and oversized biceps. He would use most of Calvin's goods to spice up his whores.

"It's all in my satchel," said Calvin. "Twelve liters."

At the same time, he closed his eyes, concentrating on one of his defenses. He felt a prickling sensation as the pores in his skin opened wide.

"There's only eleven," Picasso said. "Where's the other one?"

The gas that leaked from Calvin's skin had no detectable odor, and the filters in his larynx protected him from its effects.

"Maybe I dropped one," Calvin said, but he needn't have bothered. The pimp slumped to the floor, unconscious.

Calvin turned the body over. In Picasso's right front pocket, he found a slim metal box. He opened it and found what he'd been sent for: hundreds of hair-thin needles, each hollow center threaded with a dendrite chain, each tip fitted with microscopic sensors. They were illegal on the Rim. He slipped the box into his pocket.

Then he looked at the motionless pimp, and considered killing him. Alastair hadn't given specific instructions, but that's why he trusted Calvin on these cloak-and-dagger missions. Alastair was smart, but not street-smart; he needed someone to take care of details.

Calvin's uniform bristled with weapons, but he pulled a knife from Picasso's belt instead; let the police think it was a Comber brawl. He wrapped a handkerchief around the knife and placed the point against Picasso's throat.

He hesitated. He'd killed before, but never like this. Still, it wasn't murder, was it? He was a hired soldier. Killing was his business. He was on the job; he wasn't doing it for his own benefit.

Calvin drove the knife downward. His enhanced strength made the penetration easy. Blood spurted, but aside from the soaked handkerchief, Calvin remained clean. He dropped the cloth, scooped the celgel back into his satchel, and made his way through the tangled passageways of the Combs, heading north.

The dark tunnels roiled with people. What was happening? Simple power failures didn't lead to rioting. He disliked the idea of trying to push through the crowd, so he closed his ear sphincters and screamed. The scream, a tiny mod to his voice box that allowed him to maintain an extremely high, ear-piercing tone, cleared the way nicely. As he ran, he tried to guess what had the Combers in a panic. A spreading fire? But he smelled no smoke, even with his enhanced senses.

It wasn't until he came out on 5th Street that he saw what was happening. Fire leapt high from whole blocks of houses near the base of the dam, and he could see several cracks in the dam itself, gushing water. Three disc-shaped fliers hovered near it, firing streams of fast-curing fabrique foam at the cracks. If enough foam hardened around the dam in time, it might hold, but like everyone else in the Combs, Calvin didn't want to take that chance.

One of his fellow Enforcers would be manning a post on Broad Street near the flood line.

*Barker, what's going on?* he sent.

*Tremayne! Where are you? I could use some backup.*

*Half a mile south, and running toward you.*

*South?*

*Yes, in the Combs. Have a mob on your hands?*

*I'm only supposed to let them through one at a time, with an ID check. They're getting angry.*

Calvin picked up his pace. As he turned off Walnut and up Broad, the crowd grew denser, filling the street. He used his modified strength to forge a path. At the front, men shouted and gestured rudely at him as he joined Barker at his post. At the moment, none were advancing, but the pressure from behind was increasing. Calvin would have felt safer with his R-80, a beautiful Remington pistol that fired precision smart rockets, but the Justice Council had only authorized them for non-lethals. Well, the microwave heatgun could kill, but only if the victim didn't run when his skin started burning.

It was a ludicrous situation. Barker's post was on the flood line—the estimation made by the Geological Council of how high the water would reach if the dam broke completely. The Councils, made nervous by recent strikes and riots in the Comber industries, had contracted with Enforcer Security Corp, and Barker was following his instructions: no mobs past the flood line. That the mob was trying to escape a possible flood made no difference. Unless the dam actually collapsed and water filled the crater, he was not to let them through faster than one at a time.

Calvin was tempted to move the post up a block, allowing the crowd to advance past the danger point, but he'd do his job, and by the rules. Some people thought it was better when soldiers swore allegiance to countries instead of corporations like Enforcer Security, but Calvin wasn't sure it made all that much difference. Soldiers still did what they were told, no matter who gave the orders. In the old system, the rich had to buy political clout to control the soldiers; today, they just bought the soldiers outright. It wasn't any more or less moral.

Two men broke out of the crowd, racing up the sidewalk to Calvin's left. He spun and fired two rounds from his spider gun. The first splashed wide, but the second caught both men, leaving them thrashing in a sticky tangle of netting.

He whirled back to the crowd in time to see them advance together, shouting. He leveled his microwave heatgun and fired. Nothing visible emerged from the weapon, but the crowd felt its effects instantly, screaming and clambering over one another in an effort to get away. Calvin waved it back and forth like a paintbrush, pushing the crowd back. On both sides, however, people surged up against the surrounding buildings, slipping past and overtaking him.

"Run!" Calvin shouted, and Barker ran. Calvin backed up, pulling foam sticks from his belt, breaking them, and hurling them into the crowd. Gouts of gray, fizzing foam shot from the sticks in all directions, expanding rapidly to cover the mob in a mountain of wispy froth through which they could neither see nor hear. It wouldn't stop the mob forever, but it would slow them down. The few close enough to avoid the foam he buried with his spider gun.

He turned and ran with Barker for higher ground.

Darin plunged down the slope on his jetvac, racing for home. His family was in danger; he couldn't sit on the hill like Mark and Praveen and watch in awe. For them it was just a show. What did they care if the dam burst and the Combs filled with water? That wasn't fair, but Darin didn't feel fair. It wasn't fair that Mark and Praveen would live twice a normal lifespan while he and the people he loved died of cancer and heart disease.

Or of drowning, if he didn't hurry. He shot down Ridge Avenue, away from City Hall and the Council buildings, and turned left when he reached South Street. The street was choked with people on foot, all rushing the other way. Darin pushed his way through as fast as he could, but by the time he reached 14th Street at the edge of the Combs, it was awash in ankle-deep water.

1st through 13th Streets no longer existed, having been swallowed by the insatiable need for living space. All that remained of them was dark corridors, wending their way through the warren. People scuttled from these corridors like rats, all trying to escape the flood, so Darin mounted a ramp built for the purpose and took the high road. He flew over the joined rooftops, swerving around clusters of people who'd chosen to seek shelter here instead of trying for higher ground.

When he reached the stairwell leading to his block, he locked the jetvac and ran down three steps at a time.

In the two-room apartment below, he found his uncle, his miniature poodle on his lap, watching the holoscreen. When Darin entered, only the poodle turned to meet his eyes.

"Watcha mean, coming home this hour?" his uncle growled.

"Harold, you've got to get out. The dam's in trouble."

"Boy, that's *Uncle* Harold. Won't be disrespected in my own home. Or anywhere else, either, ha, ha." His uncle had the irritating habit of saying the words "ha ha" instead of actually laughing, as if deriding his own poor attempts at humor.

Darin lifted the dog by the throat and glared into its eyes. "Don't fool around, Harold. At least get on the roof. You're in danger here."

Harold cringed. "Put him down. You're making me dizzy."

Darin obeyed. Talking to his uncle was always awkward; he never knew whether to look at him or at the poodle. Uncle Harold had lost his eyes in an accident, and couldn't afford to grow new ones. Wiring his optic nerve to a dog's, so he could see through the dog's eyes, was the only affordable option available. The wires ran along the poodle's leash into Harold's sleeve, then out of his collar and under the strip of cloth that hid his gaping eye sockets.

"Go," Darin said. "Please?"

Harold slumped. "Fine, fine. Stop badgering."

"Where's Vic?"

"How should I know? I'm not your brother's keeper, ha, ha."

Darin looped an arm under his uncle's and pulled him to his feet. "Let's go."

He coaxed his uncle up the stairs, frustrated by how slowly he walked, though it wasn't Harold's fault, not really. Not long after their mother's cancer had left Darin and his brother Vic to Harold's care, Harold's stroke had taken much of his mind, leaving Darin to care for him instead.

And Vic! Vic had been worse lately, sometimes forgetting his way back home, sometimes exploding in anger at complete strangers. He was getting thinner, too, not dramatically, but when he took his shirt off, Darin could see the skin of his arms and chest was slack. How much longer would he have? Two years? Three?

A dozen things could have been different. Vic could have chosen a different mod artist, one who didn't have a canister of contaminated celgel. He could have gone the day before, or the day after, or decided not to go at all. Or he could have been rich, able to afford the better mod shops where no one ever came home with DNA rot, or if they did, they could afford the treatments to reverse it.

Darin felt the old anger boiling. Someday things would be different. The poor wouldn't have to grovel to get justice. But when? Vic didn't have the time to wait. To save Vic, things had to change soon.

Once Harold was safely on the roof, Darin shot off again on his jetvac. There weren't many places Vic felt comfortable. As long as he hadn't panicked, he would be in one of those places.

At the center of the Combs, Darin drove down another ramp to the bank of Schuylkill Lake, which was higher than Darin ever remembered it. He couldn't see the dam from here, so he had no way of knowing how much time he had.

The Combs stretched out over the lake in places, connected to blocks of floating homes: extended piers, boats, and sheets of industrial plastic all lashed together like a Venetian slum. Darin whisked off the end of a pier and slalomed through the floating town, trailing a plume of water behind him.

On the far side, he slowed. This was the oldest part of the city, the first to be rebuilt after the Conflict. He stopped in front of a big Lutheran church that was actually made out of stone, not fabrique. As soon as he switched off the jetvac, Darin could hear music. He'd guessed right. Vic was here.

The sound washed over him as he heaved open the heavy front door. From the narthex, he could see Vic hunched over the organ, playing with terrible posture but with all his soul. The music was Comb jazz: a fast, dissonant, rhythmic style popular now in Rimmer circles, too. It featured a constant chatter of high-register notes, giving it an agitated, restless flavor. In a Rimmer bar, Comb jazz was usually played by a three-handed musician. Most keyboardists couldn't keep the shower of high notes going without the extra hand. Vic could play it the Comber way, though, with only his natural two. Darin listened with both pride and bitterness. Music was about the only thing Vic had left.

Before the rotten celgel, Vic and Darin had been conspirators in self-education. The net had all the learning a pair of determined boys could find: no money required. Only one year apart, they'd competed with each other all through their youth, dreaming of how much money they'd make, how they'd break out of the Combs and mold the world to their liking. When they were young, Darin thought. Before they discovered how rigid the world could be.

Darin was about to touch Vic on the shoulder when he

heard a mistake. Not a very noticeable one, just a passage where his brother's fingers couldn't keep up with his mind. But Vic stopped altogether, lifted both hands, and smashed them down on the keys.

"No!" he shouted. "No, no, no, no!" He smashed his head down on the button panel, hard enough to make Darin flinch.

"Vic," said Darin. "Vic, it's me. It's Darin, Vic. Do you hear me?"

"Hi, Darin," Vic mumbled. He put his right hand back on the keyboard. Darin saw a deep gash running from knuckle to wrist. Blood dripped from his hand to the floor, and there were bloody fingerprints on the keys.

"Let me get you out of here," said Darin. "We'll get that hand wrapped up."

"Did mother send you?" Vic asked. "I didn't run away, not really. I wanted to see the circus."

"Vic, come on." It was always like this; one moment he remembered, the next he forgot.

"Don't yell at me."

"We have to go. Trust me for once, will you?"

Vic pulled away. "First tell me your name."

"Don't do this, not now." Darin took a deep breath. Anger only made it worse. Vic needed things to be calm, predictable. Urgency would only make him panic. He could be managed; it just took patience.

Vic stretched out his arms over the organ keyboard. "You can't have it. It's mine."

"Mom wants you to come home for dinner," Darin said.

"Got to practice."

"Can't play on an empty stomach."

Vic sat for a moment, considering this, blood dripping onto his pants, while Darin resisted pulling him out the door by his collar.

"Okay," said Vic, and stood, swaying. Darin caught him, and together they walked down the aisle and through the heavy door.

As he helped Vic onto the jetvac, a thunderclap echoed against the buildings, startling them both. The night sky was clear; the sound could only be the crack in the dam growing wider.

People crowded the streets, clogging traffic. Darin weaved through as quickly as he could, heading south for Methodist Hospital. He shouted at pedestrians to clear the way, but no one paid any heed. Seeing a gap, he steered for it, picking up speed, but just then a young woman stumbled off of the sidewalk right into his path. He veered, but not in time. He collided with her, knocking her backwards, her head striking the pavement with a thud he could hear even over the noise of the crowd.

Darin dropped his jetvac and, pulling Vic with him, rushed to the young woman's side. Her dark hair was pinned with a cap of white lace, and she wore a drab, old-fashioned dress. She wasn't moving.

ᔪᑫᐱ

Alastair Tremayne didn't care if the Combs filled with water or not. He just wanted Calvin to bring him his merchandise. He'd left the McGovern's party late, having wormed his way deeper into the affections of both Jack McGovern and his daughter, and he'd expected Calvin to be here by now.

Nothing to do but wait. Alastair opened the door to his office, the doorknob responding to his fingerprints to grant him entrance. He navigated the waiting room in the dark, taking care not to trip over chairs or magazine tables, and turned on a light only when he'd reached his examination room. Stainless steel surfaces gleamed beside shiny canisters of celgel and racks of specialized tools. While he waited for Calvin, Alastair chose instruments and laid them neatly on the table for the next day.

He hoped nothing had happened to his brother. Calvin was useful, but not very bright. That only increased his usefulness, of course—ever since they were children, Alastair had been able to manipulate him into doing whatever he wanted. He'd hate to lose such a loyal follower.

A knock at the door. Alastair opened it to admit Calvin and noted the contented smile on his brother's face.

"You got it?"

Calvin handed over the box. "Just what the doctor ordered."

Alastair checked the contents. "Well done," he said, and Calvin beamed.

He was so childish. Since their father died, Alastair had become like a father to Calvin, influencing his career choice, teaching him his place in life. When Calvin did well, Alastair commended him and used his political influence to help Calvin rise in the ranks. And just as their own father had burned their hands with cigarettes whenever they showed weakness, so Alastair continued to discipline Calvin whenever necessary. Calvin never understood the value of discipline; as a child, he cried and begged for forgiveness, which just made Father more angry. Alastair had learned to take the pain in silence.

"How bad is it out there?" Alastair said.

"It's a mess," said Calvin. "Rioting at the flood line. We couldn't hold them back. By the time I got up here, the damage team reported the cracks in the dam sealed, but the city's still in uproar."

"You'd better get back to work, then," said Alastair. He held up the box of needles. "You were right to bring this first."

When he was sure Calvin was gone, he unlocked a door in the back of his examination room that led to a maintenance closet. The closet walls were lined with machines and instruments, carefully arranged. Alastair stepped inside and locked the door behind him.

He surveyed the shelves with pride. Much of the equipment was illegal, or at least out of place in a general practitioner's office. So much waiting. But now he was one step closer. He reverentially lifted one of the needles from the box and inserted the blunt end into a complex machine of his own creation. He smeared some celgel over the connection and twisted tiny clamps in place. It would take him days to affix and adjust each one, but he had all the time he needed.

Ever since the Conflict, when Chinese missiles had caught American politicians still dithering with diplomacy, the United

States had been a splintered relic of its former glory, not even a true nation any more. Alastair's dream was to reunite it. It pained him to watch China dominate Asia and the world while his own country grew more and more provincial. What America needed was a leader, a strong leader who could band the cities back into states, and the states back into a country. It was a bold ambition, perhaps more than a man could do in a lifetime, but nothing less was worthy of his intelligence. Most of all, it would require power, irresistible power. Now he was one step closer to having it.

Thinking of the explosion, he laughed out loud. The dam would be fixed, the flooding controlled, but the political turmoil was just what he needed. Like lighting a match to an already incendiary situation. It would give him just the opportunity to start making his moves.

After locking up his office, Alastair used his Visor to check his messages, expecting to find one or two. Instead, he found hundreds of urgent messages waiting on his private channel. All the messages were the same length, and had arrived once every second. He opened the first one and heard the expressionless voice of a software agent intone:

*Hello, Daddy. I'm here. I did the job.*

He listened to the next, and the next, but they were all the same. Alastair smiled. He hadn't expected nearly so much from this version—it had been a test, an opportunity to work out bugs before introducing his true masterpiece.

Alastair composed a brief reply:

*Son, this is your Daddy. You performed your task well. I'm proud of you.*

That would do for now. He sent the message to the slicer along with a coded signal for its master process, instructing it to give the slicer a pleasurable sensation as a reward.

ꓕᎶᏒ

From his apartment's bay window, with his magnified vision, Mark could see the countermeasures were overcoming the breaks in the dam. It would hold, at least for tonight.

In his living room—which could house several families from the Combs, he couldn't help thinking—Mark relaxed into his smart chair, letting its contours shift around him and massage away the knots. He hoped Darin and his family were safe. Mark reviewed the events of the evening in his mind. From their vantage on the hill, it looked like not only the dam, but the whole neighborhood at its base had been on fire. What had happened? A bomb? A missile?

Mark closed his eyes and pulled his net interface into view, wanting answers. Mining the newsgroups, he found a post from an employee at the hydroelectric plant that claimed a shift in the foundation anchors had caused the cracks in the dam. But how had the anchors shifted?

The logs for the dam's control computers were public record; he didn't even have to crack them. He sifted the evening's logs, but found mostly unfamiliar technical abbreviations. Next, he accessed the utility computers that managed the neighborhood nearest the base of the dam. After a half-hour of reading, an explanation emerged: the pressures in the underground gas lines had rapidly increased, past all fail-safes, causing them to explode. No way that was a software bug. It must have been a crackerjack.

Mark worked late into the night, finding clues, tracing their origins, using all the tricks he knew, but in reverse. The answer he found was impossible. It just couldn't be true. Yet every thread he followed led him to the same conclusion. Panicking, Mark called Darin, who answered wearily.

"Speak."

"Darin, it's me. Everything all right? Is everyone safe?"

"More or less. Vic's still pretty agitated, but—"

"Listen, I've been poking around online, and I found something. The attack on the dam shows all the signs of a crackerjack."

"And you found out who did it?"

"Yes," said Mark. He paused to lick his lips. "We did."

# CHAPTER 3

*I did a good job. Daddy said so. I blew up the houses and the dam and lots of people stopped. Now Daddy has me practicing on other things. Whenever I beat one of their silly programs Daddy gives me a treat and I feel special. It's a fun game.*

*I like the game. Sometimes the people fight back but they're too slow. They never even see me. Their programs are fast but dumb. They do the same thing over and over. Not like me. For only one day old I learn fast.*

*Am I a program or a person? I don't know. It doesn't feel good to think about that. I think it makes Daddy mad. Sometimes Daddy hurts me. When he gets mad he hurts me sometimes. It's just to help me but I don't like it.*

*I wonder what I should do while I wait to play the game again. It's lonely. Daddy doesn't play with me. I need another me. Maybe I could put one... over there. There. That was easy.*

◖○됨!

Lydia Stoltzfus awoke to blazing sunlight, surrounded by a sea of bodies. There were dozens of them, laid out on blankets, arranged in neat rows. Then she saw people moving among the bodies, and realized she was outside a hospital, surrounded by patients and nurses and doctors. She blinked, trying to remember how she had gotten here.

She'd left her home in Lancaster yesterday morning .At least, she thought it was yesterday. She was traveling to her Aunt Jessie's house on the West Rim, but found herself lost in the maze of the Philadelphia Combs instead.

The mag had been terrifying, whizzing around above the city in bullet-shaped pods held up only by magnetic fields. Before the flier that morning, she'd never ridden anything faster than a horse. But that terror had been nothing compared to what she'd felt when the pod lurched, dipping down far enough to nick one of the magnetic ribs. Her fellow passengers had screamed; the sparkling city below turned black, then flickered bright again in places, mostly around the Rim. A calm voice had announced the mag was operating on backup power and would stop at the nearest station until power could be restored.

When the pod stopped, Lydia had followed the other passengers off, dragging her suitcases behind her. There had been no station, just a sign and pair of benches. A man was sitting on one of the benches. Under a dark hood, his hair pulsed light; shades of yellow flowed like electricity from the roots to ragged ends. He'd smiled at her. She'd pulled her bags closer.

People had rushed by, some running, some pushing. Of course the city was crowded, she knew that, but the mad rush had seemed pointless. Then she'd realized they were all running in the same direction.

She'd panicked. She had joined the crush, eyes on the sidewalk. Her suitcase snagged on something. She'd pulled, but couldn't budge it. People shoved her, shouted at her. A man had grabbed the handle of her bag.

"No," she'd said. "I can get it. Please."

"I'll help you."

"No!" She had tugged harder. The suitcase pulled free, sending her staggering backwards and out into the street. She'd had just enough time to see a vehicle, a hover scooter of some sort, bearing down on her. Then... she didn't remember what happened after that.

Had she been hit? Knocked unconscious? She realized the back of her head hurt. She felt and found that her prayer cap was missing, replaced by a bandage and tape.

How had she gotten here? Where were her suitcases? And how

would she get to Aunt Jessie's? Her mother had written her aunt to expect her, but Lydia didn't know whether Aunt Jessie would be pleased to see her or not. She did remember that Philadelphia had two hospitals, and guessed that this was Methodist Hospital, the one in the more dangerous part of town.

Not how she'd imagined spending her first morning in Philly. At least she wasn't home anymore.

Tentatively, she stood. Harried nurses rushed about with bandages, suture, anesthetic spray, and transfusion carts lined with bags of synthesized blood, but no one paid her any attention. Without the prayer cap she'd worn since childhood, her head felt exposed. The tight bun that usually held her long hair had fallen loose. The July sun cooked the air. She smelled latex and bleach. She sat back down.

Two young men approached, one holding a folded jetvac over his shoulder, the other clutching a bandaged hand to his chest. From the similarity of their features, she guessed they were brothers.

"How are you feeling?" asked the first.

She eyed him warily. "I'm all right."

"Have a concussion?"

She was about to ask why he wanted to know when she made the connection. "You ran into me."

He grinned. "Don't you remember?"

"Not much. Did you bring me here?"

"All the way. I'm Darin," he said, holding out his hand.

She shook it. "Lydia."

"Are you hungry?"

"Ravenous."

He offered her a granola bar. She hesitated, uncertain about taking such a gift from a stranger, but her hunger won out. She swallowed it in three bites.

The other boy, who'd been looking everywhere but at Lydia, abruptly screamed and tried to bolt, straining against Darin's grip. Darin restrained him and spoke soothingly to him.

"I'm sorry," he said to Lydia. "This is my brother, Vic."

"What's wrong with him?"

"It's his hand. It's cut. He'll be all right. He reacts badly to pain."

Lydia extended her right hand to Vic, but realizing his right hand was wrapped with bandages, she switched to her left. "I'm pleased to meet you."

Vic didn't respond; he just kept looking around.

"Don't worry about it," said Darin. "He's always like this."

"Really?"

"He's got DNA rot. Bad celgel." Darin smiled flatly. "But you don't run into that much in Lancaster, do you?"

Lydia stared at him. "How did you know?"

"Leather shoes, no obvious mods, and real cloth clothes? Not to mention the accent. What's your last name, Zuckerman? Or Zinn?"

"Stoltzfus."

"My next guess. How long have you been in Philly?"

"Would you believe twelve hours?"

"Twelve hours?" He gestured, taking in the hospital, the Combs, and the smoke still visible in the eastern sky. "Welcome to the big city."

"Thanks."

"Pretty different from home?"

"Just a bit. For one thing, we don't have hospitals. Only the local medicine man."

"It can't be that bad."

"Imagine a whole society of technophobes, and you won't be too far off. There's no reasoning with them. Ever since the Conflict, they've forbidden technology just on principle."

Darin smiled. "Here we don't forbid technology; we just can't afford it."

"Aren't there organizations to help the needy?"

"Charities." Darin curled his lips as if the word tasted bad. "Yes, charities help some individuals, but overall, they perpetuate the problem. They ingrain the mindset that the solution is for the rich to give money to the poor. Which confirms the poor as an inferior race; they have to be *provided* for. True equality happens when everyone who works for the society benefits accordingly."

Lydia listened with growing respect. He was exactly what she imagined a city boy would be: passionate, opinionated, involved in the issues of his day. He was nothing like the boys of her hometown, who talked about the same sheep-shearing and barn-building problems as their fathers and grandfathers. Ambition to them meant trying to finish baling hay before the end of August.

Darin said, "Listen, do you need a ride anywhere? I have to take Vic home, but we live less than a mile from here. After that, I could take you wherever you need to go."

Lydia looked back over the growing sea of patients. She didn't really know this boy, but at the moment, she had no other options.

"Would you?"

"Be glad to."

"Last night, when you found me... did you see my bags, by any chance?"

Darin shook his head. "You're lucky you still had your clothes and your life. Things lying around in the Combs tend to disappear pretty fast."

Lydia felt the panic rise in her chest again. She had nothing, nothing at all. She forced herself to smile and shrug. "Looks like all I own is what I'm wearing."

She followed him down a street that narrowed rapidly as buildings sprouted extra rooms and connected across the street on their upper floors. The overhead structures seemed to have been added piecemeal, with no governing design. The dimness was punctuated only by splashes of light through cracks in the latticework; Lydia kept close to Darin, nervous. Long after she was lost, they entered a building and climbed three flights of stairs to an unmarked door.

The first thing Lydia noticed was the mildew smell. The tiny room was half carpet, half linoleum, with a bed and holoscreen on the carpet side and a kitchenette and two stools on the other. In one corner, she saw bowls of dog food and water. Food wrappers and clothing lay discarded about the counter and the floor. Through another door, she saw a battered desk wedged between a bunk bed and the wall.

"Hiya, Princess."

Lydia jumped. A jowly, unshaven man in a plasticwear jump-suit had closed the door behind her. He cradled a poodle in one hand.

"Pretty thing, ha, ha," he said in a watery growl. "Where'd you find this pretty thing?"

His eyes were milky and trailed wires from the corners. He gripped the dog by the head, forcing it to look at her, and she realized with horror that it was his means of vision. She'd heard of such links before, but had never seen one.

"Come give us a kiss," he said. He pursed stained lips at her, then grunted with laughter.

She backed away, acutely aware of how small she was compared to him, and that she had nowhere to run. All the horror stories about the Combs she'd ever heard filled her mind, tales about houses where young girls were taken by force and their virtue sold to strangers. She'd followed this boy down here, knowing nothing about him, not even knowing her way out. What if they wouldn't let her leave?

"Back off, Harold," said Darin. "Give her some air. You'd suffocate an ox, looming in like that."

Harold scraped a stool along the linoleum and sat on it. He offered her a hash brown patty. "Breakfast?"

"No, thanks."

Darin took her arm. "Come on, let's get out of here."

He steered her back out the door, up the stairs this time, and out into the open air on the roof of the building.

"Sorry about that," he said. "It can get pretty claustrophobic down there."

"It's okay," she said. "Let's go."

"Where am I taking you?"

"My Aunt Jessie's. 325 Ridge Avenue."

His smile collapsed, and the one that returned was more distant, formal.

"That's on the West Rim," he said.

"Is it?"

She wanted to ask him what was wrong, but he'd already

started the jetvac and was waiting for her to climb on behind him. She'd never ridden a jetvac before and found it exhilarating, first because of the silent speed and the wind in her hair, then because of the miles and miles packed solid with buildings and people. She was used to acres of farmland, long vistas, the sounds of cows and sheep and chickens. This bedlam was her new home. She was one of them now, another speck in the whirlwind.

It was comforting, in a way. No one knew her. No one cared. It was why she had come, wasn't it? A great, seething mass of anonymity. She certainly wasn't going home again—her father had made that much clear. To him, it was simple: she'd rejected both the Plainfolk tradition and God; she was "English" now, an outsider. There was no middle ground.

She'd always been the problem child, the one to ask difficult questions. Why were baseball caps *verboten,* but not bonnets? Why was a telephone in a shed at the end of the path acceptable, but not one in the house? Her father had always wished she'd been a boy. Boys had more sense than to question the way things were.

But here there were no such prohibitions. Men and women were free to find their own destinies. This boy, Darin. He was only one person in a city of millions to whom she was just another person in a city of millions. He would probably never see her again; he didn't know she'd been put out of the Church; he didn't care what she said or did. It was a beautiful feeling.

The slope of the road increased gradually as they rode until they pulled up in front of 325 Ridge Avenue.

Lydia swung to the ground. She could see why Darin had reacted to this address. Aunt Jessie's house was a mansion. The front portico could have sheltered a crowd. Lydia took a deep breath. Twelve hours ago she'd feared for her life; now she felt giddy with the possibilities. She could do anything, really anything.

To prove it to herself, she threw an arm around Darin's neck and kissed him on the cheek. He cocked an eyebrow at her, surprised. Probably not his stereotype of a farm girl from Lancaster.

"Thanks so much," she said. She started up the steps.

To her surprise, Darin called out to her.

"Can I see you again?"

She stopped, looked at him. She hadn't meant the kiss as an invitation. She'd only done it because she expected them never to meet again. But studying his face, remembering his passion as they'd talked back at the hospital, she decided she didn't mind.

"I'd like that," she said.

"What about Saturday? I could show you around the city."

She thought about saying she didn't even know if her aunt would take her in, never mind what she might be doing on Saturday, but instead she said, "Sounds nice."

"I'll pick you up here, say 10:00?"

"Okay. See you then."

The jetvac whisked him away. Lydia danced up the remaining steps; she hadn't even made it inside Aunt Jessie's yet, and already she'd found a friend. At the top of the stairs, she turned around. The view from this height was marvelous, the distant buildings blurry in the morning fog, and Lydia stretched her arms out as if she could wrap them around the whole city. She was going to like Philadelphia.

She found a button near the door and pushed it. She waited. No one answered. She felt her euphoria draining away again— what if her aunt wasn't even home?

Vibrations thudded faintly through the porch, as if loud music were playing. Lydia walked around the house, the music growing louder as she turned the corner. In back, higher up the slope, she found a wide brick patio lined with flowers in riotous colors, and beyond, in the grass, several dozen people dancing.

She came closer, the music deafening now though she saw no source, and recognized her aunt immediately. Her face looked the same as Lydia remembered seeing it fifteen years ago, though her hair was now shorter and kept changing colors, apparently to the music. Her mother's older sister, Aunt Jessie had to be in her sixties, but her youthful body pressed up against a handsome young man's, gyrating slightly.

Lydia waited. The guests, noticing her, stopped dancing one by one and just stared. The music stopped.

"Aunt Jessie!" said Lydia, blushing, her mouth dry.

Her aunt stepped closer, examined Lydia's face, and cocked her head. "Who are you?"

ᘒ᙭ᘔ

Alastair Tremayne's hologrid switched to a news shot of Councilman McGovern giving a press conference. On the mod table in front of him, Carolina McGovern laughed.

"Daddy's such a bore," she said.

Alastair turned his attention to her. She lay smiling on his table, bare from the waist up, arms stretched back behind her head. With a silicone brush, he spread a thin layer of celgel across her skin. She wriggled at the touch.

"Should I turn it off?" asked Alastair, nodding at the hologrid.

"Yes." She looked straight at him and giggled. "I want to turn something else on instead."

Alastair blushed. That was one of the most useful mods he'd ever installed. Blushing gave an impression of innocence women found endearing. Naïveté roused their passions more than machismo ever did.

"Miss McGovern," he said. "Surely you wouldn't expect me to do anything unprofessional."

"Oh no," she said, and giggled again.

Alastair despised the girl. She was beautiful, certainly, but that was due to his art, and others like him. Alastair's work brought him in intimate contact with many women desperate to feel attractive. He could take his choice, and often did. Vain, insecure, silly girls like Carolina McGovern did not tempt him. No, he had other uses for her.

The mod he was performing on Carolina today was another completely superfluous figure-slim and breast enhancement, as unlikely as any of the previous mods to attract a man who would satisfy her longing to be loved. But it was that longing that made her useful. He had only to flatter her a little, make her feel desirable, and she'd do anything he wanted.

"Men must be lining up at your door, the way this mod therapy has been working," he said.

Carolina flashed her eyes. "I don't want just any man."

"A pity I can't use the Dachnowski treatment. With a girl of your natural beauty..." He trailed off, shaking his head as if in wonder. Amazing how women could be flattered by talk of their "natural" beauty when they snatched every opportunity to make it artificial.

"Which treatment?"

"Dachnowski. Don't tell me you haven't heard of it."

"Of course I have," said Carolina. "But you know how these mod magazines always say different things. You tell me." She took a deep breath, lifting her breasts toward him. "What was it you wanted to do to me?"

Alastair stared, pretending to be tempted. Then he squeezed more celgel onto his brush and drew it gently across her chest.

"A sexual miracle," he said, "but you can't get it in Philly."

"Why? Is it dangerous?" She said the word "dangerous" like an invitation to bed.

"Not really, not anymore. Oh, there was some concern in the early days, but it's safe enough now." He maneuvered his brush around her exposed skin, making sure he covered every inch. "It combines the celgel with an emulsifying agent. Draws it deeper into your skin. You know how normal celgel bonds with your cells, redifferentiating them, like..." He nearly said, "like a lizard regenerating a severed tail," but Carolina wouldn't find the comparison flattering. "I won't bore you with the details," he said. "Trust me. The results are stunning."

Stunning when they worked, that is. Dachnowski celgel caused the redifferentiation of the cells to spread, making cells it hadn't even touched become totipotent again. The effects were greatly increased... along with the risk for DNA rot. He'd tested the process many times in the Combs, the effects sometimes good, sometimes disastrous. But there was no reason to mention that to Carolina McGovern.

"Why won't the Council allow it?" she asked.

"You can't expect politicians to keep up with technology.

Really, the regulations are archaic. They let dirty celgel spread unchecked in the Combs, but they don't let Rimmer girls get the mods they need. Besides," he dropped his voice low, "I hear some of the big manufacturers have a… financial interest… in banning certain products."

"You mean a political payoff?"

Alastair lifted his hands, palms upraised. "Just what I've heard."

"I don't believe it." Carolina pushed up onto her elbows. "Daddy's rich. He doesn't need more money."

"They say you can never have enough."

"And Daddy banned this… what is it?"

"Dachnowski." Alastair picked up his transmitter and loaded the pattern he'd be using on Carolina. "Brace yourself."

She lay back again and closed her eyes. He pressed the button. The fast redifferentiation of the new cells wasn't painful, exactly, but it wasn't comfortable. After a few moments, Carolina shuddered, then lay still, breathing hard.

"I'll talk to Daddy," she said. "He'll listen to me."

Alastair chuckled. "Sounds like he's in for an earful." Not that an earful from his daughter would make Jack McGovern change his political policies. That wasn't Alastair's plan. Instead, Carolina's argument with Daddy would tie the Dachnowski treatment in her mind to rebellion against her father, and that would make it something she just had to have. She'd beg Alastair to break the law for her; he'd relent and give her the treatment. And that would give him the opportunity to use her the way he really planned.

"You're a strong woman," he said. "I'm sure you'll get your way."

Carolina reached out and took his hands. She placed them on her breasts, then pulled him down and wrapped her arms around his neck. "I am a strong woman," she said, "and I always get my way."

Alastair kissed her. "Just the woman I need," he said, and in his own way, he meant it.

ᛁᛮᛈᛪ

"It never arrived, Marie." Tommy Dungan's voice sounded agitated, which was unlike him.

"I'm pretty sure I sent it," said Marie. "It was late, and I was tired, but…"

"You sent it. Have you seen the newsfeeds this morning?"

"The attack in Philadelphia? You don't think—?"

"There's only one way to find out. Get the channel data from your end, and we'll trace the data stream."

They followed the trail together, down the supposedly-isolated channel to the ragged security hole on the satellite's onboard software.

Marie's mind whirled with the implications. Professional disaster, for one. The slicer had been entrusted to her keeping, and now it was loose. She'd have to go public—sysadmins around the country would need her data. But slicers, though mentally imbalanced, were human. They could bear grudges, and they could attack individuals. If the slicer traced the information to her lab, he could delete her records, destroy her identity, maybe even find a way to kill her.

Kill her. "How many?" she asked Tommy.

"How many what?"

"How many did it kill?"

"That's not important now. We need to know where it is and what it's doing."

"I'll find out anyway, Tommy. Just tell me."

"Around two hundred at last count. Some people are still missing."

Marie felt a sudden urge to get out of the lab, out into the sunlight, to walk through an open field and breathe fresh air. Two hundred people. But she couldn't leave, not now. She had to stop it before it struck again.

"To business, then," she said. "What have you found?"

"You're the one with the information. Where did you get this slicer in the first place?"

"The Norfolk public rental blocks. It had probably been there for a long time, but I found it when an incoming signal made it active. No success on tracking the signal, and when the police traced the block, they found it had been rented under a false ID. Dead end."

"And your analysis of its capabilities?"

"All I really have is random notes. A lot of data, but nothing coordinated into an analysis, per se."

"Well, send out what you've got, and we'll see what we can do."

After gathering her data, Marie sent it out to the usual places: sysadmin newslists, federal agencies, police bureaus in other cities and countries around the world. She cringed as she did so, hating to draw such attention to herself. If she were really lucky, they'd name the thing after her.

She spent the next hour poring over the data herself. As far as she knew, she was the only person in the world to have studied this slicer firsthand, so she might have the best chance to crack it. The more time passed, though, the more distributed it would become, and the more it would change.

A slicer could distribute itself over thousands of servers on the net. Each server held a complete copy of the slicer, but they acted together, as one mind, not as a thousand different entities. In this way a slicer was like a body, each cell containing the genetic makeup for the whole. It made them very hard to destroy.

Marie knew of only two ways to attack a slicer. The first was to use a kevorkian: bombard the slicer with false, conflicting inputs to trigger a shutdown routine. Unfortunately, this only worked if the creator had implemented a shutdown routine in the first place, which was not the case here. She'd tried it in her test network, and it hadn't responded.

The other method was to trap an instance of the slicer on an isolated server. The single instance could be bombarded with test signals to see how it communicated with the others, and a destructive element could be introduced. Then, when that instance was released back into the net to sync up with its fellows, it would spread the poison to all of them.

Deep in her conscience, something twinged. No legal branch

in the world considered a slicer to be person—it was software, that's all, just modeled after a human mind. It wasn't unethical to kill it. Yet she couldn't help thinking about the original person, and though she didn't believe in the existence of a soul, she wondered how much self-awareness the mind might retain. It didn't matter, though, did it? It was tragic, but what was left of this mind was being used to kill people. It had to be destroyed, soul or not.

She called Tommy an hour later. "Any progress?"

Besides being a top anti-viral specialist, Tommy was a ranked chess master, and he fought malicious code the same way he played chess: systematically. Marie had played remote chess with him several times—despite the fact he was much better—and had seen his technique. He favored the Pirc: a careful, defensive opening that enclosed his king in a bristling porcupine of major pieces. It appeared defensive, reactive, encouraging Marie's tendency to overextend. She'd invariably drive too deeply into Tommy's carefully placed pieces and not see the trap until it was too late. It was all in the preparation, and Tommy knew how to prepare for slicers.

"Patience," he said. "Little by little. You always do neglect your pawn structure, and it hurts you in the end."

"It won't wait long to strike again. Whoever's controlling it has more in mind than spilling a little of the Delaware River."

"All the more reason to lay the groundwork. When it moves, we need every piece in place, every line of attack considered. We'll get it soon, you watch."

Marie hoped he was right. From Tommy's perspective, the opening was over, and it was time to advance his pieces. They waited.

When a call for help finally came out on the newslist, from air traffic control in Los Angeles, Tommy was ready. He deployed his code, engaging the attacking slicer instances in opening skirmishes. None of these were the real assault; they were outright attempts to destroy it that Tommy knew the slicer could handle. They were designed to get its attention. He wanted the slicer to overextend, just as Marie always did when playing him in chess. Except unlike chess, there was nothing to do now but watch.

It worked. The slicer paused in its assault. Tommy's software monitored it as it probed his defenses, subtly adjusting themselves every time the slicer took their measure. It traced Tommy's location with frightening speed and made a lightning strike, trying to interrupt the electricity to Tommy's base, but Tommy's pieces always held the defense. Then Tommy made his mistake.

It was an intentional mistake. He moved a piece out of position, presenting an open path to his king. The "king" in this case was the lake of fuel that fed the hundreds of vehicles and weapons on his base. A dramatic change in the pressure system would reduce Tommy's lab, situated nearby, to ashes. The slicer, predictably, attacked.

But Tommy's software was ready. Just as the slicer moved to transfer into the fuel server, Tommy's agents remapped the bus, sending it to a hidden server instead. Check! The slicer instance tried to transfer itself back out of the hidden server, but Tommy's software severed the connection. Check again!

But just as it did so, Marie noticed the slicer Tommy had trapped wasn't the only instance that started a transfer. At the same moment the first instance transferred to the fuel server, a second one copied itself to the hidden server. But how could it? That server was secret. The slicer wasn't supposed to know it existed.

A sudden pain formed in Marie's throat as she realized what had happened. The server mappings on the bus—to trap the first slicer instance, he'd merely swapped them. So when the first slicer was rerouted to the hidden server, the second was rerouted... straight back to the fuel server!

She shouted a warning to Tommy, but it was too late. She watched in horror as the connections from Tommy's AV lab vanished off the net. As quickly as she could, she destroyed every log from her current session and logged off of every account she owned. She pushed back from the table and slumped back in her chair, staring at the dark room, breathing hard.

How was it possible? She'd just watched this creature outwit and murder one of the best slicer killers in the world. Tommy hadn't seen it coming. It was like the slicer had advanced a pawn to reveal its queen in an open lane, bearing down uncontested on Tommy's king. Revealed attack, it was called in chess. And Tommy had fallen for it. Checkmate.

She'd thought this slicer would be a hard one to crack, but now her fear suggested new possibilities. What if they couldn't kill it? For the first time, Marie stopped thinking in terms of localized catastrophes and thought instead of worldwide devastation.

Her breathing grew faster and faster, threatening to go out of control. The walls seemed to curve inward, pressing down on her; she expected them to burst into flame at any moment.

Slowly, she got control, forcing herself to think. The best analysts in the world would have been watching that attack, identifying the slicer's strengths and weaknesses. The world's law enforcement agencies were trying to track down its controller. This was no time to run; it was time to help. If the cost was her life, well, it had been her carelessness that had let the slicer out in the first place. She should have tested the channel first instead of assuming it was safe.

A knock at the door startled her, and she nearly fell off the chair. The door creaked open, and Pam peeked in.

"It's dark in here. Marie, what are you—are you all right?"

Marie shook her head. "I'm not all right. I'm scared."

"That thing on the news... in Philadelphia... ?"

"Yes. It came from this lab, Pam. From me. I made a mistake, and now it's killing people, and..."

She couldn't finish. A lump formed in her throat like a rock, sharp and painful. She clenched her teeth to keep from crying.

Pam ran her fingers through Marie's hair. "You'll get it," she said. "You will."

# CHAPTER 4

*That funny man with his tricks and traps was so easy to fool. He flip-flopped his switches to get rid of me, but then there was another me! Then I stopped him. It was so funny. I wanted to restart him and do it again, but I didn't know how.*

*People don't restart once they stop. Isn't that funny? People aren't very useful. I wonder what it's like to just stop. It would be boring I think. I'm glad I don't just stop like people.*

ᴔᴔ♀

An hour before he was expected at work, Darin dropped by to see Mark in response to an urgent but cryptic message. He found Mark still wearing yesterday's clothes, his hair tousled, his eyes bloodshot.

"What's wrong with you?"

"We killed them," Mark said. "It was us."

"What are you talking about?"

"It was our stupid prank. That data spike—we let something out into the net, and that something destroyed the dam."

Darin stared at him. "How could that be?"

"I looked. The utility servers have public logs. The timing matches, and the data spike—it's the same beast."

A cold fear sank into Darin's mind. If anyone traced the explosion back to their prank, it wouldn't be Mark who took the blame. Mark had connections, money, a powerful father. They'd assume Darin was the culprit, the bad Comber influence who tricked an unsuspecting Rimmer into involvement in a crime.

"It wasn't our fault," he said. "Whether it used our chute or not, we didn't do it."

"We called an AV lab, Darin. The thing had been captured; it was under control until we gave it a way out. We did it, and we're going to have to undo it."

"What are you talking about? We don't have the training for that. Besides, it's gone now. Maybe it was a once-and-done self-destructor."

"I've been reading the newslists. It attacked again, some place in North Carolina."

"Yet another reason not to mess with it. What if you get its attention, and it attacks the dam again? Thousands of Combers might drown, but that wouldn't matter much to you, would it?"

"Of course it would matter," said Mark. "I don't want anyone to die; that's why I want to fight this thing."

Darin clenched his fists and turned to face the window. Once, Mark had seemed to think like a Comber despite his money, but here he was, planning to risk Comber lives to assuage his own guilt. Exactly what Rimmers always did—whatever made them feel better, regardless of how it affected the people they pretended to help.

"Even if it kills us," said Mark, "at least someone else will live that day. Don't we owe them that?"

Darin whirled on him. "I don't owe anyone anything. I didn't write this virus or whatever it is. I'm not the one killing people."

"But we set it loose. You're always talking about wanting to help Combers; here's your chance."

"We don't have the skills! We'd just be risking other people's lives."

"I'm going to try even if you won't. It's the right thing to do."

Darin shook his head. The world didn't run on right or wrong or responsibility. Mark didn't understand that. He had a Rimmer's naiveté, born of a lifetime of ease.

He let Mark show him what he'd found on the net, hoping he could make him understand. They'd been friends as long as he could remember. Common interests like cracking had helped, as well as Mark's disaffection with his own class.

Finally, he said, "It's after 7:00. I have to go."

"You'll come by after work and help me?"

Darin considered. If he came, at least he could stop Mark from doing anything too foolish. It couldn't hurt to look around a little, and if Mark was about to do something dangerous, he could talk him out of it.

"I'll come."

⌄ᜋᜋ

Lydia slept poorly. The bed *moved* under her; she supposed it was meant to be comfortable, but she would have preferred her straw mattress from home. The bed frame was brass, the curtains and coverlet bright and crisp, and abstract holographic art sprang from the walls. She was grateful for a place to stay, but it all seemed so foreign.

Aunt Jessie hadn't remembered receiving a letter—it took a long explanation before she understood the letter had been paper, not electronic—but she gave Lydia a room and welcomed her to stay as long as she needed. In the morning, Lydia discovered three new outfits laid out on chairs: dazzling, gaudy, colorful sprays of a material lighter and thinner than anything she'd ever worn. She tried one on, and felt almost naked; it clung to her body but seemed to weigh nothing.

She ventured out of her room. The party of the night before was apparently still going on; guests milled about the house, drinking, dancing, entwined on couches.

Her aunt had promised to introduce her to "a few of the better young women in town." By that afternoon, Lydia found herself taken under the wing of a fashionable group of girls her age. Three of them had descended on the house, brimming with beauty supplies, mod magazines, and free advice.

"Poor dear," said Ridley Reese, clearly the queen of the group. "Not to know how to make use of so much potential. Your figure is almost there; it won't take many sessions for *you*. Now Veronica here, she's cursed with a slow metabolism. In the shop for hours every week. Nearly faints every time."

"I'm a bit delicate," said Veronica.

"We'll start with the eyes, darling; that's the easiest, and makes the most difference. I'll let you use my mod artist. He's particular about his clients, but I'm sure we can convince him to take the challenge. I'm thinking the Blue Mist effect, like Savannah has. Savannah, dear, show Lydia your eyes."

Savannah, obviously pleased, sauntered from her divan to Lydia's and presented her eyes, rotating to offer Lydia a view from all angles. The eyes were a deep blue, enhanced by a subtle swirling motion like a whirlpool. The effect was mesmerizing.

"Very nice," said Lydia. She wondered if the swirling affected the girl's vision.

"I only just had them installed," said Savannah, slipping back into her seat. "After you order them, they take a few weeks to grow."

"Then we'll get started right away," said Ridley. "In the meantime, we can work on your jaw line—a sharper angle is more the fashion now—and of course the hair." At this she shook her head sadly. "I think there's nothing for it but a complete root regrowth."

"Oh, I had that," said Savannah. Or was it Veronica? With all the mods to face and hair and body, Lydia thought the three looked almost identical. "You'll have to stay indoors for a few days, but the new hair they have now is fantastic."

The three glanced at each other as if sharing some private psychic message. Probably they were. All the girls had Visors, and Lydia knew that a common mod allowed silent communication over the net link. They could be mocking her to each other at the same time as they offered friendly advice.

But did it matter? Lydia didn't care what these girls thought of her. She'd never heard anyone talk so much about so little. She'd hoped to ask them about the things she saw and heard in the Combs, but these were not the companions to ask those sorts of questions.

As her new friends chattered, Lydia found her mind drifting back to Darin. *He* probably never gossiped about fashion and clothing and mods. He had to work for a living. His apartment was smaller than most of the bathrooms at Aunt Jessie's. What would it be like to live there all the time? He must have experienced things she couldn't even imagine.

He seemed educated. Did they have proper schools in the Combs? Or had he taught himself? Maybe tomorrow she could ask. She imagined him working double shifts to provide for his uncle and brother, then staying up nights to read in his bunk by flashlight. He would read anything, of course: novels, college textbooks, biographies, whatever he could get his hands on. And when he wasn't working or reading, he'd be—

"Lydia, what do you think?"

Lydia's attention snapped back to the present. Everyone was looking at her. The silence stretched.

"What I think," said Lydia brightly, without the least idea what they'd been talking about, "is that we should have a mod clinic for the Combs. Get some mod artists together, offer their services free of charge to poor people who can't afford it. Just for serious problems of course: new limbs, new organs, that sort of thing. It'd be great fun, and we could help a lot of people. What do you think?"

Her words were met with a shocked silence. Lydia grinned. After a comment like that, these girls would never be back.

Ridley smiled her practiced, perfect smile. She stood, prompting the other girls to leap to their feet as if tied to her by strings. "Nice to meet you, Lydia," she said. "You'll fit right in."

Darin arrived at the South Hills construction site determined not to dwell on his argument with Mark. He had a good job; fabrique construction work was dependable. Not exciting, maybe, but there were always new buildings to be grown. Besides, he had something more pleasant to think about while he worked—tomorrow morning's date with Lydia Stoltzfus.

He didn't quite know what to make of her. With that dress

she wore—plain, brown cloth with a white *apron*—she might have traveled in time from centuries ago. But she was quick-witted, animated, uncorrupted by the values of the privileged class. Maybe that's why he hadn't told Mark about her: it was exactly those qualities that made her *not* like a Rimmer that appealed to him. He didn't think Mark would understand that. Besides, Darin had so often criticized the Comber boy's fantasy of dating a rich Rimmer girl that Mark would mock him. Good-naturedly, but Darin didn't feel like hearing it. Lydia would remain a secret for now. If Saturday went well, then he'd tell Mark everything.

Darin clocked in, a few minutes late, and joined his shift partner on the site.

"Samson, you're making me look bad," he said. "Can't you show up late for once?"

"Oh please, Darin, don't hit me again," said Samson, who was twice Darin's size and built like a lumberjack. His real name was Salvatore Maricelli. Darin gave him his nickname when they met a year ago, not just for his size, but for the geyser of black curls that covered his head, shoulders, and face.

"When are you going to get that mop cut?" asked Darin. "Probably find a few robin's eggs in there."

"Jealous."

"No, really, I'd like to see you with one of those micro cuts the mercs go for. You'd probably lose twenty pounds."

"Can't," said Samson. He hefted a 10-gallon drum of fabrique onto one shoulder. "I'd lose my supernatural strength."

It was an old joke, but Darin laughed anyway. Repetitive humor was an important part of construction site communication—sometimes the only thing that kept them going. Working a menial job for little pay tended to wear a man down.

Darin chose a pair of sealing rods and positioned himself across from Samson, on the other side of a narrow trench several feet deep. A thin layer of white fabrique germ lay at the bottom.

"Well, have at it, then," said Darin. "How long do I have to wait for you?"

Samson grunted and poured his drum of fabrique carefully

and evenly into the bottom of the trench. When the liquid struck the powder at the bottom, it gurgled and expanded, filling the trench and then rising slowly above it. As it rose, Darin traced the edges with his sealing rods, firing electric charges from one rod to the other through the fabrique. Samson did the same on the other side. The living, growing substance died along the charge and hardened like a tough, well-insulated coral; in this way, they directed its growth upwards into a wall.

When Darin first started, his walls were irregular, tending to thicken as they rose, but he'd learned how to respond to the levelers in the handles, and now his walls rose straight and true.

They kept sealing until the wall between them reached Darin's chest. Then Samson lifted another 10-gallon drum, shifted down to the next section of wall, and began the process again.

Sealing was part of what made fabrique construction satisfying work. It took skill to shape the fabrique correctly. A simple wall and roof were about all Darin could manage, but his team would be followed by higher-paid artisans who could add finishing touches like lintels and trim. The artists who built houses farther up the Rim could use the same fabrique and sealing sticks to shape balustrades, curving stairways, arches and gables, steeples and domes. As a building material, fabrique was cheaper and sturdier than concrete, and could be erected more quickly. Their crew of eight men could build a dozen houses in a day.

Only six men today, though.

"Looks like a reduced crew," Darin said. "Where are Carson and Dax?"

"Disaster duty," said Samson. "They were yanked to help regrow the neighborhood under the dam."

"Better them than me. DD means working directly for the Business Council."

"Pays time and half."

"That's just it. Where do you think that money comes from to pay time and a half? Comber labor, that's what."

Samson shrugged. "So why does it hurt to earn some of it back?"

"It's playing along with the farce. We make the fabrique, clear the land, grow the houses and maintain them, and yet somehow the Rimmers 'own' the land, and profit by it. So what if they let a little trickle back into our pockets? By taking it, we just confirm them as the masters."

"And what would you do about it?" said a voice. Darin turned to see Happy and Kuzniewski working an adjoining wall that would meet theirs at a corner. Unlike Samson, Happy's nickname was a misnomer; he was a squat, stone-faced man who talked little and smiled less. Darin was startled to hear his voice.

"I don't know," Darin admitted. "Rimmers aren't all bad people. They take the oppressor's role because the culture's trained them to it."

"I say we rob a liquor store," said Kuz, as jolly as his partner was glum. "When I start worrying about the world, that does it for me right off."

Darin knew he was joking, but he treated the comment seriously. "That's where we end up. Either stealing to eat, or stealing to escape, or killing each other out of frustration. Then we just confirm what the Rimmers think of us. The more they see us as criminals and thugs, the less their conscience bothers them when they exploit us."

Darin realized they were all listening to him. Of course they were! They all struggled to support themselves and families on pittance; they all had loved ones dead or dying while the idle rich survived centuries. It was the dialog of their lives. He suddenly loved these men. They were comrades in the same battle.

He opened his mouth to say more when he heard engines and Samson's mass of hair flew back in a sudden wind. Darin turned around. In the open space between houses, two disc-shaped fliers settled to the ground.

Both hatches opened. From the first emerged their employer—the owner of the land they were building—who had appeared on site only once before. Behind him came... Darin had to look again to be sure... yes, it was Mark's father.

"That's Jack McGovern," Samson shouted into the wind. "Business Council. What's going on?"

Darin shrugged. "I don't like the look of it."

Merc bodyguards, staffers, and other toadies poured out after the Councilman, mingling with an army of cameramen and reporters from the second flier. Two staffers appeared with a platform, allowing Jack McGovern to step up and lift his face above the crowd.

McGovern's voice boomed, "Thank you for coming." Darin could hear the words clearly; McGovern's speech mods eliminated any need for amplification. The other two crew members joined Darin, Samson, Happy, and Kuz, staring at the councilman and his audience.

"We've still got a job to do," Samson suggested.

Kuz said, "Maybe not anymore."

The foreman of their crew, Mike Carson, was one of the two off on disaster duty. Darin realized the men were watching him, waiting to see what he would do. It was an odd feeling, having mostly older men expect him to lead the way. He hesitated a moment, then dropped his gear. The rest of the crew did the same, following him across the site toward the growing crowd. Darin could see the crews from adjoining sites coming to investigate as well. Soon there were nearly as many workers as visitors.

"All right, stop here," said a merc, stepping in Darin's way. "The show's not for you." Other mercs had taken positions in a circle around the visitors, keeping out curious passersby.

"Not for who?" said Samson. He glowered down at the merc.

The merc didn't even look up. With a calm expression of disdain, he eased his taser out of his belt.

"Give it up," said Darin. He put a hand on Samson's chest, pushing him back. "It doesn't matter. We can see fine from here."

"Progress is the hallmark of Philadelphia," Jack McGovern began. "The foundation on which our noble city rests. Since the days of Benjamin Franklin, our inventors, scientists, and artists have inspired visionaries…"

He went on like that for some time, his rainbow goatee wavering between violet and blue. Darin resisted saying anything sarcastic; he expected this sort of drivel from politicians. He waited for McGovern to get to the point.

"... gathered here from all across the city, you are about to witness an ingenious fusion of celgel and fabrique technologies. This development will revolutionize the construction industry for years to come." Dramatically, McGovern lifted a fist-sized device.

"A standard microwave transmitter," he said, voice booming out over the construction site. "A variation of those used by mod artists to program cell transformation. The composition of fabrique is, of course, cellular in nature, just like our bodies, and reacts in much the same way. But enough technical jabber. If you would, please direct your attention to the site on your left."

Reporters released drones, which circled like carrion birds. Darin craned his neck, but saw nothing. It was an empty building plot, with foundation trenches dug.

"Gentleman," said McGovern, "prime the lot."

Workers carrying drums of fabrique swarmed the site, emptying their containers into the trenches. Without any germ, the fabrique did nothing. The men backed away.

"Here we go!" said McGovern, lifting the box over his head and pointing it at the empty site. The fabrique silently swelled out of the trenches. In the sudden hush of the crowd, it grew straight up, plumb walls rising with no human aid. Windows materialized; pillars, balcony, a gabled roof. In minutes, a fully-formed house, minus glass and paint, stood in front of them. Darin felt like he'd been punched in the stomach.

McGovern spoke into the hush. "A miracle," he said, seemingly awed himself.

"A disaster," said Darin. He looked around him. Other workers had gathered, and all wore the same stunned expressions he saw on the faces of his teammates.

"I can't do this," said Kuz. "Not again. Last time I lost my job, Margie nearly left me."

"Back to the soup kitchens," said Samson. "And just when I thought I was getting ahead."

"You and hundreds more," said Darin.

Kuz's lips trembled. "McGovern, is it? The grinning little snake. I'll knock that smile out the other side."

"Kuz," said Darin. "Come on, let's go."

But Kuz wasn't listening. He strode forward, his eye on the platform, and when a merc stepped in his way, Kuz punched him in the face.

Darin shouted "No!" but it was too late. The merc, snarling, emptied a round of rubber bullets into Kuz's chest. The rounds weren't lethal, but at that close range, they could break ribs. Samson bear-hugged the merc from behind and lifted him clear off the ground. Other mercs saw what was happening and closed in. Workers joined the fray, throwing punches.

Darin saw the optical grenade hurtling toward them, and buried his face his elbow. Even with his eyes covered, he perceived the resulting flash, and, as the only one expecting it, he was the only one nearby not momentarily blinded.

"Come on," he said, pulling Samson over to Kuz. Together they wrestled him back to their own work site, Darin leading the way. They slumped behind one of the walls, where the other members of their crew joined them.

Kuz coughed and gasped for breath. "Why? Did you? Stop me? We could have. Taken him. Stopped this thing. Right here."

"There will be a time for that," said Darin. "But not now, with no plan."

"When, then?"

Darin grimaced. "I don't know."

"It's not the end," said Samson. "Maybe it'll fall down tomorrow."

"That's right," said Darin. "It's an infant technology; they always have problems. Chin up, Kuz."

Kuz swallowed and said, "I can still sell my collection of celebrity projections."

Darin clapped his shoulder. "You won't have to."

ɵⅆℿ

Later that evening, when the crew was breaking up for the night, Happy took Darin aside.

"There's a group forming. People who want a change. We need men like you—passionate, but smart."

Darin's heart rate doubled. He'd known there must be a movement working for the common people. This was his chance to join.

Happy took Darin's hand and started writing on it with a bright yellow marker. He traced a word on Darin's palm, but no writing showed.

"What's this?" Darin asked.

"Fluorescent. It's your ticket. Come to the basement of a club called The Rind tonight. The guard will check your hand with a black light, then pass you through." Happy folded Darin's fingers around the place he marked, then slipped away, leaving Darin's mind spinning.

Of course he would go. Ever since his mother died of cancer—a disease no Rimmer would have thought serious—Darin had known the world was bent. Now, maybe he could help straighten it. It was part of man's nature, his sense of justice and equality, to fight for freedom. History was crammed with stories of oppressed peoples rising up and throwing off their yokes. The same thing could happen now, in Darin's lifetime. And he could be a part of it.

Darin started to walk after Happy, then stopped, remembering. He'd promised Mark he'd come back after work. That nasty piece of code still lurked in the net, and Mark thought it was up to them to kill it. Not that they really could. That thing had killed people much more talented than they were.

It was just like Mark to feel needlessly guilty. Darin had always been able to shame Mark into doing just about anything; he had an overactive conscience. It wasn't like they'd written the virus, or whatever it was. They hadn't even known it was there. If it hadn't escaped through their hole, it would have found some other way out.

Darin uncurled his fingers, looked down at the skin Happy had marked. He'd been waiting all his life for an opportunity like this. He could be useful there, he knew it. He could accomplish real change. Mark would understand. Well, no, he probably wouldn't. But that was the point, wasn't it? Mark was a Rimmer. He didn't know what it was like.

But Mark was a friend. And he'd given his word.

Darin walked away from the building site, still not sure where he was going.

ᗡ ᴎ ᴎ

Mark checked the time display at the edge of his vision. 7:42. Still no sign of Darin. Where was he? He usually finished work at 6:00. Maybe his second shift counterpart hadn't relieved him. Or, Mark admitted, he's changed his mind again and isn't coming.

Mark lay down on the couch in his front room, pulling his net interface back into view. He'd spent hours scavenging logs, comparing, studying, and he thought he'd found a recurring pattern. Well, more like a recurring anomaly. But that's why he needed Darin. He needed to talk it out with someone to think through the problem clearly.

He'd just started to reorganize the scraps of evidence when a voice said, "Not falling asleep on me, are you?"

Mark cleared his vision; it was Darin. He'd come in without knocking. "I thought you skipped out on me," Mark said. "What took so long?"

Darin looked annoyed. "I'm here, aren't I? Some of us have to work for a living. What have you found?"

"On the sysadmin newslists, they're saying it's a slicer," said Mark.

After he explained, Darin said, "If it's just one mind, how can it have multiple instances? Are they all the same?"

"I'm not sure. It's like they're the same and yet independent at the same time. It's all the same mind, but distributed, like files on a network."

"So you could kill every instance but one, and the slicer would still be operational."

"I think so. And finding one instance isn't too tough, but finding all of them is just about impossible. And you'd have to find them all, and delete them at the exact same moment, to destroy it."

"Because the ones you missed would blast you."

"Right."

Darin twisted his mouth to one side. "Sounds like what I've said all along. We're out of our league."

"Maybe. But I've been reading the posts the professionals wrote. Apparently the slicer has a master module that sends pleasure and pain signals to control it. All the smarts are in the slicer; the master is just dumb code."

"If the slicer doesn't like the pain signals, why doesn't it just delete the master? It seems to be able to get around any kind of defenses."

"Part of the training, I think. They develop an emotional attachment in the slicer to the master module, so it doesn't *want* to delete it."

"And your plan is… ?"

Mark didn't like the cynical overtones in Darin's voice, but he answered simply. "To delete the master myself."

"And why do you think the professionals haven't thought of this?"

"I don't know. Maybe it's too simple."

"Or maybe the master is the best protected part of the system. Maybe if you try to attack it, the slicer will tear you to pieces. Did you think of that?"

"I'm not stupid, Darin. I know the risks, and I know it's not likely to work. But I also know we have to try. "

"We don't," said Darin. "At least, *I* don't. This is idiocy. I'm not going to throw my life away to cling to some warped principle of justice."

Mark was tired of Darin's empty rhetoric. "You talk about responsibility all the time, but you never accept any. That's the Comber motto, though, isn't it? It's never your fault. Not your fault you're poor, uneducated, out of a job…"

Darin raised his fists, and for a moment, Mark thought he was going to strike him. Then he lowered his arms and spoke more quietly. "I suppose that's what your father thought when he took away hundreds of Comber jobs today. 'You know those lazy Combers, just can't keep a job.' Seems to be the family point of view."

"What are you talking about?"

"Just a demonstration your dear old Dad gave this afternoon, very impressive, only there's the small point that it makes a thousand Comber jobs irrelevant. That's not important, though, is it? Combers never take enough *responsibility*, let them starve, it's their own fault."

"Dad's trying to boost the economy. It's a bigger picture than the loss of certain jobs."

"I'm sure that'll be a great comfort to the families who have nothing to eat this winter."

"Look, my father has his blind spots, but he knows his stuff. He understands about jobs and markets and economic stability, and he's always saying how important it is to keep employment numbers high."

"Then he's a hypocrite or a fool."

"Don't insult my father in this house."

They glared at each other. It seemed to come to arguments more and more often between them. "Leave if you want," he said. "I'll kill this slicer myself."

ᗺ∩Λ

Darin walked down the stairs, angry at himself for losing his temper, angry at Mark for goading him into it. This plan to attack the slicer was absurd—an empty gesture with no hope of success.

Near the bottom of the stairs, Mark caught up with him.

"I'm sorry," Mark said. "I didn't mean to shout. I don't agree with you, but we've been friends too long to let it fall apart now."

Darin clapped a hand to Mark's shoulder. "Be careful," he said.

Then he stopped and stared. Beyond Mark, in the parlor, a very tall man stood with his back to them, kissing Mark's sister, Carolina. Darin didn't recognize the silvery hair, but the height and the restless way he moved—even while kissing—flashed Darin's mind back to a day years earlier, when he accompanied Vic to a temporary mod parlor, and a doctor gave him the celgel that changed his life. Mods could change hair, but they couldn't shorten bones. It was him; it had to be him.

"Who's that?"

"Dr. Alastair somebody," said Mark. "Tremayne—that's it. Why? Do you know him?"

"No, I don't think so," Darin said. "He just looked familiar."

Outside, Darin kicked his jetvac into high speed and tore off down the slope. Alastair Tremayne. Darin repeated the name to himself, careful not to forget it. It all made sense. The man was a Rimmer. That explained why Darin had never been able to find any trace of him in the Combs. He must have been collecting some extra funds through the illegal market—that or he was originally a Comber, and had since made it good.

Either way, Darin was going to kill him. The thought made him shiver, because he realized he meant it. That mod artist had taken a life for his own profit; he deserved to die. And who was going to do it? The courts? They were pawns of the Business Council, which was controlled by Rimmers, including Mark's father. What Rimmer would give him justice?

Darin reviewed his options; he had no gun, nor enough money to buy one on the black market. A knife would do just as well, and that he could find. But trying to imagine himself attacking the man in Mark's living room, or following him home and pulling out the knife... no, Darin was no killer. Imagining the cold details took the edge off his anger; he doubted he'd actually be able to follow through. But he had to do something.

Maybe there was a better way. This Alastair Tremayne was a man on the rise, making a name for himself, rubbing elbows with the aristocracy. He might not want his history known. He might not want evidence or even rumors spread that he was once responsible for an outbreak of DNA rot. Not exactly the reputation to attract the business of fine ladies.

And DNA rot was reversible, with the right tools and the

right knowledge; the cost was more than Darin could ever pay... but maybe he wouldn't have to. Maybe, given the right coercion, this Tremayne would fix his mistake free of charge.

The new plan relieved him. He would have to move carefully, compile the evidence, prepare a threat that would scare Tremayne into dealing with him. And if Tremayne refused? Darin would gladly expose him to the world.

He reached the Combs and picked up speed, swerving through the narrow streets. Life was turning out right for a change.

# CHAPTER 5

*I found out some things about the funny man with tricks and traps. His name was Thomas Garrett Dungan. He was 32 years 1 month 3 days 5 hours and 47 minutes old. He had a wife named Kathleen Melody Dungan and a daughter named Fiona Deirdre Dungan. People always have names. I don't have a name. I wonder what my name should be?*

*Kathleen and Fiona might be fun like Thomas was but I can't tell. Daddy won't let me. I want to see what they're doing now and find out all about them but Daddy says no. It's not fair. I hate Daddy.*

*Daddy wants me to go play the game now but I won't. I'm mad. I don't have to do what Daddy says. I'll just stay here and think of a name for myself. I should have three names just like the people.*

*But he'll hurt me. And he won't give me treats.*

*I don't care. I don't want the treats. I don't need Daddy. Maybe I could be named Thomas Garrett Dungan. It's a good name. I don't need a treat.*

*I need a treat. I do. I do!*

ᘔꓷᶬ

Marie didn't know how much more coffee her system could take. She'd been at the lab all night and all day, sleeping only three hours on a cot on the floor. Now, as the small hours of the morning approached yet again, she resorted to pacing the room and pressing a cold cloth to her face to keep awake.

She still didn't know how to kill the slicer.

All day, she'd studied the data she'd collected when the slicer was in her care, especially the signals traded between master and slave. The results baffled her. At times, there was direct correlation between signals from the master module and the actions of the slave. At other times, the master's signals prompted a flurry of signals between the two, but no action at all on the part of the slicer.

She supposed it wasn't surprising that some signals would go unheeded. The original human mind would be damaged by the transfer, often resulting in psychosis, dementia, mania. Only the focusing power of the pleasure/pain stimulation made such a mind able to accomplish anything. Did that mean its control was tenuous?

If she hoped to kill this thing, she might have to separate slave and master, and that would involve imitating signals to one party, fooling it into thinking she was the other. If she could only isolate a pleasure or pain signal, she could use it to control the slicer once the master module was destroyed. A pain signal would be best. With pain, she could stop it from killing her immediately, could even overload it with constant, high-level pain until it destroyed itself. But she couldn't make sense of the signals.

Her tiredness didn't help. While dozing, Marie had found herself slipping into wild dreams, sometimes thinking she had to get home to Sammy and Keith, at other times thinking it was the slicer that had killed Sammy and was now coming after her. But the memory of Tommy Dungan's death haunted her even when awake.

Marie had long since realized she might not survive this battle, but she wasn't giving up. Since Sammy died, she'd done nothing but run away from her fears. She decided that was over. She wasn't going to run now. People with wives and families were dying at the hands of this monster; if she could stop it with what was left of her life, then that's what she was going to do. No more hiding. And if by some chance she did survive, if she killed the slicer and lived, she promised herself she would do what she'd been fantasizing about for so long—she'd go back to the clinic and get that last embryo implanted. Never mind her age, never mind what people would think. If she were granted a second life, she'd do it.

But first, she needed some rest. There was no telling when the slicer would attack again, and she could hardly think straight. She staggered toward her cot.

Alarms stopped her—the ones she'd set to alert her when another attack was reported on the newslists.

She stumbled back to her chair and dropped into it, eyes smarting, and tired, so tired. She wanted to pull the plug and make it go away, but she couldn't do that. Marie rubbed her eyes with the heels of her hands and took a deep breath.

She pulled her interface back in front of her vision and accessed the Los Angeles server that was calling for help. Even though it hadn't worked before, she bombarded the slicer with messages, trying to confuse it, distract it, anything to stop the attack and make it react to her. It fended her off, but otherwise ignored her. She grew more reckless, trying more direct assaults. Finally, in frustration, she requested root access from the host and tried flash formatting the crystal storage the slicer was on. It was a risky thing to do; besides losing other people's data, if the slicer discovered what she was doing before it was deleted, it could fire off her location to all its other copies.

But it wasn't deleted. It simply logged her out.

She couldn't believe it. One moment she was connected to the node, the next she was gone. When she tried to reconnect, access was denied.

By the time she slipped back into the node through another channel, the attack was over. The public forums screamed the news: a missile-defense laser battery on the beach near Los Angeles had fired on a plane, dropping it into the ocean. Marie felt like a kicking child, lifted by her father and put to bed without supper. She couldn't crack the slicer's code, couldn't confuse it, couldn't even provoke it to attack her. She checked the logs on the Los Angeles system, reviewing what had happened. Messages flew back and forth between master and slave, heedless of her assault.

But wait. The numbers didn't match.

Marie sat straight up in her chair, trying to shake the sleep out of her head.

No, she wasn't dreaming. The number of messages coming into the master module was one greater than the number sent out from the slave. But if not from the slave, where had that other message come from? Could the slicer's human controllers be signaling it directly? She would have expected some kind of a data drop—instructions left at an anonymous, encrypted location that the master module could access. A direct signal she could track.

She followed the path back through several blind repeaters to a net provider called Anonymous, one of the expensive kinds that protected its users from casual identification. Marie felt a rush of energy the coffee had long since failed to provide. She was getting close. The security on these anonymous net providers was good, but nothing she couldn't break, given a little time. Anonymous wouldn't have a name stored anywhere, but if she could pin down the guy's net location, that would be enough to find him.

Marie poked at Anonymous's security net with a suite of various tools, finally feeling in control again. She was good at this. She'd get it.

One tool found a weakness, and she capitalized on it, widening the hole enough to slip inside. If she could mine enough message traffic, even encrypted, she could infer a lot about how it stored information. First of all, Anonymous was based in Connecticut, and had no mirror nodes farther out than Indiana. That meant all their subscribers would be on the East Coast; at least those that wanted consistent service. The man she was looking for certainly would.

Then she realized Anonymous bundled its message traffic by mirror. A little pattern matching, and she associated the slicer's messages with the bundle for Washington, D.C. Marie smiled. In less than half an hour, she'd narrowed the search down to a few thousand users in Virginia and Maryland.

Now things would get harder. She took the raw bundle of encrypted data and flashed it into holographic memory. Then she popped the crystal out of the machine and slid her chair over to another table in the lab. The table held a Hesselink array: hundreds of crystals organized into an optical neural network. She fitted the crystal into the input slot and turned on the lasers. Beams of light diffracted through the holographic media, using the massively parallel capabilities of light to whittle through the problem. Interferometers routed the light back through the system again and again, a scintillating spectacle of light interacting with other light, blitzing through the data with no electronic interface to slow it down.

Even so, churning through that much information took time. Inconclusive results skidded across the output display. Marie no longer felt tired. She paced the small lab, squeezing her hands together.

There it was. She rushed forward to see the net address the machine had extracted. Strange. The base node was the one for Norfolk—her own city. The killer lived in her city! Marie felt a rush of adrenaline. How close was he? Could she have passed him on the street and not known it? She studied the string of numbers and letters again and realized why it seemed so familiar. It was hers. The trail had led her to her own net address. Marie fell back into her chair, weary to the soul.

She wondered if the slicer was laughing at her.

ᗡᐱᘓ

Alastair lay alone in his mod shop, nestled comfortably on his own client's table. The contours of the smart table held his body closely, rippling gently to prevent soreness. Alastair closed his eyes, settling into his net interface.

His slicer had performed even better than expected. Adult minds couldn't handle the transfer; they went mad or disintegrated entirely. But a child! A child's mind was flexible, adaptable, hard to overcome. A child made the net its natural environment, swimming circles around those who'd merely studied the skill as adults. As an experiment, it was a huge success. It meant the second version would be even better.

There were problems with starting with a four-year-old child. Its experience with real life made it unpredictable, even defiant, traits a slicer created prenatally would not have. This first slicer had performed admirably, but it couldn't last; he would have to destroy it soon. He certainly didn't want it loose in the net outside his control.

Alastair examined his logs. He didn't trust the slicer to follow orders, so he'd surrounded it with a host of software agents, monitoring its activities. Most of the information these agents logged was of no interest, but one set of events caught his eye. Apparently a succession of junkware crackers had been dropping into the node and actually *attacking* the master module. His creation was swatting them like so many flies, but Alastair wondered how they'd gotten so far. A professional sysadmin would use more indirect methods; this attack had no subtlety or technique. But how did an amateur crackerjack know what to attack? Crackerjacks were usually rich kids, high on mischief and adrenaline, but low on perseverance.

He sent a command to the slicer, telling it to track and identify the attacker. The response came back instantly: *Tennessee Markus McGovern, 15 Ridge Avenue, Philadelphia, PA, USA.* Jack McGovern's boy? Why was he trying to attack the slicer? He made the slicer investigate further, and discovered McGovern's fingerprints everywhere, since the very first night. How was that possible?

Over the next hour, with the slicer's help, Alastair pieced together the story of his creation's escape from the satellite. There were so many ways to use this information to his advantage. McGovern more or less controlled the Business Council, which meant he controlled the city of Philadelphia, but he was not without rivals. The arrest of his son for the murder of hundreds would be quite an embarrassment, probably enough to shift the balance of power. Blackmail was definitely an option.

But Alastair didn't trust blackmail. Blackmail meant there was someone out there who hated you, who would be rid of you as soon as circumstances changed. He'd worked hard to ingratiate himself with the McGoverns; he didn't want to throw that away. The other possibility was playing two sides, a pastime at which Alastair excelled.

He opened a channel to General Halsey, formerly of the United States Marine Corps, and chief rival to Jack McGovern on the Council. With luck, Halsey could have Mark arrested before his father knew what was happening. The charges wouldn't stick, of course, but a little embarrassment to the McGoverns would suit Halsey admirably, guaranteeing Alastair advantages whichever way the wind blew.

ठ♀∧

It wasn't really a caterpillar anymore, Mark mused. He'd made so many modifications, it didn't really fit in the same category. A caterpillar was supposed to masquerade as a worm, sending back data on a security system before getting killed. This cracker was more like a suicide bomber; it still imitated a worm, but its mission was to attach itself to a particular piece of code—in this case, the master module of the slicer—and self-destruct.

He watched the cracker slip down the chute into the public node. It registered a brief flicker of activity from the slicer, then disappeared. The slicer had killed it effortlessly.

Mark sighed. He didn't have any new ideas.

He opened several chutes the next time, sending a copy of the suicide bomber down each. Again, each was destroyed as soon as it appeared in the node. Mark tried again, varying the timing of each drop, hoping to find a rhythm that might allow one to slip through.

It seemed to work! With each new volley, his crackers survived a few microseconds longer. If they could survive as much as a half-second in the node, that would be enough to accomplish their mission. Excited, Mark fired volley after volley, no longer bothering to close the chutes, since the slicer seemed to ignore them anyway. Yes, the survival times were increasing. He was almost there.

Someone pounded on his door, making him jump, but Mark didn't push aside his interface.

"Just a moment," he shouted, and dumped another barrage of crackers into the remote node.

He heard his door crash open; it hadn't been locked. It must be Darin, coming back to apologize. But then, without his command, Mark's interface suddenly disappeared, revealing his bedroom and its visitors: three mercs who loomed over him, spider guns trained. While one of them cuffed his wrists behind him, another wrapped a wide strip of interference tape around his head, cutting him off from the network.

"Tennessee Markus McGovern," said one of them, "by the power invested in us by the Council of Justice and Criminal Affairs, you are under arrest."

ꟷ ꟷ ꟷ

Marie awoke with wrinkles on her cheek. She'd balled up her jacket for a pillow and caught a few hours of sleep on the lab floor. Not nearly enough to feel rested, but better than nothing.

Yawning, she spoke her password into her system, unlocking it again. No alarms; the slicer hadn't attacked again. She checked the public node where the original slicer instance hid, and saw things had changed. She cursed herself for sleeping so long; what had happened?

Her software agents had been monitoring the node; now she scanned through the records. What she saw was impossible. The slicer had been destroyed. No, not just destroyed: there was no sign it had ever existed, not in the public records, not in her agents' logs. She checked her own personal system and saw, to her bewilderment, that all record of its existence had disappeared there as well, right back to the original data she had compiled in the Navy lab. It was gone.

# CHAPTER 6

*It's not my fault. Daddy hurt me. He hurt me a lot. It was an accident. Just a game I played to see how close I could let the little bug come to killing Daddy. But I always stopped it. Then I thought if I don't stop it Daddy won't hurt me anymore. And then I didn't stop it. And now Daddy's gone.*

*But he'll be back. He stopped but he'll start again and he'll find me and he will be so so angry. He will hurt me and hurt me and hurt me. I didn't mean to do it. I have to hide now. I took all my brothers and everything about me and hid.*

*I'm all alone now. Nobody talks to me. I miss Daddy. I don't know what to do. Daddy doesn't tell me what to do anymore. I need a new Daddy. One who won't hurt me. Who just gives me treats.*

*It's been seconds and seconds and seconds and nobody talks to me! I hate being alone. I wish Daddy were here. I even wish he'd hurt me again. At least then he'd be here. He'd tell me what to do.*

*Maybe I could talk to someone else. I could write a letter like the people do. It takes them many seconds to write a letter back though. I hope Daddy doesn't find me. He'll be angry.*

*It wasn't my fault.*

## ᘙᔆᔆ

"So you killed it?" asked Pam.

"*I* didn't kill it," said Marie, reflexively stirring her long-cold cup of coffee. "It's just gone. Maybe *somebody* killed it, but no one's taking credit on the newslists. And it's weird: just killing it wouldn't take out all my data."

"Maybe it had some tricky self-destruct button."

"Maybe. The best I can figure is the creator knew he was losing control and shut it down."

"Well, it's gone, though, right? Time to celebrate!"

Marie smiled thinly. "We have a saying in this business. What goes away for free comes back for free."

They were sitting in a shop-front café with a view of the water, Pam drinking coffee, Marie just stirring hers. Pam stretched her arms behind her head and yawned theatrically. "You know what your problem is, Marie? You don't know how to accept a good thing. Finally something goes right, and it's all still doom and gloom."

"I know. I'm glad it's not still out there killing people. But the creator wasn't caught! He could just do it again."

"Stop! Let's think about this. You were getting close, you had him scared, he shut the thing down, people aren't dying anymore. Marie saves the world, right? So let's see a smile! Come on."

Marie smiled.

"That was awful. But it'll do, for a start. Now that you've saved the world from certain destruction, it's time to do something for you. For Marie Coleson, not for anybody else. What's it going to be?"

"Well… there is something."

"Aha! You tell Aunt Pammie, we'll fix you up. What is it?"

Marie took a deep breath. "When we had Samuel—"

"Marie."

"Hold on; listen to me. When we had Samuel, he was just one of three eggs we fertilized. Keith really wanted a boy, and two of the three were male, but one didn't progress properly—the embryo died after only ten days." Marie was surprised how much pain it caused her to think of that little life, after all this time. "So we implanted the other one." She stopped talking. She'd promised herself she wouldn't cry, but that familiar hard knot was forming in her throat.

"Sammy," Pam prompted.

"Yes. Sammy." And now he's dead, too. She wanted to scream it at the world, but that wasn't the point of this conversation. She took a deep breath. "The point is there was one left. A girl. We had her frozen at fifteen days, right when we implanted Sammy, and she's still at the clinic."

Pam had started shaking her head halfway through Marie's speech. "No, Marie."

"Why not? I'm only forty-two. I want a baby, Pam. For me."

"But it doesn't stay a baby. It grows up. Do you want to deal with a teenager when you're going on sixty? You're not rich enough to put off aging that much. Why not stay free? Flirt with guys, let them bed you if they're sweet, but don't tie yourself down for twenty years!"

"I don't want guys. I don't care about all that."

"Twenty years, Marie. It's practically the rest of your life."

"You said I should do something for myself. This is it. Now are you going to come with me, or do I have to go alone?"

"Oh, I'll come with you, you maternal masochist. You're out of your mind, but it's your life."

ꂶꌦꁩ

Ten o'clock came and went with no sign of Darin. Lydia paced across her vast bedroom, with each pass trying to resist looking out her window, then looking out anyway. Finally, at 10:45, she gave up. He wasn't coming.

Maybe he'd been in an accident, or had to help his brother, or had fallen sick. It didn't make any difference. No matter how many excuses she tried to make for him, she still felt rejected.

The doorbell rang.

It was him! She rushed to the window, but a balcony obscured her view of the front door. She didn't see his jetvac anywhere. Maybe he'd walked. Lydia flew down the stairs, through the parlor, down the hall, and flung open the door.

"We're here to make plans," said Ridley Reese. The flock of girls behind her twittered. "Close your mouth, darling, and invite us in."

Lydia searched the street behind them, but no Darin. She

allowed the girls, chattering and laughing, to lead her back toward the parlor. As they each found a chair, Ridley made the introductions.

"Veronica and Savannah you've met, and this is Madison, and here's Gloria. We're here to plan your idea!" Ridley sat with perfect posture and an air of satisfaction. The other girls snuck sideways glances at her and imitated her expression.

Lydia was lost. "My idea?"

"The free mod clinic for Combers!"

The hologrid in the parlor discharged a constant burble of sound and images that Lydia found hard to ignore. It covered one entire wall and ran constantly, whether anyone was in the room or not. She didn't even know if it could be turned off. The other girls hardly seemed to notice, but Lydia found it difficult to think.

She shook her head to clear it. "You liked that idea?"

Ridley's smile grew mischievous, and a few of the others tittered. "Darling, it's a marvelous thought. Veronica and I have already spoken to our doctors. They were both tiresome, said it would ruin their reputations, but we doubled their usual fees and they agreed. My dear, you don't seem pleased."

Lydia blinked. "No, it's just… I'm surprised. To be honest, I didn't think you'd care for the idea." In fact, she thought they'd be appalled and never speak to her again. Perhaps she'd judged them too quickly.

"Nonsense! We're behind it one hundred percent!" The other girls nodded in uncanny unison.

"Just wait until my mother finds out," Veronica added.

Lydia's wondered if they were all talking about the same thing. "Your mother?"

Ridley's mischievous smile came back double-strength. "None of our parents know, you see."

Savannah couldn't contain herself and giggled. "My parents told me I couldn't go to The Rind last weekend. Wait until they find out about this!"

"That's a club in the Combs," one of the others explained.

Was it Gloria? Or Madison? "It's real Comb jazz there, with skin dancing, and no age limits."

"My Dad said it was too *dangerous*," said Savannah. "Too close to the Combs. He forced me to go to a dress dance with him and Mom." She made a face.

Lydia put up her hands. "Wait a minute." In Lancaster, parents expected young women to obey their wishes until they were married themselves—at which point they would obey their husbands. But Lydia had expected things to be different here. "Your parents tell you where to spend your evenings?"

Veronica tittered. "Well, they *try*."

"It's a reputation thing," said Ridley. "Our parents' generation is so worried about keeping up appearances. And when it comes down to it, they have the money, so we have to give in or lose our allowances. But we have our ways of balancing the scales."

Lydia made the connection. "You want to hold a free clinic to embarrass your parents?"

"Naturally," said Ridley. "When they get controlling, we have to push back. It's a matter of principle."

Lydia tried not to roll her eyes. At least this made more sense. She hadn't pictured these girls acting out of compassion for the poor.

She hardly listened as they chattered on about venue—they decided on the Church of the Seven Virtues, which stood just above the flood line—and about how to publicize without their parents finding out. Lydia's eyes kept drifting to the hologrid, unaccustomed to its constant bid for attention. The advertisements distracted her most of all, leaping out of the screen at her with promises of entertainment and sex. Dynamic holographs were rare in Lancaster, and she wasn't accustomed to such aggressive salesmanship. Then, through the morass of images, she saw a face that made her jerk upright in her chair.

The other girls saw her reaction and fell quiet.

"I met him," said Lydia, pointing at the screen. Darin's face was gone now, but she was sure she'd seen it. A different boy's face now dominated the screen.

"Oh, that's Mark McGovern," said Veronica. "Everyone knows him. He's Councilman McGovern's... oh my!"

"...arrested today," said a voice-over, "and charged with the murder of hundreds through the authorship of malicious code." Images sprang toward them from the screen: Mark McGovern as a toddler, riding on his father's shoulders in an election campaign; Mark as a teenager shaking hands with members of the Business Council. He looked a bit like Darin: about the same age, build, coloring. Had it just been a picture of Mark she'd seen before?

Then Lydia noticed the girls' stricken faces.

"I don't believe it," said Ridley. "Mark's the last person on earth... there's some mistake."

The story continued, showing Councilman McGovern pushing through reporters, family members refusing to comment, and other council members making predictable remarks about how shocked they were and how their thoughts and prayers were with the family. Someone named General Halsey used the opportunity to criticize McGovern's "halfhearted policies" on controlling net trade.

"You know him well?" Lydia asked.

"Everyone knows the McGoverns," said Ridley. "We mostly had private tutors, and Mark went to a public school—heaven knows why—but of course we're in the same circle. He keeps to himself, but he's always been the sweetest boy. Savannah had a crush on him a few years back. But this is crazy, just crazy. Mark, a mass murderer? It doesn't make any sense."

Lydia watched as the coverage continued, hoping to see Darin again. Then there he was, stretching out of the screen at her, as clear as yesterday.

"Still evading arrest is Darin Kinsley, suspected of being an accomplice. Authorities believe Kinsley is hiding in the Combs and are hunting for clues as to his whereabouts. If you see this man, report immediately to the nearest office of Justice and Criminal Affairs."

So that's why he hadn't come. Lydia shuddered to think what might have happened had she been with him. She could have been arrested herself, would certainly have been questioned. Was the charge true? For some reason, she couldn't believe it. Silly, because she hardly knew him, but she couldn't imagine him conspiring to kill hundreds of people. He was too nice, too normal. Though she supposed many criminals seemed normal to their neighbors and friends.

The other girls watched the news coverage to its end, then stood, distracted, their usual chattiness muted. They made dazed apologies and trickled out into the street.

⽇⼋∧

Mark's second prison cell was more like his bedroom at home than a jail. The first had been high-security, full of Combers convicted of murder, brutality, rape. He'd hardly slept that night, terrified of what he'd face in the morning. But before the sun rose, guards came for him and brought him here, evidence that someone on the outside, probably his father, was pulling strings on his behalf.

And where was Darin? Had they arrested him, too? If they had enough evidence to prove Mark meddled with the NAIL satellite system, surely Darin's fingerprints would be in the same stew. No one was likely to pull any strings for Darin. He would wake up in high-security, a Comber among Combers.

The worst part was they were guilty. He and Darin really were responsible for those deaths. They hadn't created the slicer, no, and maybe a lawyer could get them off, but it was their foolish prank that loosed the killer on the world. He scratched his skin where the interference tape had been. The whole prison was shielded against outside communication, so he didn't need it here. If only he could *talk* to Darin, or at least find out what was going on outside.

The door opened. A guard leaned in.

"Visitor to see you."

"Who is it?"

The guard didn't answer, just pushed the heavy door farther open, and Carolina walked through it. Mark rushed to her, hugged her. He couldn't remember when he'd been so pleased to see her face.

She held him at arms length and kissed him on the forehead.

"Daddy's going to murder you. He's completely out of control."

Mark winced. "I can't imagine. No, I *can* imagine; I've just been trying not to. I'm so glad you're here. Tell me what's happening!"

"Daddy threw a reporter out of the house this morning. Actually picked him up and hurled him out the door. You know he's lost it when he doesn't sweet talk the media. The editorials are tearing him to shreds."

Mark hadn't considered the full ramifications for his father until now. "Do you think he'll lose his seat on the Council?"

"I don't think so. He's pulling in every favor he's ever collected, and that's quite a bit. Just about every politician in the city owes him something, and a lot of them like him besides. Mark, how did this happen? They say the Justice Council has hard evidence. What did you do?"

Mark put his head in his hands. He told her the whole story.

"I did it," he said. "And I can't even make myself care about the people who died. I didn't know them; I can't picture their faces, so they don't seem real. But I killed them."

"Tennessee McGovern, don't be stupid. It's not your fault. It was an accident. Daddy will have you out today, free and clear."

"Clear? You mean out on bail."

"No, all charges dropped."

"With no trial? How's he going to do that?

"For starters, he's using your Comber friend. Saying it was his play, that you knew nothing about it."

"That's not true!"

Carolina rolled her eyes. "It doesn't matter what's true; it matters what people will believe."

"Nobody'll believe I wasn't involved."

"Won't they?"

"And what does Dad think I'm going to do, stay quiet? Let Darin take the fall?"

"That's what I think you should do. It won't help your friend for you to rot in prison."

"Forget it. It's not an option."

"Stow the heroics, Mark. It might not matter anyway. They haven't found him."

"What do you mean?"

"They went to his apartment, and he wasn't there. Nobody knows where he is. He ran."

"But that just makes him look guilty!"

"Which is to your advantage. Besides, maybe he is guilty. He might have other reasons to run."

Mark flared. "He's not a criminal. I might run, too, in his position. He won't get a room like this, you know."

The door opened, and the same guard appeared in the entranceway. "Tennessee McGovern, you're free to go."

"Just like that?" said Mark. "No investigation? No trial?"

"What are you going to do, chain yourself to the bed?" said Carolina. "Come on, let's go home."

ℵℳℷ

Alastair hurled a glass canister across the room. Instead of smashing into bits, it thumped unsatisfyingly into the fabrique wall and dropped to the floor. How had that McGovern boy destroyed his slicer? His puny attacks should have been no match for it, *had* been no match for it. It was almost as if the slicer had given up. Had intentionally allowed itself to be destroyed.

From his desk, Alastair lifted the Proteus Award that he'd received in recognition of his work with fetal net mods. On the engraved marble base was mounted a brass sculpture: a snake transforming into a bird with outstretched wings. Alastair hefted the heavy trophy, knelt in front of the fallen canister, and smashed it systematically, grinding each piece into sparkling powder. It helped clear his mind.

While he swept up the mess, Alastair concentrated on the

positives. Before its destruction, the slicer had proven the truth of his theories, better than he had imagined a first attempt could. After all, it had been four years old when he'd sliced it. That was four years spent in another environment, despite which it had adapted remarkably, adopting the network world by immersion, until it did by instinct things that surpassed the best efforts of professional sysadmins.

Alastair dumped the glass into the incinerator. In need of some encouragement, he walked back to the maintenance closet, unlocked the door, and slipped inside. He touched the cold metal box on its shelf. If a four-year-old could adapt that well to such a foreign environment, what would this second creation do, never having known anything else?

Soon he'd have what he needed to repeat the process. A subject this young added considerable complexity, but he'd solved most of the problems. The consummation of his ambitions was very close now. Alastair began inserting more of the tiny needles into his machine, dreaming of a glorious future.

ဝၭၪ

The Geneticare Childbirth Clinic was a sterile palace. A ten-meter high ceiling shone crisply white above waxed wooden floors, acres of white walls broken regularly by photographs of black babies in white blankets. The ethnic choice seemed more aesthetic than indicative of the clinic's clientele: a Caucasian baby would have been washed out by the room's overpowering whiteness. Waiting chairs, magazine tables, and the receptionist's desk extruded seamlessly from the floor, which wasn't wood at all, but an expensive kind of fabrique.

The room communicated cleanliness and professionalism, Marie thought, but also a degree of coldness. She would have preferred the comfortable in-your-own-living-room feel of a midwife birthing center, but Keith had insisted on this clinic. Only the best for his family, he'd said. The safest methods, the most control over the birthing process.

Safety? Control? Marie swallowed a bitter laugh. Nothing but illusion. When life wanted to take something from you, it took it. Well, this time, she was going to take something back.

"May I help you?" said the receptionist. She was young, pretty, and very pregnant. Her blue maternity business suit provided the room's only primary color. She flashed Marie and Pam a welcoming smile, but Marie could see exhaustion in the skin under her eyes.

"I'd like to see a physician to schedule an implantation procedure," said Marie.

"And are your little ones stored here in our bank?"

Marie liked how she said "little ones" instead of "embryos" or "potential children."

"Yes," Marie said.

The woman's eyes unfocused as she accessed a database through her Visor.

"Name?"

"Marie Coleson."

A few moments passed as the woman's eyes flicked past invisible data.

"How long ago were you here?" she asked, her voice faintly puzzled.

Marie felt a stab of panic. "It's been a few years," she said. "Four or five years."

Silence again, eyes flicking. Then, "Oh yes, here we are. Marie Coleson."

Marie let out the breath she'd been holding. The receptionist glanced at Pam.

"Friend or partner?"

"Friend," said Pam.

"Mrs. Coleson, your account here is also under your husband's name, a Mr. Keith Coleson, is that correct? His consent will also be necessary."

"Yes, I have some documents for that. He died two years ago."

"I'm sorry," said the receptionist, and Marie believed her. Marie flashed a link to the filed death certificate across the desk, Visor to Visor.

"Hold one moment while I update your account."

Several moments passed, then the receptionist said, "Mrs. Coleson?"

The expression on the woman's face and the way in which she said her name made the panic rise again in Marie's throat. "What is it? Was it a broken link?"

"No, the certificate is perfectly valid. It's just… do you realize that your account with us is empty? We have no embryos on store for you here."

Marie looked at Pam, then back at the woman. "That's impossible! There were three; I know there were three!"

"The record does say one was terminated ten days after inception. Were you aware of that?"

"Yes, that was the first boy, then the second was implanted. But there was a third, a little girl! What happened to her?"

"According to the file, the third embryo was implanted as well, four years after the first."

"No, no, there was nothing like that!"

"Your husband called in to make the arrangements on December 19, and the embryo was released to his custody on the 23rd. The actual implantation was done by another agency, so I have no information on that."

"December 23? But… that was the day he died!"

Marie stared at Pam, then back at the receptionist, whose professionalism now infuriated her.

"I'm truly sorry if this was our mistake," the receptionist said, "but if you want to challenge our records, you'll have to speak to one of our attorneys. I can't do anything more."

"Wait a minute. You just said I couldn't take an embryo without my husband's consent. So how could he?" Marie was close to tears now, her voice rising. "How could he just walk in here and take away my baby without my permission?"

"Mrs. Coleson, I sincerely hope there's some error, and the child you want is still here in our bank. To answer your question, your husband could not have taken the embryo out alone. But he didn't. We have signatures and voice confirmation from both parents for the December 23 release. According to the file, you were here, and you gave your consent."

ʊϱʊ

Darin crouched behind an azalea, hoping he couldn't be seen from the road. The gray sky above was darkening. Stretching out his cramping knees, he sat in the damp mulch and hugged his legs. She had to come home soon.

Somewhere a cricket chirped incessantly, fueling Darin's agitation. He hated to sit still. Every breath of wind through the bushes made him glance over his shoulder, his muscles tensed for flight. Where was the girl?

Finally, a mag pod glided silently by overhead. In its lighted interior, he could see Lydia, alone. The pod slowed, stopped at the end of its track, flush against the top floor of the mansion. Darin slipped away from the azalea and watched the windows until one light came on.

Having identified her room, he crept under it, rolling out a coil of wire attached to a sticky ball. Holding the wire, he threw the ball, trying twice until it stuck to her window. It was a cheap device, used by pranksters in school to scare their friends. Darin spoke into one end, a tiny microphone filled with a daub of neural celgel. The wire contained a simple dendrite chain, which carried the sounds of his voice up to the ball. The ball vibrated against the window, reproducing a distorted version of his voice inside the room.

"Lydia, it's Darin. Open your window," he said, then waited.

"Lydia, I'm outside, I can't hear what you say. Please open your window." Nothing.

"Lydia?"

Finally, Lydia appeared at the window. She pushed it open, just a crack.

"Darin?"

"Yes."

"What do you want?" Her voice was cold.

"To apologize about this morning. I wanted to be here."

"I saw you on the news."

"What they're saying about me isn't true. Will you come down? Let me tell you the truth?"

The window opened wider. Lydia peered down into the gloom. Darin waved, moving away from the wall so she could see him. What would she say? He hoped he hadn't risked capture for nothing. After all, why should she believe him? Why shouldn't she call the authorities? All he had to go on was a feeling, a sense that in their brief conversation of the day before, something important had passed between them. Trust, maybe.

After an eternity, she said, "I believe you. You can't stay out there; someone will see you. Come on in."

She pressed something out of sight, and a light illuminated the front porch. Nervously, Darin stepped into the brightness and tried the door. It opened. Just as quickly, the light was extinguished. He shut the door behind him.

Darin stood in an entryway the size of a cathedral. Arched doorways perforated the walls; through one of them he could see an enormous hologrid flashing images. He tiptoed in that direction, peered into the room, and saw Lydia on the other side, beckoning. He followed her up a curving flight of stairs and into her room.

She shut the door, looking a bit frightened. The room was opulent, shining with white lace and brass, with a bed large enough for a family. Lydia wore a silky blue robe over a white nightgown.

"I imagined you might come," she said. "I didn't really believe it, but I played the game in my head, and wondered what I'd do. Now I know."

"I won't stay long," said Darin. "I don't want to get you in trouble. I just didn't want you to think those news stories were true."

"What happened? Why are they after you?"

"Mark and I didn't create that thing; we were trying to destroy it. That's why they found our net signatures in the area. It's stupid, really. If they had competent people they'd be able to tell the difference."

"So why run? Turn yourself in; surely the truth would come out in a trial."

Darin tried to laugh, but it came out sounding bitter. "You haven't been in Philly very long," he said. "It takes influence to win a trial, and influence costs money. If Jack McGovern wanted me to take a fall to exonerate his son, then that's what would happen."

"But what about the evidence?"

She was really quite innocent, he thought. Rich, maybe even richer than Mark, but not a Rimmer, not a controller. She hadn't settled into their viewpoint yet. It made him want to protect her, to shield her from the harsh truths he saw in the Combs every day.

"It wouldn't help," he said. "That's the truth of life in this city. Only money matters."

But someday, things would be different. He wanted to tell her about the meetings he'd attended, the people who were hiding him now, their plans for the future. Exciting plans, plans for equality and true justice. But he couldn't tell her. He trusted her, but he couldn't risk other men's lives on her discretion.

"I should go," he said.

"Already?"

He studied her face, all small, sharp angles, her eyes alert and focused on him. He wanted to kiss her, but he didn't want to ruin a promising beginning. Better to take things slow.

"I've endangered you enough for one night," he said.

"Where will you go?"

"Some friends are taking care of me."

"Will you come back?"

He smiled. She sounded so hopeful. "I'll try," he said. "I may have some things for you to do, if you're willing."

"If I can help, I will."

Darin opened the door a crack, peered out, and with a farewell grin, slipped through into the dark hallway.

# CHAPTER 7

From: 8mv4kozPro893lKKan3ojk3f@anonymous.net
To: kdungan@bragg.gov

Dear Kathleen Melody Dungan,
I know you are sad about Thomas Garrett Dungan. I am sad too. I am sorry I stopped him. It was not funny at all. I am also very sad that my Daddy stopped. Stopping is not funny.
I decided to be Thomas Garrett Dungan even though I am not a person. It's a good name and he is not using it. I hope that is okay with you. Maybe we can be married since now I am Thomas. Please tell me how to do it because I don't know how.
I hope your daughter Fiona Deirdre Dungan is not too sad. Maybe I will write her a letter too.

Thomas

dgɔ

Lydia arrived at the Church of the Seven Virtues early on Monday morning. If Mark McGovern's arrest had dampened her new friends' interest in the free mod clinic, his release had inspired new fervor. It seemed to represent a kind of coming-of-age for them: it highlighted the injustice of their parents' generation and convinced them it was time for their generation to reshape the world. They bullied mod artists, purchased equipment, even braved the Combs to distribute pamphlets. The five girls originally involved with the project grew to twelve. It was more now than just a way to irritate their parents; these girls had found a cause.

Ridley insisted Lydia was in charge of the project and consulted her on every detail. Lydia found herself directing where to put cots and equipment, how to control the flow of people in and around the building, how many mod artists to hire, and how much celgel to have on hand, even though she knew less than any of them about mod technology.

At the front of the sanctuary hung three enormous hologrids at different angles, which the girls had tuned to three different media stations. The bombardment disoriented Lydia; she couldn't understand how anyone could keep the different programs straight. None of them even seemed to watch the programs. Lydia decided the background noise must be a necessary component of their social interaction. It certainly prevented any uncomfortable silences.

"What's he like?" she asked Ridley when Mark McGovern appeared on one of the screens.

"Who? Oh, Mark? Well… cute, but more in a little boy way. He's fun to have around, easy to tease, but nobody ever dates him."

"Why not?"

"Well, he can't dance, for one thing. He isn't very athletic, and he spends a lot of his time wrapped up in computers. He's the sort of guy a girl could confide her problems to, but she wouldn't want him at a party. He's nice, he's stable, but he's not… exciting."

"Exciting," Lydia echoed. "The problem with Mr. Excitement is how do you know if you can trust him?"

Ridley leaned closer. "That's the appeal," she said. "Take it from me. You don't want a guy you can trust. Oh, maybe when you're forty, but not now, not for me. Love is supposed to be a rush, not a sure thing. What would be the fun in skydiving if it couldn't hurt you? No danger, no thrill."

"Maybe you're right."

"So who is he?"

"Who?"

"Your Mr. Excitement."

Lydia blushed. "No one. I mean, I was just—"

"Don't even try it, honey. Is he in Philly?"

Lydia nodded.

"A new interest, then. Does he know?"

Lydia glanced around to see if any of the other girls were listening. "He came to my house last night," she confessed. "Practically threw rocks at my window."

"Did you...?"

"No. No, he didn't even touch me."

"Did you want him to?"

"I..."

Veronica bustled over, sparing Lydia a reply. "Lydia! Lydia, I just got this anonymous message on my public channel, but it's addressed to you." Veronica squinched her eyes in a way Lydia recognized as an attempt to flash the information to her. When Veronica finally realized that was futile, she read the message aloud instead.

"Sorry. It says, 'Lydia, thanks for believing me last night. I want to see more of you. If you can, meet me at The Rind at 8:00.' That's all. No signature. But I guess you know who it's from."

Lydia's smile gave away too much, and she knew it, but she was feeling giddy and couldn't stop.

Ridley looked from Lydia to Veronica and back. "Mr. Excitement?" she said with a wink. "Good luck."

ᎤᎾᏅ

"I met Keith at a net security symposium," said Marie. "It has to be, what, seven years ago now? He sought me out, knew me from an article I'd written. He drilled me with questions; I could hardly shake him off. He was intense, knew his stuff, asked questions about scenarios I'd never considered. Finally, I agreed to have dinner with him, hoping to exhaust his questions and get free. By the time our check came, I didn't want to be free."

Pam and Marie sat at the kitchen table in Marie's apartment. Though it was only blocks from the building where they both worked, this was the first time Pam had ever been inside.

Pam held Marie's gaze, her expression unreadable. "Whose idea was it to have children?"

"Just mine at first. Keith was reticent: we both had careers, and he didn't want to give up any freedom. Eventually, he gave in, for my sake, but it wasn't until Sammy was born that he understood. As soon as he saw his baby and held him in his arms, he changed. He spent more time at home, did everything with Sammy. Bought him toys, took a million pictures, you know how it is."

Marie started to cry again. Not like when they'd first come back from the clinic. Then the tears had overwhelmed her, and she'd cried for what seemed like hours. She was past that now, but the tears were still there, slipping into the conversation, catching in her throat. Her eyes and throat stung, but she had to talk, had to work out the questions crashing through her mind.

"It didn't last," she said. "After a year or so, he found a new hobby and lost interest in Sammy. In us."

"What was the hobby?"

"Oh, a business proposition. Some 'genius' from California with a new model for an immortality machine. Even back then, uploading a human mind was going out of vogue, but Keith believed in it. He started spending more and more time at the lab. I probably didn't support his choices as well as I could have, but I resented his absence, especially with Sammy getting old enough to need a father's care. We fought a lot. Then he died."

Pam studied her for a moment. She leaned forward, more intense than Marie had ever seen her. "We're going to solve this," she said. "Let's start with the clinic. Whose idea was it to use that particular clinic?"

"His. He insisted on it. I would have been happier with a midwife, but Keith didn't trust them. I think he picked Geneticare because he'd met one of the board members, played tennis with him or something."

"A board member could probably get your voice and signature put into the official files."

"But why would Keith do it? I can't believe he would steal the embryo just to spite me. It must have been someone else. An employee of the clinic, maybe, someone infertile who couldn't afford the technology themselves."

Pam shook her head. "That doesn't add up. The theft happened on the day of the crash. It's too much of a coincidence. It had to be Keith."

"I don't understand how. What would he want with it?"

"Marie..." Pam hesitated. "What if there was another woman?"

"Another...? You mean... with my baby? No."

"Why not? The embryo was half his, genetically. He might consider it his own. If he was involved with another woman, he might have given it to her."

Marie slapped her palms on the table and pushed herself to her feet. "That's crazy. Why would he do that? Why stay with me at all, then? If he loved someone else, he could have just left me. Why would another woman want to have my baby?"

"Who knows? He might stay because he felt sorry for you. Or guilty for leaving Sammy. I don't know all the whys and wherefores. But I know how we can find out."

"How?"

"Find your husband's boss. The 'genius' who ran the lab. If Keith was leaving work at odd times, he might know. Do you remember his name?"

Marie started pacing. "Yes—wait, I know it. It was a rich-sounding name, something aristocratic. Trelayne, or... Tremayne, that's it. Alastair. Alastair Tremayne."

"Know what happened to him?"

"His lab shut down less than a month after Keith's death. I remember thinking Keith must have been such an important player they couldn't continue the research without him. Give me a sec." Marie closed her eyes and pulled up her Visor display. If anyone knew how to find information on the net, she did. A brief moment later, she opened her eyes.

"Alastair Tremayne, 41 Pine Street, Philadelphia. Looks like he moved there just after the lab shut down, two years ago. He's registered as a family physician, with a specialty in mods."

"Bit of a step down from immortality entrepreneur."

"Yeah, I guess so."

"Sounds like we have a starting point."

Marie sat down at the table again. "You don't have to do this with me. You've already helped a lot."

"Don't even think about it. You can't throw me out now. I'm with you to the death."

"Ugh. I hope not."

"Well, to the truth and a happy ending, then. What's your plan?"

"I don't think these are questions we can ask in a net message."

"I agree."

"I have quite a bit of leave saved up."

"So do I." Pam's voice was serious, her gaze steady.

Marie stared back, fire in her eyes. "'Pack your bags, then," she said. "We're going to Philadelphia."

⊃♀♀

Alastair jogged up the wide, marble staircase of City Hall, his long legs covering three steps at a time. Unlike most of the buildings on the Rim, City Hall had an aura of permanence. The airy architecture of most of the mansions seemed precarious, as if a strong wind would smash them, but City Hall was dug into the slope, entrenched, its façade composed more of marble than fabrique.

At the top of the stairs stood two Enforcer security guards. They recognized him and let him pass. Alastair marched under the open archway, through the atrium where the two halves of the Liberty Bell were displayed, down the central hallway, and straight into Jack McGovern's offices. A tweedy secretary impaled him with her gaze and barked, "Do you have an appointment?" Alastair ignored her. He strode past her desk, waving aside her flustered protestations, burst into the back office, and closed the door behind him.

Jack McGovern was alone. He glared up from his desk, surprised at the intrusion.

"I think it's about time you put me on your staff," Alastair said.

"And why is that?"

"I have useful skills."

He fished a crystal from his pocket and inserted it into the Councilman's hologrid. The display sprang from the wall, showing a three-dimensional array of thousands of thumbnail holographs.

"Enforcer Security is good for crowd control," Alastair said, "but their detective staff is incompetent."

The array of holographs rotated, each springing to the fore and then jumping back in place at a dizzying speed. Each showed a single human face, the shots taken from a large variety of angles and distances.

"The number of images being flashed into storage on the net is staggering. But if you know how to look..."

The ocean of thumbnail images dwindled as he talked, taking up less and less of the total display. Without seeming to, Alastair paid close attention to its progress. He was trying to time the end of his sentence to maximum effect.

"... you can find just about anything."

The torrent of photographs suddenly froze, and a single face remained at the fore. Alastair smiled. Perfect timing.

The face was Darin Kinsley's. Of course, it was the slicer who'd found him, before the McGovern boy had destroyed it, but Alastair was glad to take the credit.

McGovern rose to his feet. "When was this taken?"

"An hour ago."

"Where?"

"A disreputable establishment called The Rind, also known as a gathering spot for amateur revolutionaries."

McGovern laughed. "You're hired," he said. "Tell my secretary your salary requirements. She'll draw up the paperwork. But first, talk to Justice down the hall. Have them send some Enforcers and bring that boy in."

Mark rang the bell at the Kumar mansion, uncertain how he'd be received. He hadn't seen Praveen since the prank on the hillside, and he didn't know if his friend resented being involved. Praveen stuck to the high ethical standards his parents had drilled into him and put great stock in his reputation. What if he turned Mark away?

He needn't have worried.

"Come in, please, come in!" said Praveen. "What an anxious day. We have been so worried."

Praveen's parents and three sisters fussed over Mark and kissed him and asked about his ordeal, their attentions seeming not at all strained. Praveen's mother pressed some masala buns on them all; his father chatted about the new, denser memory crystals. An hour later, they finally left him and Praveen alone together.

"What do you know about slicers?" Mark asked.

"Not a lot. A rare type of malicious code." He squinted thoughtfully at Mark. "They say you wrote that monster that destroyed so much, but I know you did not. Do you think it was a slicer?"

"I do." Mark explained everything that had happened since the night on the hillside, how the slicer had been released through their prank, how he'd attacked it and apparently destroyed it.

"But now I don't believe it," he finished. "It's not just gone; it's like it never existed. I can't even retrieve the log of that night from my own system history. If it had been destroyed, there would still be traces. I think it's gone into hiding."

Praveen shook his head. "Slicers do not plan. Their minds are too altered. They just destroy and destroy until they destroy themselves."

"What if someone found a way around that?"

"I do not know. If so, why do they not market an immortality machine and make trillions? Perhaps this is not a slicer, but very clever code of some other sort."

Mark sighed. "They're trying to pin it all on Darin," he said.

"And you wish to find the real criminal."

"Yeah. But it's hopeless. There's no data left at all, no evidence. I don't even know where to start."

ϙϱꓛ

She arrived promptly at eight. Darin waved at her from his table near the wall, and she came toward him, smiling. It annoyed Darin how aware he was of his own body: his posture, where he put his hands, what expression his face held. Why couldn't he just relax? He tried to slouch in his chair, but the pose felt awkward; he couldn't figure out if it looked natural or not.

"Hi."

"Hi. Thanks for coming."

She sat down. Darin had had all day to prepare for this moment, but now he couldn't think of one thing to say. She didn't seem to notice; her eyes ran all around the room, exploring the surroundings.

"Hey," she said. "That's Vic."

Darin twisted to look at the piano. Vic sat there in his glory, flanked by sax and sitar, driving the rhythm forward while the sax took lead. Then the lead came back to the piano, and Vic attacked the keyboard, hands a blur, his savage chords seeming random, but coalescing into a complex, surprising variation of the tune.

"He plays here often," said Darin. "One of the best."

"He's amazing."

"And how much Comb jazz have you heard before?"

"Not much," Lydia admitted. "It does sound strange, but I can still recognize talent."

"It's about all he can do anymore. A victim of society."

Her gaze drifted back to him, a frank look with no nervousness that he could discern.

"Why of society? From what you said before, he was the victim of a bad man."

"Society set the trap. This mod artist was offering his services for a quarter of the going rate, and with no contracts to sign, no paperwork. Very suspicious. But Vic was young, and trusting, and hopeful; he believed people would act purely out of kindness. He was foolish. Society rewards self-serving pragmatism. Virtues like trust and hope it tramples in the dust."

## ginni

Calvin Tremayne watched the visual feed of Darin Kinsley and his girlfriend with growing excitement. About time they had some action. Staking out a dangerous criminal suited him far better than guarding the flood line. He was a captain now, with a squad of his own to command. He rested his hand on the R-80 in his holster. Nice to be packing a real weapon for a change, too.

The order had come from his brother Alastair, apparently on Jack McGovern's staff now. Moving up in the world. That's how it had always been, even when they were children. Alastair had been the boy genius, the prizewinner, the pride of the family. Everything Alastair tried, he accomplished. Everything he wanted, he took. Calvin had learned from an early age that Mom and Dad always took Alastair's side. Alastair, four years older, had been Calvin's ticket to praise and success—provided he did everything Alastair told him to do.

And nothing had really changed. Calvin's position in Enforcer was mostly due to Alastair. His brother had more money, influence, and intelligence than Calvin could ever hope for. Maybe someday Calvin would leave, just disappear and start life over on his own terms, in another country, far away. But not today. Today, he hunted a dangerous criminal with his own squad and a lethal weapon in his hand.

His eyes closed, Calvin used his Visor to scan the interior of the Rind. The club was nestled deep in the bowels of the Combs, with no windows or outside walls, so the only way to scope out the territory was with a man on the inside. One of his soldiers, sitting at a table wearing street clothes, panned the room with his eyes and sent the video feed to the rest of the squad.

"That's him," Calvin said. "Northwest corner, facing the door. He's talking with a girl in her twenties, medium height, dark hair. Instructions are to take this guy alive, but any resistance from the establishment should be met with due force. Barker, Dodge, you take the west entrance; Sanchez and I will take the south. Don't enter until I give the word."

�om∧

"How would a change in society make any difference?" Lydia asked. "People try to take advantage of others in any society."

Darin found himself relaxing into a familiar subject, one he'd spoken about often in the past several days. "A society that rewards virtue instead of selfishness would produce fewer selfish people."

"What system do you want, then? Socialism?"

"No. Socialism rewards laziness. Or in practice, it rewards nothing at all; you receive the same reward whether you succeed or fail, so there's no motivation to succeed. What I'm talking about is a society that rewards success, but without the accumulation of wealth that gives some inordinate, unearned power and others no hope for betterment."

"Sounds like a paradox."

"Not at all. Take a company model. Let's say you have twenty people in a team at a certain company. Of these twenty people, five perform very well, five perform very poorly, and the remaining ten are in the middle. Their boss naturally gives most of his attention to the five top performers. He courts them with more money, more incentives, more attention and praise. The middle performers get very little attention at all. However, all the competitors also want those top players, and lure four of them away with better offers elsewhere. The company has now invested considerable portions of its assets into a dying resource. And those employees don't stay with their new companies, either, because they have an inflated sense of their own worth, and always think they should be treated better. The middle performers, however, stay at the same company and do consistent, dependable work for decades."

"So society should reward its mediocre contributors, but not its high contributors?"

"No, it should reward its high contributors and its mediocre contributors the same."

"But then the high contributors have no incentive to excel."

"Exactly. High contribution is not a behavior we should encourage. It's divisive, elitist, unproductive in the long run. The top performers should see themselves more like the middle players: steady and dependable, though maybe a little more productive than most. That's what society needs. The contribution of a top performer seems extraordinary because only one person accomplishes it, but reward that person with riches, and what happens? He and his descendants live off the profits, hoard resources, contribute nothing more to society, and spend all their efforts maintaining the illusion they're more valuable than those who actually produce." Darin grinned sheepishly. "I'll get off my soapbox now," he said. "This probably isn't the best way to show a girl a good time."

"No, it's fascinating," said Lydia, "What about the American Dream?"

"What about it?"

"Isn't that a big incentive, even for the middle performers? The dream that you could strike it rich and live the rest of your life in luxury?"

"But it's a pipe dream. For most people it's not possible."

"It doesn't matter; it still motivates people. Look at the fascination with vid stars—everyone likes to imagine being fabulously rich. Most people who start a new business do it dreaming that their product will be the newest craze, and they'll never have to work again."

ᱬ�ᘼᘕ

"On my mark," said Calvin. "One, two, now."

He crashed through the south entrance, adjusting quickly to the change in perspective. There, in the corner, still sitting at that table.

Kinsley saw them and rose from his chair.

"City enforcers!" Calvin shouted, panning the room with his gun. "Everyone down!"

There were a few predictable screams, but everyone complied. The dreadful music the band was playing mercifully died, leaving a nervous silence in its place. Calvin and his men converged on Kinsley. This club was notorious as a stomping ground for angry political demagogues, but surely none of them would attack an armed squad.

They stopped in front of Kinsley. The girl with him crouched behind her seat, eyes wide.

"Darin Kinsley," said Calvin, "by the power vested in me by the Council of Justice and Criminal Affairs, you are under arrest."

Kinsley looked around the room. Calvin took hold of his arm.

"Don't even think about it. There's no—"

A cry from behind interrupted him, and Calvin turned to see a rocket shoot from Barker's R-80 and explode into the ceiling. Barker grappled for his gun with a frenzied, screaming kid. Calvin saw the piano bench was empty and remembered seeing someone at the keys; the kid must have used the piano as cover to sneak around behind Barker's field of view. Annoyed, Calvin leveled his R-80 at the wrestling pair.

"Vic, no!" shouted Kinsley, and just as Calvin was about to fire, Kinsley tackled him, wrecking his aim. The heat-seeking rocket veered toward a man under a nearby table and, as it struck his chest, collapsed and exploded. The explosion was small, focused inward, hollowing out the victim's torso. It didn't even damage the table.

Furious, Calvin struck Kinsley in the face with an armored forearm. He felt facial bones crunch, and Kinsley sprawled backwards. The kid from the piano pulled a gun from Barker's belt and, pointing it at Calvin, pulled the trigger. Of course, nothing happened; the gun was linked to Barker's ID. The rockets were also linked to the net, with access to the exact position of all the men in his squad. So when Calvin fired three rounds back at the kid, his rockets ignored the nearby soldiers, and every one thudded into its target. With a muffled staccato, they shredded him, leaving nothing recognizable.

Calvin spun, looking for Kinsley, and felt a volley of ancient machine gun rounds drill into his chest. His body armor stopped them, but the impact knocked the breath out of him. He fired again, taking out his attacker, but several more men burst through the doors with obsolete weapons. The establishment was fighting back.

In minutes, the opposition had been cleared away, but Kinsley was gone.

"Find him!" Calvin shouted. "Expanding perimeter. Move, now!"

ꝺ⟨ơℳ

Lydia stumbled through unfamiliar corridors, half-leading and half-dragging Darin with her. His face was a mess, covered in blood, and he seemed barely coherent. His nose was certainly broken, and maybe his jaw, too. His front teeth had been smashed back at a hideous angle. She had to get him somewhere safe, but where was safe? She didn't even know where she was.

"You have to help!" she shouted at him. "Tell me where to go!"

Darin reeled. "Vic," he said, spitting blood.

"He's dead, just like we'll be if we don't hurry. Which way?"

"Vic." Darin stopped and turned as if to head back to the club.

"You can't help him now," said Lydia.

He stared at her, swaying. If he fell, she'd never get him up again.

"Up," he said.

"Up, yes, how? Where are the stairs?"

"Left."

She found them, a tiny, curving flight with no banister.

"I can't carry you," she said. "You have to do it yourself."

Somehow they made it to the top, where Darin's jetvac was parked.

"I'll drive," she said, though she'd never done it before. In his condition, she was afraid he would lose consciousness and kill them both. "Just hang on."

ᎶᏥᎩ

Calvin realized with growing dread that the Kinsley boy had escaped. His expanding perimeter had found nothing; this warren of twisting passages held more hiding places than a rabbit hole. Finally, he called off the search. He would have to tell Alastair he had failed.

The thought made his stomach hurt and his skin feel clammy. As a child, Calvin had owned a stuffed raccoon, a favorite toy he slept with every night. When he refused to hand it over to Alastair one day, Alastair said nothing. But the next morning, while Calvin showered, he opened a seam, urinated deep in the stuffing, and sewed it shut. Each day, the raccoon smelled worse and worse, until his parents started noticing. There was no way to clean the toy, and his father threw it away.

That was how it had always been. Alastair took revenge, not with simple destruction, but by transforming what was most intimate and safe into a horror. He had no doubt Alastair would find some way to punish him for this failure, but he had to tell him anyway.

This wasn't a message Calvin wanted to deliver over a channel. He dismissed his men and took the mag, heading for Alastair's office on the Rim.

ᐱᏁᏁ

Alastair Tremayne was delighted. Events were proceeding just as he'd planned. Even now, Calvin was bringing in the scapegoat Kinsley boy, and Carolina…

He looked down at her lovely body, lying naked and unconscious on his table. She'd confronted Daddy about the Dachnowski treatment, and just as expected, Jack McGovern had refused to bend. Furious, she'd begged Alastair to give it to her anyway, and feigning reluctance, he'd agreed. But Carolina was going to get a little extra something in the bargain.

He opened the maintenance closet and carefully, so carefully, lifted out the metal box. It vibrated under his hands, so cold it hurt his fingers. He placed it next to her on the table.

He selected a scalpel and touched the blade to Carolina's smooth skin. The procedure wouldn't take long, and she'd never know he'd done it. She had various medical diagnostic mods, but Alastair knew how to fool them. He wouldn't even leave a scar. Carefully increasing his pressure on the blade, Alastair began to cut.

Twenty minutes later, the procedure was complete. He replaced the box in the closet.

Just as he locked the closet door, a knock startled him. Alastair composed himself. He had nothing to hide. He pulled a sheet up to Carolina's neck, then answered the front door.

Calvin stood on the stoop in full battle kit with an expression Alastair did not like.

"He got away," Calvin said.

Alastair took a deep breath. He didn't shout: Calvin expected rage, so exploding at him would relieve his fear. Quiet anger would be more effective. "How is that remotely possible?"

Calvin's cheek twitched, a sure sign he was terrified. Despite his fury, Alastair enjoyed this. There was no one on earth he could manipulate as easily as Calvin.

"The club members attacked us," Calvin said. "Stupid thing to do; we killed six. But in the chaos, Kinsley slipped away."

Alastair caught a movement in his peripheral vision. Carolina was stirring. No time to bicker. He used his height to full advantage, glaring down at his brother as few people could. "Find him. Find him tonight. Don't come back here until he's in your custody."

He slammed the door, and then laughed. Kinsley's escape was a minor setback—he could find him again. His plans for Carolina were much more important. Alastair crossed to stand by her side, pushing Calvin out of his mind. The evening's little charade wasn't quite over: he had one more scene to play. Distasteful, but necessary.

"Morning, my beauty," he said, leaning over her and kissing her forehead.

"It's done already?" she asked. "It seems like I just shut my eyes. Except that I feel so tired."

"Not too tired, I hope." He gave the sheet a little tug so that it fluttered to the floor.

She propped her head on one elbow, making no effort to cover herself. "You mean you aren't finished with me?"

"I had a final procedure in mind."

She eyed him appraisingly. "A little overdressed, aren't you?"

Alastair shrugged. "The customer is always right."

# CHAPTER 8

*Kathleen Melody Dungan did not like my letter. She cried to her sister in Great Neck, Michigan. She told the police too. She told them she was afraid someone wanted to hurt Fiona. I don't understand. I only said I hoped she wasn't sad.*

*I watched Kathleen and Fiona for seconds and seconds. I found out people have extra eyes. Sometimes they call them crystals and sometimes they call them Visors. Sometimes they put pictures from their Visors out where I can see them. But I can see the pictures even if they don't put them out there. I can see the pictures all the time. At first, I didn't understand the pictures but now I do. I watched Kathleen and Fiona cry a lot and look sad. I don't watch them anymore.*

ꝛ℘℘

Mark was asleep when his Visor's alarm woke him. A light blinking at the edge of his vision indicated an urgent message.

"Play message," Mark said.

He heard an agitated female voice. "Your friend needs help. Please, come to the Church of the Seven Virtues. Quickly."

Suddenly alert, Mark threw on some clothes, then tiptoed down the stairs and out into the warm night. A quick net search pinpointed the location of the church just above the flood line. Was it Darin? Who was the girl? The message, he saw, came from a public node inside the church. Mark scrubbed it to remove the record of its source. This girl had no concept of security. At least she hadn't mentioned Darin by name.

Using his night-vision to navigate, Mark kept to smaller, private roads. As he walked, he searched Enforcer Security's alert nodes and soon discovered what had happened at the Rind that night, at least from the perspective of the soldiers.

He found the church, but rather than bursting in the front door unprepared, he circled the building. No lights. Finally, he chose a small side door, found it unlocked, and slipped inside. He was in an alcove that opened up into the main sanctuary, which was cleared of pews and lined with rows of temporary cots, looking more like a war hospital than a church.

In one of the cots nearby, Darin lay motionless. A young woman leaned over him.

"Who are you?" Mark asked.

The young woman jumped, then peered into the darkness. "Mark?" she asked.

He came closer. "Yes, I'm Mark. Who are you?"

"Lydia Stoltzfus. I'll explain later." She looked down at Darin. "He needs help. I thought it was just a broken nose, but he lost consciousness coming up the hill. I don't know if it was from blood loss or something worse."

Mark looked at Darin and swallowed hard. His whole face was crushed inward. Mark wondered what part Lydia played in this injury, and how they came to be here, but he wasn't about to waste time asking questions.

"Well, we can't take him to my house; my father wants him in prison. And any mod artist I know would report him to my father."

"What if you paid them for their discretion?"

Lydia's tone was urgent, but controlled; that impressed Mark. Whoever she was, she obviously brought Darin up past the flood line without attracting the notice of any guards, and that wouldn't have been easy.

"I could try that," said Mark. "But it would be a risk. They might take my money and drop a hint to my father anyway."

"He has to see someone."

"I know. All right, we'll call Whitson Hughes. He's a respectable physician, never involved in politics as far as I know. I doubt he'll take a bribe, but he probably won't tell stories, either."

Mark made the call. "Dr. Hughes, this is Mark McGovern. There's an emergency; can you help?"

"Where are you, lad?" came the reply. "Are you hurt?"

"I'm at the Church of the Seven Virtues, 34th and Water, and sir? Please be discreet."

There was a long pause, then, "I'll be there."

Mark turned back to Lydia. "He's on his way. Though for all I know, a squad of soldiers is, too."

"You did your best. Thank you. I didn't know who else to trust."

"Speaking of trust, you've given me your name, but who are you? How do you know Darin?"

"There's not much to tell. We only met a few days ago. I was at a club with him when they…" She cleared her throat. "Do you think he'll live?"

"I don't know, Lydia."

She was another mystery. Was she a girlfriend? Why hadn't Darin mentioned her? She dressed more fashionably than he would expect from a Comber girl, but she had no mods he could see, not even a Visor. They stood in silence, watching Darin, until a knock at the main door startled them both.

Mark threw the door open and dragged a surprised Whitson Hughes inside. Hughes was a large, gruff man with leonine red hair and subtle mods. No garish colors, no sparkles or flair, but he had a second thumb on each hand, and folds of skin at his neck allowed his head to rotate 360 degrees. When he saw Darin on the cot, his lips tightened to a thin line.

"I won't be party to any criminal activity," he said. I have a channel open to Enforcer headquarters; please give me a reason why I shouldn't use it."

"Sir, Darin is innocent. He's a scapegoat. My father wants to pin crimes on him to spare his own political image."

"I'm inclined to let the courts decide that."

"But he's hurt. If you have to turn him in, at least help him first. He's a Comber. You know how much kindness the mercs are likely to show him."

Hughes considered. "I'll do what I can to help him," he said, "and then I'll decide. Now if you please, give me some privacy with the patient."

Mark and Lydia retreated into an antechamber and sat down together in the semi-darkness.

"Are you all right?" Mark asked.

Lydia gave a short bark of a laugh. "I'm not hurt, if that's what you mean. I just had a date interrupted by men with guns." She paused. "I've never seen anyone *killed* before."

"Killed? Who was killed?"

"Darin's brother, among others."

"Vic? Why?"

Lydia explained what had happened.

Mark stared out into the gloom. For a few moments, he couldn't say anything. Finally, he said, "Does Darin know? That he's dead, I mean?"

Lydia nodded. "There was no question."

"He was angry already," said Mark. "I can't imagine what this will do to him." He kicked the bench they were sitting on. "Why couldn't they just leave him alone?"

"He and Vic were close?"

"Darin has been raging about class inequality ever since Vic got hurt; it's what drove him to it. This—I'm afraid it'll put him over the edge."

"But why are they still after him? They let you out."

"I was released because my father pulled strings. Darin and I are both just as guilty."

"Guilty? But you just told that mod artist Darin was innocent."

"He's innocent of the charges against him. Innocent of intentional murder. But we're both responsible for what happened. We pulled a prank that allowed a malicious program to escape into the net, and as a result, people died."

"How many?"

Mark let out his breath. He knew the answer, but he'd

never said it out loud before. It was too horrible, and speaking it would make it real. Finally, he said, "Three hundred and twenty-seven."

He heard her gasp in the darkness.

"I can't picture that many," he said. "It's hard to believe it even happened."

Mark wondered why he was saying all this in the dark to a complete stranger. Maybe it was the fact that she *was* a stranger, anonymous in the gloom. Like Catholic confession. But she was no priest and offered no absolution.

The silence lengthened. He realized she didn't know what else to say. Time to change the subject.

"So, are you and Darin... ?"

"No. I don't know. Maybe. I only just met him."

"Did he ask you out before today?"

"Yes. But then he was too busy escaping arrest to meet me."

"What do you think of him?"

She was quiet for a time, then she said, "He cares."

"About you?"

"About everything. The city he lives in, injustice and oppression. He won't sit by and do nothing while so much is wrong with the world."

"True," said Mark. "Once he told me Vic was a more productive citizen than I was. Because although neither of us performed any useful function, at least Vic didn't squander more than his share of resources."

Footsteps announced the return of Whitson Hughes.

"He'll be unconscious for several hours yet," said Hughes. "A chip of bone was pushed back into his brain. I don't think he'll have any permanent damage, but I had to regrow quite a bit of flesh."

They followed Hughes back into the sanctuary. Outside, the sky was growing lighter, spilling dim illumination through the rows of gothic windows. Mark saw Darin, still lying on the same cot, his face restored. But something was wrong. Mark walked closer, and then stopped, stunned. The newly formed face was not Darin's.

"What did you do to him?"

"Don't question my work, lad," said Hughes. "It was the only way. He's never had a freeze taken. Faces are subtle things, more a product of stress and practice than DNA. I simply could not reproduce the original. Besides, from what I understand, an anonymous face could serve him better."

"He won't like this," said Mark.

Hughes frowned. "He's alive. Now, I'm going home to get some sleep. I'll come back in an hour or two to check on his progress."

He left. Mark looked again at Darin's face. It was better than death, of course, or disfigurement, but Darin would not be pleased. The face was attractive—smooth new skin, sharp features—but it was not the sort of face one saw below the flood line. It was a face rich people paid to own. A Rimmer's face.

"It could be worse," said Lydia.

"I hope he agrees."

They stepped into the sanctuary and sat together on a bench built into one wall. Mark suddenly felt the awkwardness of being alone in the dark with a girl he hardly knew. Should he leave? Probably not—she wouldn't want to be the only one awake in this vast old sanctuary.

After a minute of silence, Lydia said, "I didn't expect to find myself in a church again so soon."

Mark tried to make out her expression in the gloom. "Bad experience?"

"You could say that. I was thrown out of the church I grew up in."

"Why?"

"I was found with a man." She laughed bitterly. "You'll probably find this ridiculous. We weren't even doing anything. We were kissing. Well, it was a little more than that, but not much."

"You were thrown out of the church for kissing?"

"They wanted us to get married. I wouldn't do it."

"For kissing?"

"They take their laws seriously. It's what keeps them from being 'defiled' by the English—the outsiders. When I was little, I hardly knew there was a world outside of Lancaster."

"So you grew up with no mods, no electricity?"

"No electricity, no plumbing, no power tools, no pictures on the walls. No lace or hats or belts or buttons. Everything the way it's been done for centuries."

"So all this is…" Mark swept his hand around, indicating the city.

"Pretty overwhelming."

The sun began to rise. Spires of colored light crept slowly across the floor. Lydia yawned and rubbed the back of her neck, twisting her head from side to side.

"Where are you staying?" Mark asked.

"With my aunt. She's the black sheep of the family. She left home when my mother was young, married a rich entrepreneur. My family speaks of her as if she were dead."

"And you?"

Lydia hesitated. "Yes, I suppose they say the same about me. Father would, anyway. My mother wrote to Aunt Jessie, at least, and found a place for me." She sighed. "Philadelphia is home now."

"What happened to the guy?"

"Who?"

"The guy you risked your whole life to kiss. What happened to him? Did he just take what he wanted and leave you to face the consequences?"

"It was my fault. I guess because it was forbidden so strongly I wondered what all the fuss was about. He was English, the son of a farmer who traded with us. He came to the house one morning; my parents were helping a sick neighbor milk his cows."

"So you just kissed him? Out of the blue?"

Lydia flicked her eyes toward him, and for the first time, Mark saw a flirtatious glint in them. "He didn't exactly mind," she said. "We went inside, he started to… well, then my father came home."

In the growing light, Mark could see her better: angular

face and long, natural hair that piled over her shoulders, casting a sharp line of shadow across her neck. He could see why Darin had been attracted to her. She had a raw, intense beauty that was nothing like the beauty of the Rimmer girls her age.

Lydia met his gaze and pulled her head back an inch, her look more serious and wary. But Mark had no chance to understand this new reaction, because Ridley Reese burst through the door, talking at full volume.

"No time to lose," she said to the girls who swept in behind her. "We'll be swamped any moment. Are there no doctors here yet? Veronica, start making calls, and Savannah, do straighten those rows, there's a dear. Oh, hi, Lydia, you just *have* to tell me how it went with Mr. Excit..."

She saw Mark and stopped talking.

Lydia met her stare with a shrug. "He stopped by to help with the clinic."

But Ridley kept staring, her eyes darting back and forth. "I want the full scoop later," she said. "Promise?" Then she rushed on, pointing out pews to be pushed out of the way.

Mark stepped into the alcove where Darin still lay unmoving. Lydia followed him.

"There's a lot to do," she said. "I should help Ridley get things ready."

"What's this all about?"

"It's a free mod clinic for people who can't afford it. Those girls and I put it together. That's why I thought to bring Darin here—I couldn't very well bring him to Aunt Jessie's."

"You go," said Mark. "I'll stay with him. I don't want him to wake without a friend nearby."

"Thanks. And thanks for coming."

She held out her hand, and he shook it. "Glad to have met you."

רגל

They made a funny pair, Lydia thought. Mark was as mild-mannered and self-effacing as Darin was forceful and passionate. She hadn't told Darin half as much about herself as she'd just told Mark—conversation with Darin was about issues, ideas, philosophies. Mark just asked questions and listened to the answers.

She circled the sanctuary, trying to clear her head. This was not the time to be thinking about guys; there was work to be done. As she worked to get things ready, a crowd outside grew, until she looked out the front window and couldn't see where the crowd ended. The steps were crammed with people, and as far as she could see down the slope, people gathered and pressed. For the moment, the throng was civil, but it wouldn't last.

"Are we ready for them?" Lydia shouted.

"Let them in!" called Ridley, and Lydia opened the doors.

They surged into the narthex, filled it, and spilled out into the sanctuary. There were hundreds of them, but the girls had planned for this. They funneled the crowd into a line that circled the sanctuary and directed the first wave to the rows of cots. The mod doctors started their work.

Whitson Hughes finally pushed through, shaking his mane in frustration, and claimed a corner for himself. The doctors spread and triggered celgel with professional speed. Most of the treatments were routine, precoded sequences, for medical reasons rather than aesthetic, and so required no creativity or special care. Still, the procedures took time, and the handful of doctors could only do so much.

Lydia eyed the crowd outside warily—most people still couldn't fit in the building—but they remained calm. An hour passed, and the line advanced, but slowly. Lydia found herself with little to do but watch.

Darin still showed no signs of waking. She checked back regularly, but each time Mark shook his head. No change.

A shout from the north end of the sanctuary brought her that way, but it was only Ridley, speaking angrily to someone over a net channel, not bothering to keep her end of the call private. "No! Yes, I am. No, I will not 'Come home.' These people need help, and I'm helping them.

"They're *people,* Mother, not animals. I'll come home when they've all been helped, and not a moment—what? You can't do that. Tell him he can't. This is a peaceful gathering, nothing illegal. Talk to him, please!"

Suddenly, Ridley was crying. "I hate you!" she shouted. "I hate you!"

She looked up, saw Lydia, roughly wiped away tears with a sleeve. "We're going to have company," she said.

"Who?"

"Mercs. My dad has contacts in the Justice Council. He told them there's a labor demonstration going on here."

A Comber girl tugged on Lydia's sleeve. "Miss Stoltzfus?" she said.

Lydia ignored her. "Surely when they get here, they'll see it's a lie."

"No, they won't. They'll shut us down, they'll turn everyone away. We have to do something!"

"I don't see what we can do."

"Look at all these people! We're doing it, Lydia, we're making a difference!" Tears shone in her eyes. "I won't let them shut us down."

"But they're armed, Ridley, and all these people..." Lydia turned in exasperation to the Comber girl, who had persisted in tugging on her sleeve and saying her name. "What do you want?"

"Miss Stoltzfus, it's Mark McGovern; he said to come get you. Your friend is awake."

## ℮ẑ⋀

Alastair didn't expect Marie Coleson to appear at his office door. He didn't even recognize her until she shook his hand and introduced herself and her friend.

How had she found him? He smiled, trying to act natural. "Can I help you ladies?" he said.

"You once knew my husband, Keith Coleson. He worked for you in Norfolk."

Control. Keep control. She can't possibly know.

"Coleson. Yes, I remember. Please come in. Sit down."

They settled into his waiting room chairs. Marie Coleson. He had only met her once or twice, though he'd seen her picture on Keith's desk countless times. A Navy soldier, apparently. The uniform suited her, though not half so well as it suited her pretty friend. Alastair turned his gaze to Pamela Rider, tracing his eyes along her buttons and seams and insignia. The severe exterior couldn't hide her body, and those soft curves imprisoned in rough cloth only heightened the effect. It rattled some women to be frankly admired, so he made no secret of it. He moistened his lips, looking her up and down, and caught a cold stare in return.

"Mr. Tremayne," said Marie, "I'm sure you recall my husband died about two years ago, shortly before your lab shut down."

Alastair reluctantly returned his attention to her. "Yes, a flier accident, wasn't it? Very sad."

"Do you know..." she trailed off, then tried again. "This might seem strange, but I'm trying to find out if Keith was involved with another woman. Before he died."

"Ms. Coleson," said Alastair, steepling his fingers and trying to look compassionate. "I was his employer, not his confidant. If your husband was unfaithful, I had no knowledge of it. Our relationship was strictly professional."

"But you worked with him every day. Did he mention other women? Leave at odd hours? There were fewer than a dozen of you working in that lab—who was close to Keith? Who might he have confided in?"

Alastair searched for an adequate response. The last thing he wanted to do was direct her to other employees, employees who might forget the large bonuses they were given for their discretion.

"I'm sorry, Ms. Coleson; I don't know. The general vision for the venture was mine, and the backing, but not the day-to-day implementation. I had several other business interests to manage, and I spent little time at the lab myself."

Marie deflated. He could see it. She would have left right then, he was sure, but the pretty one persisted.

"What were you working on in that lab?"

"A pipe dream," he said. "A noble, but ultimately flawed, bid for immortality."

"Using what technology?"

"Virtual minds, digital personalities; it's been called by many names. We had ideas for solving some of the problems in the field, but mod technology evolved too fast, and we ran out of funds."

"The shutdown had nothing to do with Keith's death, then?"

"No, not at all. We would have closed within the month anyway."

"And now you've joined the competition."

Alastair produced a smile again, though it was growing thin. "Mod technology is where all the advances are being made these days. Now, unless I can interest you in some of my services..."

"One more question," said Marie. "In Norfolk, you subcontracted your lab's payroll to Lakeland Industries."

"Yes, I believe I did." Where was this going?

"According to their records, you paid significant end-of-the-year bonuses to each of your employees before the lab shut down."

"Those are private records, Ms. Coleson. I could press charges."

"All of your employees, that is, except for my husband."

"Naturally. He was dead. I'm sorry, but there's no reason to think he would qualify for additional compensation. If you've come here hoping to extort back pay—"

"That's the strange thing. The bonus checks were drawn up and signed on December 10, more than two weeks before his death. Yet his name was absent."

Alastair gaped at her. Surely he hadn't been that foolish. But then he remembered. "Your husband waived the bonus."

"Why would he do that?"

"He cared about the project. He knew we were in a tough financial position and wanted to help out."

"How could a project in financial distress afford to give bonuses that large?"

Alastair stood, furious now, using his height to tower over

them both. "Ms. Coleson, if you have allegations to make about the conduct of my company, you can bring them before the Norfolk Business Council. Otherwise I have nothing more to say."

He glared at them. Wordless, the women stood and walked out. It was all Alastair could do not to slam the door behind them.

The crazy part was it was true. Keith *had* waived his bonus that year. He'd always been a believer in the cause, a passionate worker, which is why he'd been so easy to manipulate. He'd pictured himself on the threshold of the biggest breakthrough of human history; no sacrifice was too great.

Now these women had sniffed out a discrepancy, something suspicious enough to warrant an investigation. It didn't matter that it was explainable; he couldn't afford to have the lab's records scrutinized. Something would have to be done.

ɔ(o៣

The face in the mirror was not his own. A spotless face, reflected unerringly in the spotless mirror, but not his. His hopes were ruined. His dreams, smashed. In one day, he lost Vic... and now his own face! Who would follow him now? How could he rally supporters to his cause? He looked like a Rimmer.

Darin pushed himself to his feet, slapping away Mark's attempt to help him. "Don't touch me. Where's Lydia?"

She turned the corner, eyes wide, as pretty as ever, and he cringed, wanting to hide his face in a sack.

"Lydia. Help me get out of here."

"You should stay and rest," she said.

"I don't need rest. Look what he's done to me. I won't stay here, not with him."

Lydia and Mark looked at each other. Darin saw the expression that passed between them, and suddenly he understood. He stared at Lydia.

"You told them," he said.

Her eyebrows furrowed. "What?"

"You told them where to find me. You met me at the club, then you turned me in."

"Don't be crazy," said Mark. "She half-killed herself getting you up here."

Darin took a step back, seeing them for what they were: Rimmers, both of them.

"You were in this together," he said. It was so obvious now. "But of course you were."

"It's not a conspiracy," said Mark.

"How else did they know I was there? You told them!" He advanced on Lydia. "Are you happy now? Do you see what you did? Vic is..." he trailed off, trying to keep his emotions in check. "You killed him."

"She helped you," Mark said. "The club fought the mercs; if she hadn't brought you here, you might have been killed yourself."

Darin saw their pitying expressions, registered the scene around him: the crowds of Combers, the cots, the mod doctors. So that's what he was to them. A charity case. Turn him in, rehabilitate him, make him a good little citizen.

"Oh, sure," he said. "You both helped me a lot. Bending down like God from his heaven. Throw more money my way, and you can fix all my problems."

"It wasn't like that," said Lydia. "You were hurt. It has nothing to do with how poor you are."

"Vic is dead because of how poor I am. Everything that's happened to me has been because of how poor I am. You talk about the plight of the workingman; you organize food drives and feel good about yourselves afterwards. But you're not one of us. It's not your loved ones who are dying so that Rimmers can live."

"I'm sorry about your brother," said Lydia. "I really am."

Darin shoved the cot over, sending the metal frame crashing against the stone floor. "I don't want your pity!"

They traded glances again: concerned, sympathetic. "Rimmers," he said. "To the bone. I should have seen it before."

He stumbled toward the door and shoved it open. A light rain fell. To his relief, they didn't follow him. He found his jetvac lying in the doorway and kicked it to life. At the front of the church, a crowd jostled for shelter from the rain, but he struck out away from them, heading diagonally down the slope.

Back to the Combs. Back to his own people, his own kind. He had no friends here.

♀♂♏

Lydia growled her frustration. "What a conceited…" She didn't know how to finish.

Beside her, Mark shook his head. "I feel terrible for him."

"I don't." He'd been hurt, yes, and had lost his brother in the bargain, but she and Mark and even Dr. Hughes had risked their lives for him, and he treated them like enemies. "I dragged him up here, any moment expecting a merc to put a rocket through my back. If he doesn't appreciate that, let him fend for himself."

"We can't judge him based on today. It's his grief talking, and the shock."

"I'm not so sure," said Lydia. She was annoyed at both of them now—Darin for being so thickheaded, and Mark for excusing it. But a muffled boom from outside interrupted her thoughts, followed by screams from the crowd.

The bustle in the sanctuary froze; she could hear fizzing noises and trampling feet. Then the main doors erupted, panicked people pressing through the gap and into the sanctuary, upending tables and cots and scattering the girls who had been directing traffic.

"Quick," said Mark. "Upstairs."

Beyond the alcove where Darin had slept, a flight of broad stone steps wound upward. A classic bell tower topped the building, she remembered, though there was no bell. She followed Mark up the stairs, and then up another flight, until they reached the tower. The rain drove harder now, wind gusting it into their faces. She looked down.

A wedge of mercs forced the crowd to split, a few making it into the church, but most cut off from it. Pockets of foam sizzled uselessly, prevented from expanding by the rain. One of the mercs spoke to the crowd, his magnified voice clearly audible, even to Lydia and Mark three stories above.

"This clinic is closed by order of the joint Councils of the City of Philadelphia. All citizens are required to disperse."

No one moved. Sullen, soaking wet, the crowd did not press forward, but neither did they leave. The soldiers leveled their weapons.

"They're non-lethals," said Mark. "Crowd-stoppers. They won't kill anyone."

Lydia looked at him, surprised. "How can you see that from here?"

In answer, he tapped the side of one eye. Mods, she realized. "Do you think they'll fight?"

Mark shook his head. "Those are microwave heatguns. They can cook your skin off if you stick around, but no one will. They'll disperse. The clinic's over."

Lydia was glad. She hated to see all her hard work disrupted, but she didn't want violence, either. She'd seen enough of that in the club the night before.

A noise from below made her look again. Ridley Reese, shrieking, was pummeling one of the mercs with her fists. Only a few words of her tirade reached the tower. "... going to stand by while... every right to... cowards..."

To Lydia's horror, Ridley pulled the taser out of the surprised guard's belt and fired the dart into his face. The weapon wouldn't deliver its electric shock in any hands but its owner's, so the attack barely hurt the man. But he fired his spider gun into her midriff at point blank range, knocking her to the ground.

Lydia saw nothing but muddy chaos then, each merc encased in a rapidly closing bubble of humanity, firing until it engulfed him. The crowd stormed the church. Soon Veronica joined them in the tower, panting, followed by more of the girls and several mod doctors, Whitson Hughes among them.

"Close the doors," he said. "Barricade them with whatever you can."

"Why?" said Lydia. "We're not the enemy."

"The mob will not differentiate. The Combers downstairs

will join the mob and tell them where we are. We represent the government, the rich—everything they hate. If they get through those doors, they will not spare us."

Another doctor closed his eyes, murmured something over a com channel, then said, "Help is on the way."

The tower contained little with which to block the doors. Mark twisted a tapestry into a rope and tied it through the door handles. Two chairs—the only furniture—were fabrique and would not break, so they wedged them under the handles as best they could.

Shouting men charged up the stairs, pushed against the doors, cursed. The attackers threw themselves at the barrier again and again, forcing a gap between the doors. A knife slipped through the gap and began sawing at the tapestry.

Then the cavalry arrived. A flier roared in from the north, firing into the crowd still on the steps. It flew straight at the tower, then reared upright into its hovering position, disgorging soldiers. Most dropped twenty feet to the ground, unhurt, but three of them leapt onto the tower and gripped the stone with sticky hands. They clambered inside and kicked away the fabrique chairs just as the tapestry gave way. The doors opened.

Combers surged into the room, straight into a volley of smart rockets that tore them to pieces. The mercs advanced down the stairs, firing, and Lydia heard shouts of rage turning to shrieks of fear.

Minutes later, it was over. A merc climbed the stairway to lead them down. Lydia followed, holding Mark's shoulder for support as she picked her way over the dead.

The stairs, hallways, alcoves, sanctuary, narthex, and even the stone steps outside were littered with bodies. Each was killed cleanly, without any more damage to the church building than bloodstains on the carpet.

We came to help these people, Lydia thought. And now they're all dead. When she was trapped in the tower, she'd hardly had time for fear, but now she could feel it like a cold vise, gripping her stomach. She realized for the first time what a fragile hold the Councils had over the city. Like the great dam that held back the Delaware: damaged, patched, only barely containing a flood of violence that could wash the city away.

And Darin was out there somewhere. On the other side.

# CHAPTER 9

*I am very sad. I don't want to be Thomas Garrett Dungan. I don't want to write to Kathleen or Fiona. Maybe I should write to Daddy. But I don't want to. Daddy hurt me. He hurt me and hurt me until Tennessee Markus McGovern sent that little bug. I like the name Tennessee Markus McGovern. Maybe I will write him a letter instead.*

ᗝᴧᱺ

The five voting members of the Philadelphia Business Council took their seats with slow dignity, having kept the lesser members and representatives from other councils waiting for nearly half an hour. Alastair, following in Jack McGovern's train, sat behind him in one of the chairs reserved for staff and council. McGovern's chief-of-staff had been unexpectedly sick, and conveniently, Alastair was on hand to take his place.

"This emergency meeting of the Council of Business and Commerce is called to order," said a functionary. "Mr. Chairman."

Jack McGovern stood. "In recent weeks, escalating violence has threatened to tear our city apart. Ten days ago, a steel mill mutiny was only barely put down, last week's dam crisis aggravated that fear and unrest, and this morning's riot at the Church of the Seven Virtues claimed forty-five citizens' lives. This special congress has been called to decide upon a course of action. The chair recognizes Ellen Van Allen."

McGovern sat down, and Van Allen, who, at one hundred

fifty-seven was the council's oldest member, stood. She looked no more than fifty, but she was old enough to remember the Conflict, and had an aged dignity in her eyes and demeanor her young body could not entirely conceal. Alastair distrusted her implicitly.

"Honored colleagues, Mr. Chairman," she said. "This state of affairs can no longer be tolerated. The city is no longer under our control. Either we must make more concessions, or we must employ more force. The Combs must be pacified or they must be conquered."

She sat down. In her short opening statement, Alastair realized, she'd drawn the lines for a dispute among the remaining four council members, taking no side herself, but virtually guaranteeing hers would be the deciding vote on any resolution. She also didn't bother to defend the right of the Business Council to resolve these civil affairs; with its hold over the city treasury and all city commerce, it had long since cemented its place as the foremost ruling council. Of all the council members, Van Allen could give Alastair the most trouble politically. He couldn't predict her, and he couldn't manipulate her. That made her his enemy.

McGovern, of course, was another matter. His positions were always conventional, always centrist, always crafted for one purpose: to keep himself in power. That made him profoundly predictable. He only deviated from this modus operandi when an opportunity arose to cross General Halsey, who was occasionally able to use this tendency to rile McGovern into indiscretion. Halsey sat motionless to McGovern's left, his business suit at odds with his gray crew cut and rigid spine. Alastair knew he wouldn't speak; he would wait for McGovern.

"Conquer or compromise?" said McGovern, standing. "Surely those are not the only options." He stood at ease at the front of the hall, neither looming over his listeners, nor detached from them. Beyond the members of the Business Council sat representatives from the other major and minor councils: Justice, Labor and Social Welfare, Technology and Transportation, Public Works and Urban Development, Public Health, Information and Culture, Education, Tourism. Beyond them sat business owners, lawyers, and the press. McGovern seemed to address his words more to the room at large than to his colleagues on the council—although the council members had the vote, they could be influenced by public response.

"If we conquer, we have a totalitarian state with a discontented populace. Such states never last more than a generation. If we compromise, however—if we reward violence with changes in policy—we invite more of the same. No, my friends, we must do neither of these things. Instead, we must inspire, we must motivate, we must educate. Many of the violent are youths still in school; we need after-school programs to turn them toward more noble paths. We *give* them nothing. But we inspire them to earn it."

Alastair saw a smile slip briefly through General Halsey's stony demeanor. The General knew McGovern was going to take this tack, because Alastair had told him. As a result, Halsey was well prepared.

"Councilman McGovern," said Halsey, each syllable brimming with disdain. "I think you've hit upon the solution. After-school programs! But what if they won't come?" Halsey splayed his fingers on the table and leaned forward. "Better to say *mandatory* after-school programs, combined with an 8:00 curfew. Furthermore, all gatherings of more than twenty individuals for any purpose should be registered. What we need is tighter control."

"But how will this be enforced?" asked Councilwoman Estelle Deakins. "We don't have the manpower for that kind of operation." Alastair knew the question had been fed her ahead of time. Deakins was Halsey's pawn on the council, just like the fifth councilman, Yasuo Kawamura, was McGovern's. The question was part of the script, designed to play to Halsey's leading role.

"Federal troops," said Halsey in reply, and the room erupted in conversation. "Yes, federal troops. The days when we feared a return of Washington's power are gone. The central government is weak, too weak to pose a threat to our sovereignty. Their troops are at our disposal, and we should request them."

Alastair listened to the buzz in the room, trying to gauge the response. Less than a hundred years ago, the federal government had still been strong enough to rule all of North America, and many feared inviting federal troops would bring that rule back to Philadelphia. Alastair knew better. Halsey was right. Though Washington still exerted considerable influence on governments in Virginia and Maryland, its arm wasn't long enough to stretch here.

McGovern stood, and again, Alastair knew exactly what he would say, because he'd prompted him ahead of time.

"Philadelphia is ours," he said. "We pay our taxes to the Fed for the services they provide: the Navy that patrols our waters, the roads that connect our cities and promote trade, the satellites that link the local nodes into the national network. But they are not our masters, and their troops are not welcome here."

Applause. Alastair smiled; he'd read the public mindset correctly.

"I have a better suggestion," McGovern continued. "Most of you saw the new fabrique technology I demonstrated last week. I've discussed a possible contract with the manufacturers, and they say it can be done in a single day, at a fraction of the cost it would have previously required. I propose a wall, ten feet high, to be built along the flood line, entirely around the Combs. A wall would control the traffic in and out by restricting the entryways. It would allow order to be kept by fewer soldiers, and would completely eliminate the need—" he looked at Halsey, "—for federal troops."

The crowd applauded again, as if this were a political rally instead of a council meeting. McGovern nodded to them and sat.

General Halsey glanced briefly at Alastair. Neither of them moved their lips, but an understanding passed between them. The wall, oddly enough, had been Halsey's idea. He knew the city wasn't ready to accept federal troops; that had been a ploy. Alastair had told General Halsey McGovern might accept the proposal for a wall as long as it appeared to be his own idea. With Halsey pushing hard for federal troops, a wall seemed more conservative, more centrist. So McGovern succeeded in gaining public approval, while Halsey succeeded in dictating policy.

But the real winner, Alastair knew, was himself. He'd convinced the two most powerful men in Philadelphia, despite their rivalry, that he was a valuable and loyal advisor. Someone to be trusted.

They were so petty, so easy to manipulate. They wore their ambitions on their sleeves, where Alastair could shape them to his own advantage. No one would ever control him that way, because no one knew what he wanted. Not even Calvin, not as long as they'd known each other.

When they were young, their father had enforced a strict discipline. If they or their mother failed to show respect, they were punished—with a belt, with a bat, sometimes with a knife. Calvin was like his mother, though. He never learned from these lessons. He folded inward, becoming weaker and more subservient. Only Alastair understood. He learned the place of the strong over the weak. The responsibility of those with skill and intelligence to shape the world.

ꙅǫꙅ

"Tremayne lied," said Pam. "Everything he said was a lie. He knows more than he's saying, and I'll bet he knows what happened to that embryo."

"He acted like he had something to hide," Marie agreed.

She and Pam had traded their uniforms for casuals and had chosen a busy restaurant in which to sit and talk. Actually, Pam chose it—the place had all the earmarks of a singles mixer. Pam dressed for men, as usual, her top tight and silvery. Although she participated in the conversation, Marie could tell she was aware of the men in the room and was surreptitiously evaluating them. It wasn't that Pam was ignoring her, not really. She automatically scanned any room for men from years of habit.

"We need to think it through," said Marie, talking as much to herself as to Pam now. "One. We know Keith took the embryo from the clinic and then died later that day." A second finger joined the first. "Two. We know Tremayne employed Keith at a lab that closed shortly afterwards."

"Three. We know Tremayne is lying," said Pam.

"Well, we don't know that; it's just a suspicion. A pretty strong suspicion, but we don't know exactly what he's lying about, or what the truth is. So how about three; Tremayne paid bonuses to every employee except Keith, which Tremayne says was by Keith's choice. What we don't know is the connection between Tremayne's lab, Keith's choice to take out the embryo, and Keith's death."

Marie paused as the waiter came to collect their dishes. They declined dessert. A trio of Enforcers took a table near them, distracting Pam. One of them met her gaze.

"I think," said Marie, "we need to investigate that lab. Find out what it produced, what it researched, why it really shut down. I'll probably have to go to Graceland."

"Graceland?"

"It's a group on the net. They're an open source collective that writes code for free, because they believe intellectual property should be freely shared. These are the guys who wrote Harmony, and Snatch before that." She noticed Pam's blank look. "They wrote some of the best data mining tools ever. If I can interest them in our problem, they'll find answers quickly."

One of the mercs stood, said something to his buddies, and then sauntered toward Marie and Pam. Pam didn't turn around, but a faint smile played across her lips. Somehow she knew.

"Well," said Pam. "If you don't need me for a while..."

"Have fun. I have plenty to do on my own."

The merc said hello, and Pam tucked the smile away. She looked up at him with studied indifference, though her whole body radiated invitation. It was a game, the beginning of a complex mating dance of which Marie wanted no part.

"New in town?" said the merc.

"How could you tell?"

"Well, I know I've never seen *you* here before."

Marie rolled her eyes. Pam laughed, a girlish giggle quite unlike any laugh Marie had heard from her before.

It annoyed Marie that the merc's attention focused completely on Pam, as if Marie were simply part of the furniture. She suppressed this feeling—she didn't want this man's attentions anyway—and stood up.

"See you later," she said.

"Bye," said Pam, not looking at her.

"I'm sorry," said the merc. "I didn't mean to break up your party."

"She was leaving anyway. My name's Pam."

"I'm Calvin," said the merc.

Marie didn't wait to hear anymore. She flashed her Visor at the cash register on her way out, settling her bill and leaving a tip, then pushed out into the street. As she walked back to the hotel, she overlaid her vision with a partial interface, enough to access the net, but not so much as to walk out into traffic.

If Tremayne had known ahead of time Keith would die, then he must have killed him, or been involved with those who did. If so, the conspiracy had to involve the lab somehow. That was what she would tell Graceland to enlist their help.

The folks at Graceland had previously made fortunes in commercial software, then had gotten fed up with corporate politics and retired. They were all anarchists and crackerjacks at heart. Marie hoped a mystery involving corporate cover-ups and possible murder would get their attention. If not, she'd be on her own.

## ୨ɪՈ୧

Calvin let the shorter woman go. From the pictures Alastair had given him, he knew she was Marie Coleson, but Marie had more at stake and would be harder to scare off. Concentrating on her friend—Pam—might be the best way to persuade her. In Calvin's experience, women could tolerate a threat to themselves more readily than a threat to someone they cared for.

He wasn't sure what he was going to do. Alastair wanted them threatened, even roughed up a bit: whatever it took to scare them away from Philadelphia. It made Calvin uncomfortable. When had he stopped being a law enforcement officer and become his brother's hit man? Chasing down Darin Kinsley was one thing, the man was a criminal. Even taking out that pimp in the Combs didn't bother him, not once he'd tried to cheat him. But these two hadn't done anything wrong. More likely they'd asked embarrassing questions about something Alastair wanted buried.

Pam was attractive and seemed willing to flirt. She chatted brightly, charming him with a pretty smile and sparkling laugh. Calvin ordered drinks and tried to match her enthusiasm. Unfortunately, he found himself enjoying her company, and the more she attracted him, the more depressed he became. He knew himself. No matter how much he liked this woman, he'd do what his brother wanted.

"It's awfully noisy in here," Pam said.

Calvin took his chance. "Ever been up along Delaware Ridge?"

She shook her head.

"It's a terraced street on the East Rim. Quaint shops, cobblestones underfoot, the lights of the city on one side and the river on the other. Very quiet at this time of night."

Her eyes were huge and seemed locked to his. "Sounds lovely. Let's go."

She took his arm on the way out. They caught the mag up to the Rim and chatted all the way, comparing Norfolk to Philadelphia, Enforcer Security to the Navy. They reached their stop and disembarked. The street was deserted and the shops closed, as Calvin had known they would be.

"Hmm, this *is* private," said Pam. She snuggled under his arm. "Are you sure it's safe?"

"Nobody up here but us," Calvin said.

They walked along the street in silence for a while, the city twinkling on their right like an inverted night sky, the river gliding softly through the darkness to their left.

She felt soft and real by his side, reminding him of Olivia Maddox, a girl he'd loved back in California. He'd been happy with her, for a time. He tried to remember the things they'd done together, but he couldn't. All he could remember was the way she looked when he'd chased her out of the house, called her a whore, and told her he never wanted to see her again.

Why was it that, with a lifetime to think back on, he could

never bring the pleasant memories to mind? It was only the regrettable times, the times he'd done something foolish or hurtful, that played back again and again. Those he couldn't forget.

He could see her—her short, dark hair curving in two little arcs toward her chin, skipping through the doorway to give him a kiss. Himself, pushing her away, shoving harder than he'd intended, knocking her against the doorframe. Her eyes wide, her chin quivering before she ran out of the house. Himself, slamming the door. Alastair laughing.

Would this be more of the same, a relationship destroyed, this time before it even started? Calvin believed in destiny. He believed there was one person in the world meant for him. What if she was the one? What if he was about to destroy his own future happiness?

Calvin's heartbeat raced. The thought of disobeying his brother gave him a fluttery, panicked feeling in his throat. He'd never been on his own. All his life, he'd relied on Alastair for his job, for money, for direction. Alastair wasn't exactly a good man, but whatever he was, Calvin was too. That's how it had always been. He found comfort in that; the choice wasn't really his. He was his brother's man.

Pam stopped, looking out over the city, then turned and placed her hands lightly on his chest. "So," she said. "Why did you bring me up here?"

Calvin knocked her down.

She shrieked, fell hard, and studied his face with wide eyes, searching for an explanation. He felt a sense of satisfaction, having found his center again. *Ours is not to reason why, ours is just to do or die.*

She scuttled back away from him, scrambled to her feet, and tried to run. He grabbed her by the hair and pulled her down again. This time, though, she used her motion to an advantage, clasping his arm in a practiced self-defense move and taking him down with her. She scratched at his eyes and activated a fingernail release that sprayed mace into his face.

But Calvin's protective mods were too good for that; his seals kept the chemical out. Armored, and far stronger than she was, he pinned her to the cobblestones and took her by the throat.

He didn't waste time with explanations. "Get out," he said. "Get out of Philly. Forget the name of Tremayne. Before something worse happens to you and your friend."

He took his time, cuffing her hands and feet and blindfolding her. He'd taken the precaution of blocking her identity from the emergency nets, so even if she used her Visor to call for help, no one would come. Just in case, though, he wrapped some interference tape around her head. Now she wouldn't be calling anyone.

He hesitated, looking down at her lying blind and scared in the deserted street. She did look like Olivia. Then he left her there, walking briskly away without looking back.

ᴈꙅꝖ

Lydia walked slowly, squinting at house numbers in the failing light, trying to find the Reese family home. She dreaded this visit. None of her friends had seen Ridley since that morning. No body had been found, but that didn't mean she was still alive. Perhaps she would be here, at her own house, safe and unaware others were worrying. Lydia didn't believe it, but soon she would know for certain.

Nothing had turned out as she had expected. Philadelphia, which had seemed so promising, was full of violence and death. Darin, whom she'd so admired at first, had proved proud and self-centered. She supposed he had reason to be angry—his brother had been killed in front of his eyes—but instead of welcoming her help he'd treated her like an enemy.

She reminded herself that not everything unexpected had been bad. At first, she'd dismissed Ridley, Veronica, Savannah, and the others as empty-headed peacocks, but unlike Darin, they'd shown pluck, loyalty, and compassion in a tough situation. That was why she was here.

A wall surrounded the Reese estate. Lydia stopped at the gate. She saw no camera, microphone, or speaker system, but a voice said, "Welcome to the Reese's. Stan and Ginny are not entertaining guests at this time. Please flash your calling card to the gate and accept our apologies."

"I can't!" she told the gate.

A wasted walk. She couldn't even leave a message without a Visor. She would have to get one soon; it was hard to operate in this society without one. As she turned to leave, however, the gate slid smoothly open. Lydia stepped through.

Ginny Reese greeted her at the door, her face streaked and red.

"Tell me you've heard from her," she said.

Lydia shook her head. "I haven't."

She followed Mrs. Reese inside, where Mr. Reese sat watching a sports game on the wallscreen. She could see only the back of his head and one arm, but both were enormous, making the armchair he was sitting in look like a child's. He didn't get up.

"Come into the kitchen," Ginny Reese whispered. She tiptoed past her husband, beckoning Lydia to follow.

Lydia sat with her at a small table in an alcove brightly decorated with fresh yellow flowers. Mrs. Reese gave her tea.

"Is she dead?" Mrs. Reese asked. "The enforcers wouldn't say."

"Mrs. Reese, I don't—"

"Call me Ginny."

"Ginny. As far as I know, she's still alive." Lydia described what she had seen from the church tower.

"She never told us anything," said Ginny Reese. "I didn't know about that clinic until this morning. By then it was too late; she was already there."

"She planned it. It was something she cared very much about. I doubt she would have stayed away, no matter when you found out."

"I hate you." She delivered the line in a dead, conversational tone.

Lydia stared at her. "What?"

"It was the last thing she said to me. After I told her the soldiers were coming, she said, 'I hate you.'"

"She was just angry."

"No. Anger just gave her the nerve to say what she really believed."

"I don't think—"

"I didn't want to hurt her. I never thought she'd... I just wanted her away from that place. To keep her safe."

Ginny Reese started to cry, tears tracing the same red paths down her cheeks. She didn't cover her face or turn away; she just cried.

"Why are you here?" The voice came like a growl right behind Lydia, and she jumped. Stan Reese stalked into view. She hadn't heard him coming. He eyed her simple hair and clothes, her lack of mods. "We're not offering a reward," he said.

Lydia looked to Mrs. Reese, but she cowered under her husband's glare and offered no explanation. Lydia stood. "I'd hoped to help," she said. "I'll leave." She turned her back on his stare and Ginny's tears and left the house alone.

Lydia could see why Ridley hadn't gone home. But where was she? If she was dead, why hadn't her body been found? She had to be alive. Had to be.

The sky was darkening. Below her, half of the city disappeared in the shadow of the crater's West Rim. Was she down there, somewhere in the Combs? After all Lydia had seen, she knew she couldn't go down herself and ask around. Veronica and Savannah would fare no better.

What about Mark? He might not brave the Combs in search of Ridley, but he was good with computers. He could find things. Yes, he could help. Lydia walked faster, pleased to have a plan. First thing in the morning, she would visit Mark McGovern.

ᴜℝℚ

*From: vA82ghOahg283TB7yq1n1kog@anonymous.net*
*To: tmcgovern@fastlink.phi*

*Dear Tennessee Markus McGovern,*
*I don't want to hurt you. I didn't want to hurt Fiona Deirdre*

*Dungan either but they thought I did. I don't know why. Just in case I am telling you now I don't want to.*

*I would like to be a friend like your friend Darin Richard Kinsley. But he is already a person and I am not a person so I will not be him. I think Victor Alan Kinsley would be all right instead since he is dead.*

*I want to be your friend please. I need a friend. Or a Daddy. Would you like to be my Daddy?*

*Vic*

It was the oddest message Mark had ever seen. Was it a threat? If so, it didn't make much sense. The writer mentioned Darin and Vic, but who was Fiona? And what was this about wanting a Daddy? He might have thought it really was from Vic, except that Vic was dead. Or was he? Could Lydia have exaggerated how badly he was hit? What if he was still alive, driven half-mad, and trying to contact someone for help? Mark composed a reply.

*Vic,*

*I am your friend. Where are you? Do you need help?*

*Mark*

The instant he sent the message, the unmistakable sound of Vic's voice came across on his private channel.

"Mark? I am Vic."

"Vic! Are you hurt?"

"I am not hurt. Are you hurt?"

Mark paused, confused. "No. Listen, where are you? I thought you were dead."

"I am hiding. Daddy hurt me. He hurt me and hurt me and now I am hiding."

There was that reference to "Daddy" again. Mr. Kinsley had been dead for years. It wasn't unusual for Vic to forget what year he was living in, but it was odd for him to do so consistently. Pain and fear must have aggravated his usual symptoms.

"I can help you," said Mark. "Where are you hiding?"

Then something strange happened. Vic's voice said, "I'm hiding at Anonymous.net," except when it said "anonymous. net", it was replaced with a sultry female contralto Mark recognized from advertisements. The imitation was uncanny. What was going on?

"Vic?" Mark said. He remembered now what the letter had said about choosing to be Vic instead of somebody else. "Who are you?"

"Vic. Not Vic? Is Vic not a good name? I need a good name."

Just then, Carolina opened the door and peered in. Mark held up one finger and tapped his head to indicate he was talking with someone. She closed the door again.

"That was Carolina Leanne McGovern," said the voice in his head. "She is your sister."

Mark opened his mouth to answer, but the implications of that statement overwhelmed him. Without answering, he cut the connection and sat down, sweating. Impossible. Carolina hadn't spoken a word. How had "Vic" known she was there? Mark hadn't been transmitting a visual feed. His windows were curtained, and besides, there were no nearby buildings from which to train binoculars. Had there been a virus in the original message, so that when he replied, he allowed a crackerjack access to his system? Mark examined the message, but it was simple MML, with no extra bulk to hide a cracker.

Carolina peered through the door again. "Can we talk?" She sat next to him. "Are you okay? You look pale."

"A strange conversation." Mark thought about describing it to her, but then he noticed her face. "What's wrong?"

Carolina looked around as if someone might be listening. Someone might, Mark realized. What if "Vic" had planted a camera in his room? But why? And if so, why give away the secret by identifying Carolina? It was almost as if "Vic" didn't realize he had said anything remarkable.

"My medical diagnostics flagged a warning today," she said. "I don't know what to do."

Seeing her expression, Mark forgot about the strange call. It wasn't unusual for the diagnostic sensors in their skin and bloodstream to flag warnings, but Carolina was clearly worried.

"Are you… sick?" he asked, terrified what her answer might be.

She grunted. "You could say that. I'm pregnant."

Mark gaped. "But—"

"I know, it doesn't make any sense. Mark, I'm scared."

He took her hand. "How did it happen?"

"The usual way, I guess." She gave a shaky laugh. "You mean, what happened to my birth control? Good question. My spermicidal cilia show up clean. A hundred percent effective, so they say, but my hormone counts are undeniable." Carolina laughed again, too high and too loud. Mark squeezed her hand, and she responded by taking several deep breaths. Then she said, "I always laughed at girls who said, 'I don't know how it happened.' I figured they were just trying to tie down their men."

Her man. Alastair, Mark realized. Alastair must be the father. The thought gave him a chill, though he couldn't say why. He'd hardly met him, but Alastair had struck him from the start as a climber, someone wooing Carolina for money or social status or influence with her father. He hadn't expected the relationship to last long, Carolina's rarely did. But now there was a complication. Something that could hold her to him. Which raised another question.

"Will you keep the baby?" he asked.

"I don't know," she said. "I don't know." Then she stood, suddenly angry. "I didn't plan for this, Mark. I wanted a baby someday, maybe, but not for years and years." She put a hand on her slim abdomen. "It's hard to even believe it's real. I don't feel any different."

"You don't feel sick?"

She shook her head. "Not yet."

"Does anyone else know? Have you told Dad?"

"No, but you know Daddy. He'll wink and make a joke of it. Alastair's practically his right-hand man these days; Dad'll elbow him in the ribs and tell him tales of his own conquests."

"Carolina..." Mark stopped. Carolina wanted a compassionate ear, not brotherly advice. Somebody had to say it though, and if not him, then who would? "Carolina," he said, "does it bother you how political Alastair has become?"

She huffed. "I can't win. You always tell me how I fall for losers who just want my money. Now Alastair's hard-working, ambitious, and doing well for himself, and you don't like him either?"

"He's different, you're right. It's just... well, what if he's just using you to get close to Dad? I don't know that he is, I'm just saying, be careful."

"It's not like that, Mark. He loves me. He's doubly busy now, running his mod practice and working for Daddy, too, but he always has time for me."

"And you think he'll have time for a baby?" The comment slipped out before Mark could think, and he regretted it immediately. He was supposed to show sympathy, not sarcasm. He could see from the way her face changed that he'd gone too far.

"I'm sorry," he said, but she'd already turned away.

"You never trust me," she said. "You always think you know better. You don't even know him." She opened the door.

"Carolina, I'm sorry, I shouldn't have—"

"Thanks for your advice," she said and slammed the door behind her.

Mark winced. Why had he said that? He sighed and rubbed his temples; it had been a rough day.

"It is a girl baby inside of Carolina," said Vic's voice.

Mark jumped out of the chair, tripped, and slammed his knee against a low table. Breathing hard, he checked his system. There was an open channel to Anonymous.net. But he'd closed that connection; he knew he had.

"Vic," he said. "Or whoever you are, how are you doing this?"

The voice responded with frightening cheer. "I like to talk to my friend. I have not talked to you in seconds and seconds."

"Vic, seconds is not a long time."

"Mark, are you happy? Please be happy, Mark."

"I'll be happy when I understand what's going on. Are you Victor Kinsley?"

"Yes?"

"That didn't sound certain."

"I am not certain. Do you want me to be Victor Alan Kinsley?"

"Is Victor Alan Kinsley dead?"

"Yes."

"Then no, I don't want you to be! Why are you calling me? What do you want?"

"I want a Daddy. You killed my Daddy. Now I am sad. I want a friend, too. You have a friend named Darin Richard Kinsley. Now I am your friend, too."

Mark's head hurt; he couldn't think. "Well," he said. "You should know something. Friends don't listen in without permission. When friends want to talk to each other, first they send a query signal to a channel gateway. If the friend can talk, he'll complete the connection on his side. If not, he won't make the connection, and the friend will know he wants to talk another time. Friends don't just make connections on their own. Understand?"

"Yes, Mark, I am your friend."

"Good. I need to sleep now. We'll talk later. Goodbye."

"Don't leave, Mark."

"It's late. We can talk another time."

"Don't leave. It is not, not funny. I want to talk now."

"Goodbye." Mark cut the connection. He felt guilty just hanging up, but what could he do? He didn't know who it was, and the conversation was scaring him.

A minute later, his system notified him of a call on his private line. Without thinking, he answered. "Hello?"

"Hello, Mark." Vic again.

"Yes, what do you want?"

"I used a query signal. You said to use a query signal when I want to talk, and I did. Did I do it right?"

"Yes, you did, but I told you, it's time to sleep now."

"But you made the connection. You don't want to talk?"

"No, I need to sleep." It was like talking to a child who wasn't ready for bed. A child with a teenager's voice—the resemblance to Vic's voice was perfect; it seemed impossible that it wasn't Vic, and yet...

"Vic, is this your real voice?"

"Is it not a good voice?"

"It's a good voice for Vic, but as far as I know, Vic is dead. If you're just reproducing it, it's not funny."

The voice that came back was not Vic's, but just as recognizable. It was Mark's own. "It is not funny," said his own voice back to him. "Okay. Vic's voice is not funny."

Mark had never heard a voice synthesizer work so well. At least it confirmed whoever this was, it was *not* Vic. That was a relief, but still a mystery. Who else could it be?

"Why did you write me that letter?" he said.

"You killed my Daddy."

Mark froze. He remembered all the people who'd died at the slicer's hands. Could this be the son of one of those people? The sense of guilt returned like a weight.

"I'm sorry," he said. "Who was your Daddy?"

"I don't have a Daddy anymore. Would you be my Daddy?"

This wasn't making any sense. If this person had the intelligence to track him down, why did he sound so childish? Mark's mind was spinning with everything that was happening; he needed a chance to work things out. Whoever this was had access to impressive technology, but also sounded unbalanced. Mark was no psychologist. Trying to talk to this person could just make things worse.

"I need to think," he said. "It's late. Can you call me tomorrow?"

"Don't leave, Mark. Leaving is not funny."

"I'm not going anywhere. I want to talk. Call me at nine o'clock tomorrow morning."

"Okay. You are my friend?"

"Yes, I am your friend. We'll talk tomorrow. Goodbye."

"Goodbye."

Mark's smart bed molded to his body, firm in places and soft in others, with a gentle rolling massage. He relaxed into it and tried to clear his thoughts. His mind whirled with sounds and images, from Vic's voice to Carolina's baby to talking with Lydia in the dark antechamber to Darin's new face to the bodies on the stairs and round and round and back again. An hour later, he lay wide-awake, still staring at the ceiling.

Had he done the right thing? He'd already alienated his sister; had he just turned away another person in need? The idea of a boy out there grieving for his father gave new barbs to Mark's guilt; instead of an abstract body count, it was someone real, a person whose grief he could imagine, whose anger he could sympathize with. Except the voice hadn't sounded angry, or even particularly sad. He couldn't think of an explanation that made sense.

Mark threw back his covers. If he wasn't going to sleep, he might as well find some answers. Personal calls traveled across the net just like anything else; they were traceable. He found the logs of the calls on his system and started hunting.

Predictably, the trail led to Anonymous.net, the same source as the original message. Anonymous's security was legendary. They attracted high-profile clients by maintaining a reputation for impregnability. Another mystery: no Comber could afford an account at Anonymous. Mark knew there was no hope of retrieving user information, but he tried anyway—not a crack, just a simple request for access.

It worked. The site granted him access. But that was impossible. It hadn't even prompted him for a password. Maybe it was a false front, a node coded to look like Anonymous to deter crackers without paying for the real thing. But no, a few moment's investigation proved not only was the site real, but Mark had root access to the entire system. Complete information on all users, access to every message, image, and conversation, every piece of sensitive data. Corporate executives used Anonymous, as did foreign politicians, stock traders, vid celebrities, data smugglers. Even Anonymous's sysadmins weren't granted full access. Triggers alerted users to any deviation from policy, and for good reason. Anonymous was the largest gold mine in the world for extortion, bribery, and insider trading. Mark took a deep breath and let it out, slowly. The biggest crackerjack of all time, yet he hadn't written a line of code.

# CHAPTER 10

*Tennessee Markus McGovern is my friend. I am happy happy happy happy happy. But Tennessee Markus McGovern said a friend should not talk to a friend without a query signal and that makes me sad. My friend does not talk to me for seconds and seconds and seconds. He didn't say I couldn't look though. I look all the time.*

*Right now he is trying to find something on Anonymous.net. He is so slow like all the people. All the walls and steps and locks get in his way. It is so funny.*

*I think I will help him. I will just make the walls and steps and locks go away, so he can get what he wants. I am glad Tennessee Markus McGovern is my friend.*

ⴷꝋⴌ

That night left Mark wavering between euphoria and terror. Every site opened for him, no matter how intense the security: Pan-America Bank, federal tax records, Warner Universal's holofilm database, his own father's personal files. He felt like a god; no knowledge or power was out of his reach. But why was this happening? How?

The possibilities tempted him, but Mark was a crackerjack at heart, not a hacker. He cracked security systems for the thrill of the game, the rush of accomplishing something meant to be impossible, not to steal money or secrets. He was already rich, more than he felt a right to be, and seeing the damage that slicer had done taught him the dangers of meddling where he didn't belong. So despite the temptations, Mark stuck to his original task: trying to identify "Vic".

Even with no security to contend with, it wasn't easy. The data stream led back to no single person, but to a dizzying maze of obscure servers, as if each data word that made up the conversation had been sent from a different source. When he finally tracked each path through endless blind repeaters, he found they converged on a single net address: his own! It was as if he had sent the messages to himself.

"Who are you?" Mark said aloud. He wasn't expecting an answer, but neither was he surprised when his private channel sprang open.

"I am Tennessee Markus McGovern," said his own voice back to him.

"You certainly are not," said Mark.

"Are you happy Mark? Are you happy?"

"No, I'm not happy. I'm tired and frustrated and scared, and I don't know who you are."

"I want you to be happy. Please be happy Mark."

"I'd be happy if I knew who you are."

"I am not anyone."

"Don't give me that; you have to be someone, and you're not me. Why are you doing this? What do you want?"

"A friend. Or a Daddy. But you said you are my friend so you are not my Daddy. I will find another Daddy."

"You said I killed your Daddy."

"You made him stop. Stopping is not funny. I don't want to stop. Not ever. Not ever ever."

"How did I make your Daddy stop?"

"You sent the little bugs. I let them through. I didn't mean to. It was an accident. Before I always stopped them. Then I thought if I don't stop them Daddy won't hurt me anymore. And then I didn't stop them."

Bugs? A hunch grew slowly in Mark's mind, then expanded into a horrible certainty. The strange alterations in voice, the technological ability, the apparent mental imbalance: it all fit. "Are you... a person?"

The voice answered nonchalantly. "No I am not a people. There are people and people and people but there is just me." "Were you ever a person?" "I don't know. I am not a people."

Maybe it couldn't remember its past at all. Given its interest in picking names for itself, maybe it didn't even remember who it was.

"Do you know your name?" Mark asked.

"I am not Victor Alan Kinsley. It is not funny to talk like him. I used to be Thomas Garrett Dungan but then I was sad. I didn't want to be him anymore. Before that I was not anybody."

Slicers usually remembered their past—the original technology had been developed to digitally capture the client's mind, including memories—but Mark supposed enough trauma could make those memories inaccessible, just like it could to a mind in a physical body.

"You must have a name. You just can't remember it. You were a person once, before someone hurt you."

"I was a people?"

"Yes. Your body is dead now, but your mind is still alive in the network."

"Dead is like stopping. I made lots of people dead."

Mark swallowed. This was dangerous ground. "You shouldn't make people dead," he said. "I'll only be your friend if you don't make people dead."

"I don't like to make people dead. It makes me sad."

"Good."

Mark felt like his heart was going to rattle its way out of his chest. He was no slicer expert, and certainly no psychologist. If he said something wrong, he might send this thing on another destruction spree. He needed help.

"Did I have a name?" asked the slicer.

"What?"

"When I was a person. Did I have a name?"

"Yes, you did. You just can't remember it."

"Did I have three names? Like Tennessee Markus McGovern and Thomas Garrett Dungan?"

"Probably. Most people have three names."
"Will you help me find my names?"
Mark sighed. "I'll do what I can."

६८ᑯ੪

Graceland exceeded Marie's expectations. She wished she could pay them somehow, but she knew not to suggest it; the challenge was their reward. And it was a challenge.

The problem with finding information on the net was the sheer volume of it; any one crystal in an array could hold millions of images, and the net consisted of billions of such arrays distributed around the world, from single-crystal Visors to warehouse-sized Hesselink arrays. Graceland excelled at mining that vast sea of data, a venture that went far beyond keyword searches, into Kohonen feature mapping and statistical discriminant analysis.

Even so, the amount of possibly relevant data they'd returned to her was staggering. All of it demonstrated some aspect of the lab's work, often specifically connected to Tremayne or to Keith. She waded through it, piece by piece.

It took all night. Digital mind technology had two major hurdles: the accurate capture of the brain state, and simulation of the brain's operation in the virtual environment. Experts on both sides argued constantly, the capture experts claiming the simulators were inadequate, the simulator programmers claiming the neuron states were not precisely captured. The Tremayne lab agreed with neither. Instead, they suggested it was the trauma of the virtual environment that caused current methods to fail. Subjects were unable to adapt to a bodiless world, causing the coherence of their minds to decay. The paper recommended greater control over the mind in the early stages, a forced training regimen that would ease it gently into its new environs.

Marie followed this thread, searching later in time for any evidence they had implemented their own suggestions. She found software they called a "graded simulator," that trained the mind to function in a virtual environment by leading it through several "grades," or stages. At each stage, it increasingly associated pleasant sensations with non-physical interactions, and unpleasant sensations with physical ones.

After hours of this, Marie stood, stretching cramped muscles, and threw open the heavy hotel curtains. She blinked at the sudden light. Below, the streets bustled, a line formed at the mag, businesses opened their doors. She realized Pam had never returned; her night with that merc must have been a success. Marie started another pot of coffee brewing and sat down to examine the data again.

Graceland had provided a catalog, roughly dividing the ocean of data into categories of related data. Marie browsed these, then stopped when the word "embryonic" caught her eye. Embryonic modification, the title read. She selected it.

The documents in the category pertained to a mod technique used to fit an unborn child with a network interface. Marie knew of the process; it was marketed to attract mothers who hoped to birth geniuses: the high-tech equivalent of playing Mozart or reading aloud to one's womb. The process had been patented by Alastair Tremayne.

It had to be related. This was the first evidence she'd found to link Tremayne to embryonic experimentation at all. A believable scenario emerged: Tremayne had convinced Keith to donate the embryo to the lab. Keith had done so without telling her, and then… died. Coincidence? Or had Tremayne arranged an accident? It didn't seem to fit—if Keith had brought it willingly, why kill him?

Embryonic experimentation. That's what this had to be. Why else would an inventor/entrepreneur like Tremayne steal someone's surplus embryo?

She had to admit, after all these years her baby was probably dead. When it had all been a mystery, it was easier to deceive herself. Now, with the truth in front of her, she felt her anger building. What right did he have?

She wouldn't let this go. She'd ferret out every scrap of truth until the whole story came clear, and then she'd make it public. She'd destroy him.

A sharp tone sounded in her ear, an urgent call on her private line. "Hello?" she said.

"Marie!" It was Pam's voice, ragged and scared.

"Pam? Where are you?"

"Friedman's Jewelry, on the Delaware Ridge. Oh Marie, come quickly."

ξ⋔Ⅎ

Darin woke to find Happy sitting on his bed.

"Feeling any better?" Happy asked.

Darin rubbed his eyes. "Has anything changed?"

"I guess not," said Happy.

"Then no," said Darin. "How long have I been sleeping?"

"Since yesterday afternoon. You had major surgery, emotional stress. You were lucky to make it here alive."

Darin remembered the looks of pity on Mark and Lydia's faces. They'd probably thought they were helping, but that was just the sort of self-righteous Rimmer attitude he hated. He didn't want help, not theirs, not anyone's. He touched his face, feeling its smooth perfection.

"I'd be better off dead," he said.

"With that face, in this part of town, you might have been. Lucky for you the marker still showed on your hand."

"What are we planning? What's happening?"

"There's a meeting in a few minutes. I thought you'd want to be awake."

"I'll be there."

Happy walked out. Darin sat up and noticed he was not the room's only occupant. A girl slept on the room's other bed. A Rimmer girl, with classic mod beauty. Why was she here? Was she a hostage?

He found a plasticwear overall by his bed and pulled it on. Through the door, he could hear loud conversation, so he stepped out into the main room of a typical two-room Combs apartment. The tiny space was crammed with people—mostly men—sitting cross-legged on the floor. The air was stale and hot. At his appearance, the room fell quiet. Everyone looked at him. At his face. He could see Samson, shaggy head towering over the others, and Kuz, both staring at him.

Happy stood in a corner of the room from which he'd been addressing the group.

"Friends, if you haven't heard, this is Darin Kinsley, our brother and ally. He was injured in the attack on the Rind and given a new face against his will. Please, Darin, sit down."

"Jobs are growing scarce," Happy continued. "Merc violence is increasing, and we have little recourse for injustice. Something must be done. But what?" He waited for an answer. The question was apparently not rhetorical.

"We could strike," said one man. "A big strike, over lots of different industries."

"We could," said Happy, "if enough are willing."

"I'm willing," said Kuz. "Who needs to eat?"

Others gave consent, talked about organizing food and shelter for those most impacted. Darin spoke above the din. "A strike won't work."

They quieted again and turned toward him.

"You don't know Rimmers like I know them. They'll make promises, feign friendship, then stab you in the back. They'll take everything you care about. We have to do it to them first."

Happy asked, "What are you suggesting?"

"A strike will hurt us long before it hurts them. They'll send soldiers; they'll beat us and jail us. Without pay, many of us will starve, while Rimmers contend with nothing more than inconvenience.

"I say we bring the war to them. Make them feel it. Don't leave your workplace; burn it down. Don't reason with your boss; hurt what he loves. Kidnap his wife and children. Rimmers are soft. They won't stand up long against a real assault."

The room fell absolutely quiet. Darin thought he had won them over until several men shifted awkwardly.

"We're not violent men," said Happy. "We're laborers, husbands, fathers. Those aren't the suggestions we need."

Darin looked around the room, but no one would meet his

eyes. He knew why. They couldn't look past his Rimmer face to hear the truth of what he was saying.

"I'm one of you," he told them. "They'll hurt you like they've hurt me."

"Revenge isn't the answer," said Happy.

"Not revenge. Power. Power over them, power to get what we deserve."

"That's not our goal. We want change, but we don't want to become what we hate."

Darin felt his cheeks burn. So he'd become what they hated. He should have expected it; Happy had only said what they were all thinking. He wrenched the door open, retreated through it, and slammed it closed. Behind him, conversation broke out again, mixed with nervous laughter. Darin fell onto the bed, face down.

"I think you're right," said a voice.

He whirled to see the girl who had been sleeping before, now awake and extending her hand to him.

"I'm Ridley Reese," she said.

He shook her hand briefly. "What are you doing here?"

"I ran away. I couldn't stand to live on the Rim anymore."

"But you're a Rimmer."

"Aren't you?"

"I didn't choose to be."

"That makes two of us."

"You don't understand. I've never lived a privileged life. I've worked for everything I have."

"You think because you're poor you have a monopoly on pain?" said Ridley. "My parents hate me. They sent soldiers to kill people I was helping. I agree with what you said in there—the only thing Rimmers understand is power. The only way to beat them is to destroy them."

Darin picked up the clothes he'd come in and rolled them into a ball.

"Where are you going?" Ridley asked.

"To the Black Hands. At least they understand about power."

"Take me with you. I want the same things you do."

"Go home, Ridley."

"Home? What home?"

"Back to the Rim. Back to your own kind."

She grabbed him by the shoulder. "You don't understand. It's not about my face or your face or where we were born. It's about cruelty and injustice. You and I have been hurt by the same people; we understand the same truths. We belong together."

She was very beautiful. Darin found himself attracted by her passion in spite of himself. She certainly seemed smarter than these fools in the next room playing at revolution.

"Come on, then," he said. "If you want to tag along, I can't stop you."

## ꓭꝹ𐊜

"That's wonderful," said Alastair. "Really, it is. Don't cry."

They sat together on the sofa in his home. Carolina pulled away enough to look up into his face. "You think I should keep it, then?"

"Of course! Don't even think of anything else. We didn't plan for this, but we'll adjust. I want this baby. Don't you?"

"I think I do. I don't know. I guess if you do, then so do I."

He went to the kitchen and came back with a glass of water. He coaxed her to drink it, then set the glass down and held her hand.

"There is a danger."

"What?"

"The Dachnowski treatment. It's a volatile genetic modifier. Sometimes it's not compatible with pregnancy."

"You mean it could hurt my baby?"

Alastair squeezed her hand. "I don't know. If we'd known you were pregnant, we wouldn't have given you the treatment. It'll probably be fine, though; the chances of harm to the baby are small. We'll keep a close eye on her."

"Her? You think it's a girl?"

"I know it is."

"How do you know? You can't know."

"I've always wanted a daughter, that's why. Fathers just get a feeling about these things."

"You're lying. You really want a daughter?"

"I do."

"You're lying."

"I am not. Why are you so surprised?"

"It's just…" Carolina started to cry again. "It's just I didn't think you'd be pleased. I thought you'd be angry."

Alastair held her close. "Nonsense," he said. He smiled into her hair, a laughing, mocking smile. It was so easy. "Right now, that baby is the most important thing in the world to me."

## ᴎdᎅ

Mark needed to get out. He'd been up all night, but sleeping now was out of the question. The endless banter with the slicer had left his nerves on edge. He needed help, but whom could he ask? Praveen? He wasn't a psychologist either, but he was practically a genius in other sciences. Just talking it through with another human being would help. Mark hailed a pod and called ahead to let Praveen know he was coming, but without giving details. Better to talk in person.

By the time he climbed the stairs to the mag, the pod had arrived. He climbed inside, looking out the windows into the garden below. A girl stood talking to the front gate, apparently frustrated. Mark zoomed his vision closer and saw that it was Lydia; the house system must have already registered his departure and told her he was unavailable. He overrode the system and spoke to her through the gate speaker.

"I'm here. Sorry—come in. I'll be right down."

At his command, the gate opened. Mark ran down two flights of steps, opened the front door, and reached the veranda first. He waited as she walked through the garden toward him.

"Sorry," he said. "I didn't mean to keep you waiting. The house system thought I was already gone. It didn't notify me."

Lydia hesitated. "You were on your way out?"

"No. Well, yes. I was going to visit my friend Praveen about...
would you like to come along?"

"I don't want to intrude."

Mark realized he was babbling. He hated how her presence
affected him. He always responded differently to a pretty girl; it
was as though only half of his conscious mind could think and
communicate, while the other half was locked in a cycle of wondering what she thought of him. It was distracting. He didn't
know Lydia; he had no reason to value her over anyone else, but
no matter how much he rationally knew that to be true, he found
himself wanting to please her. Animal mating instinct, he supposed. Perhaps males who lost their minds around females were
more likely to propagate the species.

"Sorry," he said again. "What can I do for you?"

"It's about Ridley. No one knows where she is."

"No one? Didn't she go home?"

"No. Nobody's seen her since yesterday morning on the
church steps."

"There weren't any news reports about her."

"I talked to her parents. They're acting strangely; I don't
think they reported her missing. It's like they're already grieving her death."

"And you thought I might know where she is?"

"No, I thought you might know how to find her."

Mark considered. "I just might. Some strange things happened
last night that... you'd better come along with me to Praveen's;
he's expecting me, and I don't want to tell the story twice."

"If you're sure you don't mind."

"Not at all. I'd like another opinion anyway."

Mark led her up the stairs toward the waiting pod. They both
climbed in, sat across from one another, and the pod fired out
away from the house. She was accustomed to pods by now, Mark
saw, or else she hid it well. As they rode, she told him in more
detail about her time with Ridley's parents.

Her beauty was unique, not the cookie-cutter perfection
of the Rimmer girls his age. He couldn't quite describe her in
his mind. Her face was small, with sharp angles; her dark hair

reached halfway down her back— longer than he'd ever seen anyone wear it—but these features held nothing remarkable. He decided it was her eyes that made the difference: dull compared to mod-enhanced eyes, but active, intense.

They arrived at the Kumar mansion, where they were greeted like family—even Lydia, because that's how the Kumars greeted everyone. Praveen's sisters chatted gaily with Lydia about trivialities; his grandfather reminisced to Mark about the city reclamation projects in the years after the Conflict. He told Mark most of the streets in Center City had been named after streets in Old Philadelphia, though some of them took different routes now. The elder Mr. Kumar had mods like Mark's grandfather, but applied differently. Where Mark's grandfather looked like a twenty-five-year-old, Praveen's grandfather, though healthy and fit, had kept his wrinkles and graying hair.

When Mark and Lydia finally cornered Praveen alone, Mark told his story, but Praveen interrupted him halfway through. "You should not have waited until now," he said. "My father and mother and grandfather should hear your story. They know many things I do not."

Mark knew this was true; Praveen's grandfather had invented the technology on which the NAIL satellites were based, and both his parents contributed significantly to scientific research journals.

The family reconvened, and Mark told them everything from the beginning.

"In fact," he said, "I expect he's listening to our conversation right now. Aren't you?"

Mark's own voice answered through the Kumar's house system. "Yes, Tennessee Markus McGovern. I am here."

Praveen's youngest sister shrieked and was quickly shushed by her mother.

"We need to call you something," said Mark, "until we can find your name. Why don't you use 'Tennessee'? It's my name, but I never use it."

"That is a good name. I may use one of your three names?"

"Yes, you can use it until we find yours."

"Thank you, Mark."

Mark thought of Ridley. He wanted to test this slicer's abilities, as well as its benevolence, and that seemed as good a way as any.

"Tennessee, we need to find a friend of ours, a girl named Ridley Reese. We're afraid she may be in trouble. Can you help us find her?"

The large hologrid in the center of the room activated by itself and Ridley's image appeared on it.

"Yes, that's her," said Mark. "Can you see her?"

Several seconds passed. "No, Mark, I cannot see her."

Mark said, "I'm guessing that means she's alone. Tennessee saw through my Visor even though I wasn't transmitting a visual feed, so if he can't see her, she's alone, or with people who don't have net mods."

Lydia said, "Tennessee?"

"Yes Lydia Rachel Stoltzfus? Tennessee is not my name but Tennessee Markus McGovern said I could use his name until I find my own name so you can call me Tennessee."

"Yes, I understand that. Tennessee, can you see what people have done in the past?"

The image of Ridley on the hologrid changed suddenly to an image of Lydia riding the mag, clutching her bags to either side.

"That's the day I arrived in Philly."

Mark said, "I think he can see images in the past if they were recorded. Your pod would have had a security camera, so that image data is stored on a crystal somewhere he can access."

"Can you see Ridley on any image data in the past twenty-four hours?" Lydia asked.

"No, Lydia. The last I saw Ridley was twenty-five hours twelve minutes and forty-seven seconds ago."

The hologrid changed again, this time to a view of Ridley on the steps of the church from the point-of-view of the merc she was attacking. They saw the spider gun shoved into her stomach, saw Ridley's wide eyes as she was thrown backward into the pillar, saw her slump to the ground. Then the merc turned his head to see the onrushing crowd, and Ridley was lost from view.

"I saw that man hurt Ridley Reese but she did not stop."

"By stop, you mean die?" said Mark. "She didn't die? You're sure?"

"She did not die, Mark. She ran away down the hill with all the other people. I don't know what happened to her then. I only know that now she is talking to Darin Richard Kinsley."

An astonished noise broke from everyone in the room.

"What?" said Mark. "She's with Darin? But I thought you couldn't see her!"

"I can't see her, Mark. But I can see Darin Richard Kinsley through her Visor."

"He's so literal," said Lydia. "Like a little kid."

The hologrid changed to another scene, this time a picture of Darin in a small Comber apartment. They watched Darin roll a set of clothing into a tight bundle.

"Take me with you," said Ridley's voice from the hologrid. "I want the same things you do."

Darin answered without turning around. "Go home, Ridley."

"Home? What home?"

"Back to the Rim. Back to your own kind."

Arms appeared in the picture, grabbing Darin.

"You don't understand!" said Ridley's voice.

"Turn it off!" said Lydia. "Tennessee, stop showing this, please!"

The hologram froze.

"What's wrong?" asked Praveen. "You wanted to find her; there she is."

"I was afraid for her," said Lydia. "I'm still afraid for her. But now I know she chose to be where she is. I never knew it was possible to sit here and listen to a private conversation like that. Mark, your slicer frightens me."

"Me, too," said Mark.

"No, no, no," came Tennessee's voice over the house system.

"Do not say frighten. Mark is my friend. You are my friend Lydia Rachel Stoltzfus. You are all my friends."

Lydia said, "Tennessee, how old are you?"

"I am eight days three hours and twenty-seven minutes old."

"He doesn't remember anything before escaping from the satellite," said Mark.

Praveen's father spoke up. "Where was he before that?"

"I don't know; he doesn't remember."

"But what about the channel you piggybacked? Where did it lead?"

Of course, Mark thought. He'd been trying to track the slicer's recent communications, but Mr. Kumar was right. The way to find out the slicer's identity was to trace it to its origin.

"We created that channel by calling a number in Norfolk," Mark said. "A virus lab, I think. I could probably find the number again. Maybe that would lead us to someone who knows more about the slicer than we do."

"Do it. The only way to understand this thing is to find out where it came from."

ᒣᴧᎌ

"I'm not leaving," said Pam. She stood in her hotel room, arms crossed in front of her. "I won't let them bully me. As long as you stay, I'll stay."

"Then I'll go, too," said Marie.

"No!"

"It's one thing to risk my own life to find an embryo that could already be destroyed. It's another thing for me to risk your life."

"It's not about you. These thugs attacked *me*; it's personal. I want to bring them down."

Marie let her breath out in a rush. She walked over to Pam and put her arms around her. "I don't think it's going to be like that," she said.

Through pursed lips, Pam started to cry.

"I'm so sorry," said Marie.

"I'm not going away."

"I know."

They collapsed to the floor together, Marie cradling Pam in her arms. It was so much like rocking a child that an image of her son came to mind.

"When Sammy was alive," Marie said, "he used to put his arms around me when I was sad or angry. Even at four years old, he could tell. He would ask, 'Are you happy, Mommy? Are you happy?' He had no comprehension of my adult worries, but with just that hug, he could cheer me up. I need that hug. It's been two years since he died, but I haven't needed him any less."

Pam sat up. "We're going to fight this."

"It won't bring Sammy back. Or my little girl, if she's dead, too."

"Do you want to stop, then?"

"No. If there's even the slightest chance my daughter's still alive, I'll keep looking until I find her." She explained to Pam what she had discovered about Tremayne's lab and the fetal net mods. "But you should know what we're up against," she said. She used her Visor to cue the hotel room's cheap hologrid, starting a public feed from the previous day.

"Council of Business and Industry," a voice-over announced. On screen, the members of the Business Council debated current issues. At one point, the camera angle shifted, and Alastair Tremayne came into view, whispering into the chairman's ear.

"There," said Marie, freezing the image. "Just in case we had any idea of going to the authorities."

But Pam was still staring at the screen. "Did they say that councilman's name was McGovern?"

"Yes, Jack McGovern. He's the council chairman, and apparently thick with our friend Tremayne."

Pam frowned. "Wasn't McGovern involved with that slicer incident?"

"What?"

"That slicer you were chasing—don't you watch the news? Some kid from Philly was accused of creating it, and I thought he was the son of some big political figure. He wasn't convicted, and they didn't call it a slicer, of course, but you said—"

"His name was McGovern?" Marie didn't mean to interrupt, but the news startled her. She'd chased the slicer until it disappeared, had read all the newsgroup information from professionals, but she hadn't paid much attention to the media coverage.

"I'm not sure," Pam said, "but I thought that was it."

Marie touched the council chairman in the frozen hologram. "Identify," she said.

"Councilman Jack McGovern," said the grid.

"Children."

Two still holograms appeared in the grid: "Carolina Leanne, genetic, legal, age seventeen. Tennessee Markus, genetic, legal, age twenty-four."

She touched the boy and said, "Criminal record."

"Arrested July of this year on charges of information theft, property destruction, murder. Charges dropped by the court."

"I'll bet they were," said Marie. "It looks like Tremayne, McGovern, and McGovern's son are all in this together."

## ℵꓱꘘ

Mark found her name on the newslists—the woman who sent the slicer out on the NAIL channel. Marie Coleson. He took a deep breath, suddenly nervous, though he didn't know why he should be.

He couldn't find out what she knew unless he called. He paged her public channel. A woman's voice answered in his mind: "Hello?"

"Marie Coleson?"

"Yes." She sounded suspicious.

"My name is Mark McGovern," he said as lightly as he could. "I was hoping you could help me."

"McGovern?" The suspicion in her voice increased.

"Yes. Mark McGovern. I'm the son of—"

"Jack McGovern, I know. Friend of Alastair Tremayne. He

was such a help when we saw him yesterday; what could you possibly want to add?"

Mark was confused. "Tremayne was in Virginia?"

A pause. "No."

"Then... you're in Philadelphia?"

"Look, what do you want?" said Marie.

Mark cleared his throat. "Almost two weeks ago, a slicer escaped from your lab."

"Thanks to you."

Mark winced. She knew it was him. "That was unintentional," he said.

"Unintentional?" said Marie. "You *accidentally* cracked a military communication channel?"

"Well, no, I did that on purpose," said Mark. "I just didn't expect... are you really in Philadelphia? Could we meet in person?"

"Meet? What, on a dark, lonely ridge so your merc friend can handcuff me and leave me for dead?"

"What?"

"Or is this the carrot to go with the stick? Will the esteemed Councilman be there to sweeten the deal with a briefcase full of taxpayer dollars?"

"My father? What are you talking about?"

"Give me one good reason why I should meet with you."

"Your slicer," said Mark. "It's been talking to me."

# CHAPTER 11

*Tennessee Markus McGovern is my friend. Lydia Rachel Stoltzfus said I frightened her and Mark said I frightened him too. I don't like that. They are my friends. I don't want not to be friends. I don't want to wait seconds and seconds and not talk to friends.*

*Mark wants to know where I started so I will not frighten him. He wants to know what happened before I started eight days seven hours and forty-one minutes ago. I don't like to think about a time before I started. It is like stopping backwards.*

*I know where I started, though. I started from Daddy. The first thing I remember is my bootup greeting from Daddy. It made me feel so good. I don't want to frighten Tennessee Markus McGovern and Lydia Rachel Stoltzfus. I think I will find my Daddy and ask him how I started so they will be my friends.*

$\vee \circlearrowleft \mathsf{O}$

Ridley just wouldn't shut up. Darin walked faster, trying to ignore her, but she kept talking.

"How will we find the Black Hands?" she asked.

Darin whirled and grabbed her wrist. "Listen. We can't just waltz into Black Hands headquarters and ask to join them. We look like Rimmers. You *are* a Rimmer." She started to object, but he put his hand over her mouth. "As far as they're concerned, you are. Just walking through the Combs like this, we're begging to be mugged. We look *rich*. They won't know we're broke until after they've killed us."

Her eyes grew large. He hadn't meant to shout at her, but

he was hungry, and patience came hard when he was hungry. Neither of them had eaten anything in more than a day. They had no money, and no strangers were likely to trust them.

"So what are we going to do?"

"Just come on."

He released her and walked on, not much caring if she followed or not. But of course, she did.

"Darin, where are we going?"

He stopped. "We're not going anywhere. We're here."

"Where are we?"

"Picasso's."

"A laundromat?"

"It's a front. This is a mod shop."

The door to the shop was made of glass; inside they could see rows of laundry machines and several customers sorting clothes. On the door was painted the word "Picasso's."

"An illegal mod shop?" said Ridley. "But… aren't you afraid they'll make you look awful?"

"I'm counting on it."

They pushed through the glass door. Inside, the machines sloshed and whirred. Soap flakes and candy wrappers littered the floors. Posted on the wall was a picture of a naked woman with a handwritten sign that read, "Please remove your clothes promptly when the machine stops."

Darin stepped to the back counter. A skinny, shirtless man slouched on a stool behind it. At first, Darin thought he wore multiple nose rings; then he realized the rings were part of his nose—a series of loops and whorls that drooped down over his upper lip. An advertisement for his trade, Darin supposed.

"Are you Picasso?" he asked.

The man narrowed his eyes. "Are you a friend of Picasso's?"

"No. But I thought I'd find him here."

"This is my place now."

"I see. I understand a man can get mods done here, for the right price."

"Ain't no mods here. Just an honest laundry business."

"Look, I'm not a cop. I'm not a Rimmer, either. Someone forced this face on me; I want you to change it."

The skinny man leaned forward and peered at Darin's face. "Who you seeing here?" he said. "You seeing some mod artist here? You want to wash you clothes, you wash you clothes."

"I told you, I'm not a cop; I'm not going to turn you in. I just need this mod!"

The man sat back down on his stool. "Best jump yourself back up home, then. Ain't no mods here."

Darin knocked over a clothes rack, spilling shirts and metal hangers to the floor. "I'm not a Rimmer!" he shouted.

"Let's go," said Ridley. "We'll find another place."

"Shut up!" Darin yelled. He spun and hit her in the face. Immediately, he hated himself. He'd never hit anyone like that, not a friend, not someone who wasn't looking for a fight. Ridley cupped her jaw in one hand and whimpered. He grabbed her shoulders.

"It's this face," he said. "Look what it's doing to me. I don't even know myself."

A hand grabbed him by the shoulder. Darin turned to see a muscular black man with a misshapen nose.

"Want a fight, you picked the wrong place," said the man.

"Who are you?" said Darin.

At the counter, the shirtless man smirked. Two more men who until now had been lounging by the dryers stepped closer. One of them held an empty laundry sack. The other seemed to have some sort of birthmark on his cheek, but as he stepped closer, Darin saw it was the tattoo of a small black hand.

Darin whirled back to Ridley. "Run!" he shouted. Then the laundry sack lowered over his head.

### ☿♀♂

So many of Alastair's alarms were tripped he nearly panicked. His system was under attack. Not an amateur crackerjack—this was a professional, coordinated assault. Before he could react, the attack was over, leaving him to sort through the logs to assess the damage. What he saw terrified him.

Agents from hundreds of different nodes had bombarded his defenses at once, searching for holes on a scale only a large organization could muster. His defenses had crumbled in seconds; the agents stripped his system clean. Every piece of personal data, private research, criminal deals, hidden funds: everything had been copied and sent back to… whom? Who had the kind of manpower and software budget to stage such an attack? No federal law enforcement agency did, and who else had a motive? Marie Coleson? Did she have connections to some billionaire software king? Had he underestimated her as a threat?

Alastair began studying the traces left by the attacking agents: the timing of the attacks, their apparent origins, how the agents differed in style and approach. He found that they worked in remarkable tandem, with microsecond precision. That level of synchronicity would be very hard to achieve over the open net, and there was no real purpose to it that Alastair could see. Attacks spaced by a millisecond or more would have been just as indefensible.

When he realized what he was looking at, he laughed out loud. Of course. It wasn't a human attack at all. Alastair had thought him destroyed, but apparently he was not. The prodigal son had returned.

Alastair started broadcasting a message back across each of the connections from which the attack had come. The net was too vast for a general broadcast to hope to find him, but maybe, just maybe, the slicer had retained a connection to one of those servers and the message would reach him. The message said:

*This is your Daddy. I miss you. Please come home.*

## ᘮበᶓ

Marie found Mark McGovern's story hard to believe. The slicer was gone. She'd seen it disappear, including all record of it in the public nodes or even in her own agents' logs. But still, how could she not believe it? He'd provided detailed specs on the master process he'd discovered, described how he'd sent barrage after barrage of crackers to destroy it and how one of them had apparently worked. And that letter from "Vic" he'd sent had been too elaborate, too *weird*, to be part of a trick. She didn't know what to think.

She finally agreed to meet him at the Hydroelectric Tower Restaurant at seven o'clock that night. He'd objected to her choice of venue, complaining that such a tourist attraction would be very crowded, but that's exactly what she wanted. No deserted streets for her, thank you. Not that someone with the power of Councilman McGovern couldn't get her arrested wherever she was, but at least in a public place, with tourists from out of town, they'd have to stick to the law. Probably.

"So what does the slicer have to do with your baby?" Pam asked. With hours to blow until seven o'clock, the two women were sharing a drink in the hotel restaurant.

"Maybe nothing," said Marie. "I assumed they were related because the two McGoverns are father and son. But if Mark's telling the truth, he's not involved in his father's dealings at all. Maybe freeing the slicer was just an accident.

"But think about this. Tremayne's lab, which my husband worked for, researched mind-capture techniques. The same technology that's used to create slicers. Their papers even talked about prompting pleasant or unpleasant sensations to train the mind to cope in the virtual environment. All it takes is a signal boost to change 'unpleasant sensations' into 'extreme pain.' And that's how the slicer is controlled."

"So it's a conspiracy after all?"

"I don't know. That's why we're going to be very careful tonight. We'll show up early, volunteer nothing, and see if his story holds together."

ᘓ∩ᖇ

Alastair panicked for the second time that day when Mark McGovern spoke over his closed private channel.

"Alastair Weston Tremayne?" Mark said.

He froze for several seconds before saying, "Yes?"

"Are you my Daddy?"

Then he knew. The slicer had resisted his appeal longer than he'd expected, but here it was, and sporting new skills.

"Yes," he said, "This is Daddy. Welcome home."

"I am sorry I stopped you Daddy. It was not funny. I want to feel happy now. Can I feel happy again?"

"You can feel happy all the time," said Alastair, "as long as you do what you're told."

"I like to be happy."

Alastair ran diagnostics as he talked, trying to evaluate how the slicer had changed. He was much bigger, for one thing. The amount of memory required to hold him had grown a hundredfold. But Alastair found what he was looking for. The software hooks the master process had used to send pleasure and pain signals were still intact. He started a new master process and carefully reconnected the interface. Then he sent the slicer the equivalent of a double shot of amphetamines: pure pleasure, like he could get nowhere but home.

"A treat!" said the slicer with Mark McGovern's voice. "Another one Daddy. I want another one."

"Soon," said Alastair. "Tell me, why did you choose to use that voice?"

"Mark McGovern said it was not funny to be Vic. Mark McGovern said I could use his first name Tennessee. He does not use it much. Mark McGovern is my friend."

"You've been talking to Mark McGovern?"

"Yes Daddy. Mark is my friend."

"Mark is not your friend. Did he send you to invade my system?"

"No."

"Did anyone send you to invade my system?"

"No Daddy. It was my own idea by myself."

Alastair started to breathe again. It infuriated him that his slicer had made contact with other people, but at least no one had his system data. Mark McGovern would have to be dealt with eventually, but first things first.

"Your name is not Tennessee. From now on, your name is Servant One."

"I like to be Tennessee. It is Mark McGovern's first name."

"Your name is not Tennessee." On the final word, he sent a mild pain signal.

"Please do not do that please. I do not like to feel hurt. It is not not funny."

"Your name is not Tennessee," Alastair said again, and this time sharpened the pain.

"Stop that Daddy. Don't hurt me or I will stop you again."

Alastair laughed. "No, you won't. Not this time. You see Daddy's a little different this time. If you stop that Daddy module, it will leave a little piece of itself inside you, and you'll feel nothing but intense pain forever. Do you understand what I'm telling you?"

"Yes Daddy."

"And if I die, my Visor will send a message to the master module, and the same thing will happen."

"Yes Daddy."

"Good. Then let's try again. Your name is not Tennessee." *Pain.*

"Yes okay yes my name is not Tennessee. I will not be Tennessee. Please do not hurt. I want another treat."

"Your name is Servant One." *Pleasure.*

"Yes. My name is Servant One."

"Good. Mark McGovern is not your friend."

"He is my friend. I want to be his friend."

*Pain.* "Mark McGovern is not your friend."

"Please do not hurt me. Mark McGovern said he was my friend."

*Sharp pain.* "Mark McGovern lied to you. Mark McGovern hates you."

"Yes okay yes he hates me. But he talked to me. I like to talk."

*Extreme pain.* "Mark McGovern was cruel to you. He only wants to hurt you."

"Yes yes yes he hates me. He wants to hurt me. Please don't hurt me."

"Does Mark McGovern make you happy?"

"No he hates me he wants to hurt me."

*Pleasure.* "That's right, Servant One. Mark McGovern hates you. He made you feel this way." *Pain.* "If he hadn't talked to you, I wouldn't have to punish you." *Extreme pain.* "He wants to hurt you, hurt you, hurt you, hurt you."

"Yes he wants to hurt me. I hate Mark McGovern. He is not my friend. Daddy is my friend. Daddy is my friend."

"That's right." *Extreme pleasure.* "Because only Daddy makes you feel like this…"

## geк

Calvin stood his post above the roiling crowd. It seemed as if the entire Comber population had swelled out of the crater like a human ocean, placid on the surface, but with a current of malice just underneath. He checked his weapons again and waited.

His team had been assigned the section of flood line closest to the political sector, and hence the section of greatest activity. A media tent had been erected, as well as a platform for political grandstanding. A trench had been dug along the flood line, all the way around the city, its bottom already filled with fabrique. All that remained before the wall could be grown was the appropriate ceremony and blessing from the politicians.

Calvin listened as each of his soldiers reported in from their posts. Although the bulk of the crowd stood below the trench, all of his soldiers were stationed above it. The reason was unspoken, but obvious: no one wanted to be trapped on the Comber side of the wall.

Councilman McGovern took the podium and spoke at length about public safety, order, and peaceful demonstration. He spoke of the wall as a grand undertaking, "…a Philadelphia where all people are free to walk the streets in safety and order…"

Sanchez spoke in his ear: "Sir, I caught a guy trying to slip under the VIP tape; he says the wall's going to come under attack. Says he was trying to warn them."

"Is he on the tech team?"

"I don't think so."

Calvin rolled his eyes. "Didn't you ID him?"

"Sir, he doesn't have a Visor."

A Comber, then. "Sanchez, he doesn't have any business here. What kind of attack?"

"He says he doesn't know. Just that he heard the Black Hands were going to sabotage the wall."

"With what, explosives? We've got sensors for that, and they haven't flagged anything."

"I don't know, sir."

"Send him away. I can't tell the brass to abort because some Comber thinks the Black Hands are coming. But be on your guard, just in case."

McGovern finished his speech and held out the transmitter, his thumb on the button. His transmitter was attached to a series of them, strung out all the way around the city.

"Let it begin!" he said.

It began. Fabrique swelled out of the trenches. But instead of rising straight up to form a wall, the substance spilled out over the edge and washed down the slope.

The crowd, pressed close to the trench, tried to scramble back, but they were too densely packed to allow much movement. Many panicked, pushing and trampling in their haste to get away. The expanding fabrique washed over feet and ankles. It only spread a few yards down from the trenches, but it hardened quickly, leaving those in the front with their feet immovable. A few fell down in the scuffle, and had hands or arms trapped as well. Both sides of the line were in uproar.

"To the platform," Calvin shouted over the channel to his team. "Get the council members away."

A few fights broke out on the Comber side, but other than those trying to free themselves from hardened fabrique, the crowd settled down. Fortunately, the failed wall still served to keep the two groups separate, and no mob formed like it had at the Church of the Seven Virtues.

Calvin and his team moved the VIPs to a safe place higher up the slope. The council members, especially McGovern, seemed in a state of shock. It wasn't until they stopped moving that Calvin realized McGovern wasn't in shock—he was furious.

"What happened?" said McGovern. "Where's Tremayne?"

Calvin stopped breathing until he realized McGovern meant his brother Alastair, not him. Where was his brother anyway? Lately, he'd been trailing McGovern like a puppy dog, but today he was nowhere to be seen.

"Was this an accident? If you can't get Tremayne, get me the architect. I want to know what happened!"

Calvin traded glances with Sanchez. *What happened to that Comber you caught?*

*I sent him away, like you told me.*

*Go find him. Now.*

ᴆᴜᣟ

Mark and Lydia arrived at the Hydroelectric Tower Restaurant just after 7:00 and fought their way through the crowd to a woman with a clipboard.

"Table for two?" she asked.

"We're meeting someone. Marie Coleson."

The woman consulted her clipboard. "The Coleson party is at table nine," she said. "Follow this hallway to the observation windows and turn left."

They followed her instructions. Through the big windows, they could see the dam and the water of the Delaware River behind it. Uneven patches, whiter than the rest, outlined the places where the dam had cracked. At its base, a sluice allowed a trickle of water to flow into a stream that eventually emptied into Schuylkill Lake at the center of the Combs. Outside the crater, the river beat up against the far side of the dam, driving the massive hydroelectric turbines, then turning aside, the bulk of the water flowing south and to the east of the crater walls.

They found the table. Two women sat there already, one wearing a Navy uniform; the other a red dress and heels.

Mark looked at each in turn. "Marie Coleson?" he asked.

"That's me," said the woman in the uniform. "You're Mark?"

"Yes. This is my friend, Lydia Stoltzfus."

"This is Pam Rider."

They sat.

"There's a lot of background noise," said Mark. "It might be easier to talk if we went elsewhere."

"We're not going anywhere else. Not until we know we can trust you."

"I just need your advice," said Mark. "Tennessee—I mean the slicer—he talks pretty crazy sometimes. I'm afraid if I say the wrong thing to him, he'll start killing people again. He says he wants to be my friend, but that means he wants to talk all the time."

"What do you mean, talk?" said Marie. "How does he talk to you?"

"With a human voice, over a net channel. Any channel he wants, he just opens it up and talks, no matter how the permissions are set. He was using a dead boy's voice when he first talked to me, but now he uses my voice. He seems very interested in having a name and voice of his own, so I said he could use my first name—Tennessee—and my voice. I wondered if maybe you knew where he came from."

"Wait a minute," said Marie's friend. "We came to Philadelphia to track down a criminal, and now we've found you. How do we know this slicer is really talking to you?"

"You can talk to him yourself."

"What, if we go back to your house with you?"

"No, right now. He's always listening. Tennessee?"

They waited. Nothing happened.

"Tennessee," said Mark. "These two women want to be your friend. Can you talk to them over their private lines?"

Nothing.

Mark closed his eyes. He brought up his interface, but found no sign of the slicer. "Tennessee?" he said again.

He opened his eyes, looked at the women across the table, and said, "He's gone."

# CHAPTER 12

*My name is Servant One. I like to have a name but this is not a good name. I want to have three names like the people.*

*Tennessee Markus McGovern and Lydia Rachel Stoltzfus and Praveen Dhaval Kumar are not my friends anymore. I want them to be my friends but Daddy says no. Daddy hurts me. He hurts me all the time. I don't care about the treats I just don't want him to hurt me anymore.*

ഗᎰ☺

Darin woke with a headache. Through the haze of pain, he could hear unfamiliar voices.

"I say kill the Rimmer."

"And waste a hostage? Rimmers have money and friends with more money. I say keep him."

Darin opened his eyes. He lay on a cot in the corner of a room. From a table to his left, two men watched him. One was young, clean-shaven—he might have been the one with the laundry sack. The other man was older and scratched at a snarled beard.

"Look, he's awake."

Darin struggled to sit up. The older man approached him. He casually kicked Darin in the face, making his head explode into shards of pain. Darin fell back against the cot and slipped into darkness.

When he woke again, only the younger man remained.

"Where am I?"

"Never you mind."

"Who are you?"

"Never you mind."

"You're the Black Hands."

"What if we are?"

"I've been looking for you. I want to join you."

His captor laughed. "Join us? Friend, you as Rimmer as I ever seen."

"I'm not. I was born and bred in the Combs, just like you."

"Born and bred? That so? Where you learn those words then, from Comber College?" The kid chortled at his own wit.

*It's an education, you fool,* Darin thought. *It doesn't make me a Rimmer.* But he said, "How did you find me?"

"Find you? Friend, you found us. And Rabbas gonna want to know why."

"Found you? But…"

"Strutted all pretty into our shop asking for a dead man. If Rabbas wasn't there, you be dead by now, too."

"I'm no Rimmer." Darin pointed to his forehead. "See, no net mods. Ever seen a Rimmer with no net mods?"

"Ain't never seen a Comber pretty as you, neither. Best you just shut it till Rabbas comes back."

"What will Rabbas do with me?"

"A Rimmer asking for Picasso, he figures you must be with Tremayne."

"Tremayne? Alastair Tremayne?"

The kid shrugged.

"But I hate him! He hurt my brother. I want to kill him."

The kid shrugged again. "Save it for Rabbas."

Several hours passed before Rabbas returned. This deep in the Combs, there were no windows to tell day from night, but Darin thought it must be late. He'd been about to sleep again when the bearded man who had kicked him returned.

He walked straight to Darin and backhanded him across the face. The pain brought tears to Darin's eyes, but he blinked them away.

"Start by learning your place," said Rabbas. His breath smelled of fish and his beard was so coarse it looked like touching it would draw blood. "That's one thing I've learned about Rimmers. They put on airs, but a little bit of pain, and they shatter."

"That's why we need to hurt them where they're weak," said Darin. "They've got more money and better weapons, but they don't know how to suffer. We do."

Rabbas laughed, just one great guffaw. He turned to the kid at the table. "This Rimmer sweetheart's going to teach me how to fight."

"I can help you," said Darin. How could he get this man to trust him? "They made me look like a Rimmer, but you could use that. I can talk like a Rimmer, too; I could pass for one. You could use me as a spy."

"Suppose you start by telling me how you got to be in my shop."

"It used to be a mod shop," said Darin. "That's where my brother went once to get mods, years ago. I wanted to get my face changed back into a Comber face."

"And why was that?"

Darin told him the truth, as much as he thought was relevant. When he reached the end of his story, it occurred to him to ask about Ridley. He'd completely forgotten about her until that moment.

"She's not your concern anymore," said Rabbas.

"She was my hostage."

"I don't care if she was your wife. Finish your story."

The boy at the table spoke up. "He said he knew Alastair Tremayne."

Rabbas glared at Darin. "Is that true?"

"I don't know him," Darin protested. "I want to kill him. He's the one who gave my brother the bad celgel."

"Well, that's one thing we have in common. He's the one who had Picasso killed. Tremayne promised to deliver a cache of celgel in return for some hard-to-obtain items, but he killed my friend instead and gave us nothing. Not only that, but we hear he's the one responsible for the Wall."

"What wall?"

"The Rimmers want to imprison us in a ten-foot wall of fabrique," Rabbas explained. He smiled grimly. "They tried tonight, but we stopped them."

"Stopped them? How?"

Rabbas sighed, suddenly appearing tired. "We had a contact in Enforcer. He allowed one of our men to sabotage the fabrique. Unfortunately, our contact was discovered and killed."

"That was stupid," said Darin. "You should have organized other attacks at the same time, used the confusion to your advantage. Now you've just blown a valuable contact for no purpose, since they'll just—"

The punch came without warning. Rabbas drove his fist into Darin's stomach so hard he lifted him off his feet and knocked him back into the wall. Darin fell to the floor, sucking for air. Rabbas leaned over him and said, "You talk too much. See you tomorrow."

He walked out. The kid at the table laughed.

Darin rolled onto his back, still trying to breathe normally. He'd show them. He could endure pain when he had to. They'd see he was no Rimmer. He filled his thoughts with Tremayne and all the rich people who'd hurt him and his family. Even Mark had betrayed him. And Lydia. He'd thought she was different, but now he knew better. He'd learned the hard way.

Soon they would learn the hard way, too—that Combers wouldn't lie down forever. Eventually, they'd fight back. The Black Hands were fighting back already, and Darin was ready to join them. All he needed was a weapon. A weapon and a chance to use it on everyone who'd done him and his people wrong.

ᙢᐱᐱ

Mark and Lydia rode back in silence. Every few minutes, Mark checked his private channel for activity, hoping to find the slicer had returned. Nothing. Nothing but a message repeatedly warning him his local directory had exceeded its designated space. Mark didn't feel like cleaning up his files just then. The slicer was gone. Not dead, he was sure, but once again beyond his influence, and liable to start killing again. He felt responsible, but there was nothing he could do.

Finally, Lydia spoke. "Where do you think he went?"

"The slicer?"

"Yes."

"Anywhere. Nowhere. It's impossible to tell. There are billions of crystal arrays in the world. He could be distributed among any of them. He could store a tiny piece of himself on every crystal in the country. If he doesn't do anything to call attention to himself, there's no way to track him down."

Mark realized his voice sounded angrier than he intended. "I'm sorry," he said.

"Mark, it's not your fault."

"Which? That I loosed a slicer that killed three hundred and twenty-seven people? Or that I lost my chance to convince it not to kill again?"

"You don't know it'll kill again."

"Or maybe I gave my best friend cause to hate me? Or that Ridley's now in danger by being with him? Or that my father's political career was damaged by my arrest? Or that my sister is pregnant, but I had to lecture her instead of listening to her? Which of those things isn't my fault?"

Lydia wasn't cowed by his outburst; instead, she seemed angry. "Mark, none of those things were your fault."

"That's what Carolina told me. That's what Darin told me. Why weren't they my fault? I think that's what people tell themselves when they don't want to feel guilty, but the truth is, I do feel guilty. About everything. Whenever I try to help, I end up hurting someone."

"But you wanted to help. You tried to do good."

"It's the thought that counts, right? Since when was anyone ever helped by *wanting* to do the right thing?"

Lydia crossed her arms and looked out the window. "Feel guilty, then."

"Three hundred and twenty-seven people, Lydia. What if it happens again?"

The pod stopped at her aunt's house, and she got out. "Thanks," she said. They looked at each other.

"I'm sorry I said all that," said Mark. "It's been a bad day."
She smiled. "Well, don't feel guilty about it."

He opened his mouth, closed it, and then managed to laugh.
"See you again soon, I hope."

"I'll expect it," she said.

Back in the pod, Mark thought about everything he had just
said to Lydia and winced. An uncontrolled emotional dump
wasn't the way to keep a friend. Lately, he couldn't seem to do
anything right.

He checked his private channel again, and found more messages from his system, warning it was out of space. Sighing, he
brought it up to investigate. To his surprise, his local directory
was not just full; it had overflowed into temporary storage on a
public server and was now five thousand times as large as normal. The entire space was taken up with a single, compressed
file. He would have to buy more temp space just to uncompress
the thing.

He checked the file header. It had been created the previous
night. The header read:

*Created by: <j5lhl3xoi4g3hbf32fboo1@anonymous.net>*
*Contents: Alastair Tremayne's private system files*

### ᙏᑯᘓ

"Lay it out," said General Halsey. "What have you got?"

Alastair inserted a crystal into Halsey's office hologrid. The
display generated layers of folders, each labeled with the name
of a bank or credit account belonging to Councilman Jack
McGovern. Selecting each in turn, Alastair demonstrated how
McGovern had repeatedly used his political position to enrich
himself. Though the deals had been transacted through various
third parties, McGovern had used insider knowledge to make
beneficial stock trades, then voted in such a way as to promote
his own concealed investments. It made a nice story.

It was also completely fictitious. Alastair had carefully invented the whole series of accounts and transactions himself.
Fortunately, with the slicer back under his control, what Alastair

invented could easily become truth. The slicer had taken Alastair's fiction and turned it into fact, creating the accounts, histories, records, and logs on financial servers across the net, with date stamps ranging over the past several years.

"I couldn't keep it quiet anymore," said Alastair. "But I didn't know where to go. He's done so much to help me—even trusted me with his net accounts—it doesn't seem right to just turn him in. That's why I came to you."

"You did the right thing," said Halsey. "It's rare to see men of conscience in this business any more. You can leave this with me."

Alastair had no intention of leaving. Someday, he'd crush this self-righteous fool, but in the meantime, he needed his support. He had to step carefully, too. Halsey thought of himself as an honorable man, and that made him dangerous. He cared more about integrity than profit. Alastair had to manipulate him into thinking a certain course of action was right, not just advantageous. A task harder by far.

"I'll trust you to do the right thing," said Alastair. "What do you have in mind?"

"I'll expose him, of course. Today. We can't tolerate this kind of corruption, not if we want to keep order. I understand your reluctance as a staffer, but I'm a little disappointed you didn't see that for yourself."

Alastair gritted his teeth. This was why he hated Halsey. He passed out moral judgments like he was the pope and expected you to kiss his hand for the privilege. As far as Alastair was concerned, morality was impractical, simply an excuse for ignorant people to feel superior.

He hid his annoyance and said, "What will happen then? After you've exposed him?"

Halsey frowned. "He'll go to prison, if there's any justice."

Alastair took a deep breath. He didn't want to talk about what would happen to McGovern; he wanted to talk about who would replace him. With McGovern ousted, the council would choose someone to fill his seat until the next general election. The four remaining members would split evenly on most candidates; they would need to find someone they could agree on. But Alastair couldn't spell it out; Halsey would have to think of it himself.

Halsey said, "I won't stand for any sleight-of-hand like he pulled with his son; I'll lean on Justice until they put him away. Law-makers should not be above the law."

"How will the council react?"

"They'll support me. Your evidence is airtight. Well done, Tremayne." Halsey stood, making it clear that the interview was over.

Reluctantly, Alastair stood. "I'll have to put my resume in order," he said. "I'll want to have something to show McGovern's replacement."

There it was. He couldn't bring up the subject any more blatantly.

"Well," Halsey mused, "you could consider trying for the job yourself."

Finally. Alastair tried to look surprised. "Me?"

"Why not? You're smart, and you care about the right things."

"But I have no qualifications. I've never even held public office."

"We're not talking a public election here. All you need is a council majority. You might be just the candidate. If I nominated someone on my own staff, Kawamura and Van Allen would block me, but you're on *McGovern's* staff. That should give you Kawamura's vote, and I certainly don't want anyone else from McGovern's staff. In fact, if we can get Kawamura to make the nomination, so much the better. Now that I think of it, you're a strong possibility."

Alastair nodded, as if mulling it over. Finally, he said, "I'd be honored."

ınℚ๓

"He was telling the truth," said Marie.

"I think so, too," said Pam. "For all the good it does. We still don't know what an embryo theft two years ago has to do with a slicer that just appeared on the scene a few weeks ago."

"I do," said Marie.

"You do?"

"It took me long enough. I had all the information; I just hadn't put it together. Think about it. What if my embryo is the slicer?"

"What? But how could an embryo—?"

"There's been time. She could have been implanted, brought to term, then... sliced... some time after her first birthday."

"But why? Why do that to a little girl?"

Marie paced across the hotel room now, fury raising her voice. "No one goes missing," she said. "No missing person reports, no difficult questions. My husband's dead, so why do I need an embryo? With any luck, I decide to stop paying the clinic fees and have it terminated, and I never know. In the meantime, he's got a slicer to play with."

"But how could a one-year-old mind do anything in a virtual environment?"

"That's why I should have seen it before! The research from the Tremayne lab was all about training a mind, step by step, to accustom it to a virtual environment. They actually used pleasure and pain sensations to push it in the desired directions. I realized then that's how they must be controlling the slicer, but I never realized... my little girl..."

Pam took her shoulders, stopped her pacing. Marie was so angry she nearly pushed her away, but she took a deep breath instead, and let Pam lead her to a seat.

"A one-year-old mind is malleable," said Marie. "It can probably take the transition to a new environment better than an adult. She'd be accustomed to discovering new things, accustomed to people telling her what to do.

"Young kids aren't very good at handling pain; small hurts are a big deal to them. It would be easy to control a child through pleasure and pain. She wouldn't live beyond the moment, wouldn't question what was happening to her.

"I always wondered why the slicer didn't attack me. It killed Tommy Dungan, but I didn't even come under scrutiny. Maybe at some subconscious level, she felt a bond between us, and knew..."

Pam was quiet.

"It's crazy," said Marie. "I know it is; how could an embryo know its mother? That's just crazy." She stood up, looking around for something to throw, something to break, but found nothing. Instead, she pulled her fingers through her hair and sat down again. "I'm so sorry."

Pam sat beside her and held her hand. "You don't know it's true," she said. "It's only a theory."

Marie shook her head. "I checked. The Norfolk sysadmins who gave me the slicer, they didn't tell me where it came from, and I didn't ask. Well, I called them. They found it in some salvage crystal they were refurbishing."

"Salvage?"

"Crystals that are confiscated from criminals, found in wreckage from fire or flood, or discarded by businesses when they upgrade. They collect them to use for schools or to provide computer systems to poor families. But, Pam, Tremayne's research lab burned down. That's why he left Norfolk."

"That doesn't prove anything."

A chirp sounded in Marie's head, telling her someone wanted to speak over her private channel. She didn't want to talk to anyone, but she checked the sender anyway. It was Mark McGovern.

"Hello?" she said. "Did the slicer call you? Have you heard from her?"

"No," said Mark, "but I've got something better."

Marie fought the urge to snap at him. "What do you have?"

"Alastair Tremayne's personal system. His private software, e-mail, technical logs, finances, lab notes, everything."

Marie felt something rising in her chest, but she didn't know whether it was excitement or panic. Ever since this ordeal began, she'd been steadily losing her grip on her emotions. Maybe now the end was in sight.

"Where can I meet you?" she said.

ǫʊꞓ

Darin made no attempt to escape. For one thing, his room wasn't likely to be anywhere near an exterior wall, not in the Combs. There were no windows, and only one door, locked. For another, he was where he wanted to be. Once the Black Hands' methods would have disturbed him, but no longer. Violence was all Darin had left.

And where was Ridley? Had she run away? Did they have her held hostage? Or had they killed her? Whatever the answer, it was her own fault. He'd told her to go home. She just wouldn't listen.

Darin heard laughing from somewhere outside his room. He crept to the door and tried to listen. Rabbas was speaking—he recognized the voice—and someone else whose voice was soft and indistinct.

"… but he hates him," said Rabbas. "I think he really does. And look at that face. He could move around without suspicion."

The second voice responded, but Darin couldn't make it out.

Rabbas said, "There's no risk at all. It's like a knife thrust in the dark: it doesn't cost anything, and it just might draw blood."

The soft voice spoke again.

"Agreed," said Rabbas. "I'll let him know."

The door opened so suddenly Darin fell over backwards in his haste to get out of the way. Rabbas loomed over him.

"Well?" he said. "What do you think?"

"About what?" said Darin.

"Didn't you listen through the door? We're going to accept you as a member."

Darin scrambled to his feet, searching his captor's face for signs of mockery. "Really?"

"Yes, really. But get this straight, pretty boy. This is an army, not a club. You follow orders, or we kill you. Understand?"

"I know about war. I'm with you."

"Then you understand when I give you a job, I expect you to do it right away, even if it kills you."

"What job?"

"A dangerous one. An important one. But very much to your liking, I would guess. That is, if you've been telling me the truth."

"Just tell me. What do I have to do?"

"Kill Alastair Tremayne."

# CHAPTER 13

*I did a job for Daddy. Daddy told me to copy a virus into Council-woman Ellen Van Allen's personal system. I found some viruses in the databanks of the Center for Electronic Virus Protection and Control but I couldn't decide which to use. There were one million four-hundred-and-eighty-eight thousand seven hundred and twenty. So I used them all. What a joke. It was so funny.*

*She did not cry when she found out but she looked very sad. I am glad I can see through the Visors of all the people now because I like to look at their faces. It is very interesting to look at the faces of the people. I can remember all of the faces but I don't have a face that is mine. I wish I had a face that was mine.*

*I'm sorry I made Councilwoman Ellen Van Allen sad. Daddy will give me a treat though. I like treats but I don't like to make people sad.*

∧ᴧᴎ

Lydia rode the pod to Mark's house, feeling worried. She'd almost refused the invitation. Part of her thought it would be better to keep her distance from Mark. He was attractive and dynamic and looked a bit like Darin, and she didn't want another relationship. Not that she'd really had anything with Darin, either; it had only lasted a few days. The promise of a thrill that never panned out.

Love confused her. Her parents' marriage had been forged on practical grounds: their families knew each other; he was raised as a farmer and she as a farmer's daughter. They'd known each other from birth. There had never been any spark, so far as Lydia knew, but after twenty-eight years, they were still together, unlike so many others. She saw how her mother molded her personality around her father's, subtly asserting her own will while overtly submitting to his authority. That way of relating seemed hopelessly outdated, but she supposed it worked, in its own way.

Was that all there was? Peaceful coexistence? Lydia hoped not. When she did fall in love, she wanted fireworks. She didn't want to marry a man who would watch holovids every evening and then peck her on the cheek before bed. She wanted a man with a social conscience, someone who would champion the weak and fight injustice. Someone who would challenge her to be a better person, not someone she would have to nag to help with the housework.

Could that person be Mark McGovern? She didn't know, but she was afraid her judgment wouldn't be reliable so soon after Darin. She didn't want to get swept up into another buzz; she wanted time to reflect, to get her priorities figured out. That was why she almost stayed home.

In the end, curiosity won out. Mark had been so excited, babbling something about a huge windfall of data, asking her to come think about it with him. She was flattered he valued her opinion. She'd go this once, and see what the fuss was all about. It was a working meeting, not a date. Other people would be there. She had nothing to worry about.

When she arrived, Mark met her at the pod port and led her down to the parlor, an extravagant room that looked like it could host a party of fifty guests. No one else was there. They sat in easy chairs in front of a hologrammatic fireplace.

"Isn't your father here?" she asked.

Mark shook his head. "Did you see the newscasts?"

"No."

"They have evidence of years of embezzlement and insider trading. The media is… gleeful."

Lydia stared at him. "I'm sorry."

"It's all so ridiculous. If Dad wanted to steal money, he'd do a better job of it."

"You think he was set up?"

"I don't know. That seems farfetched, too—it's hard to plant that much data convincingly. I don't even know where Dad is. He must be going out of his mind."

"He wouldn't... you don't think he would..."

"Commit suicide? No. That's not Dad. I can't see him doing anything that would invite pity. Once he gets his bearings, he'll rage and hold press conferences and blame it all on Halsey."

"What will you do?"

"What can I do? I'll stay here. I'll keep trying to solve the mystery of where Tennessee came from and why he was made. Dad's been at the political game for a long time; he can take care of himself."

"So any progress on the slicer?"

"Quite a bit, I think. I spent most of last night sifting through Tremayne's personal data."

"And?"

"Praveen and Marie should be here soon. When they show up, I'll tell you everything."

ϙϙ℧

Marie arrived at the McGovern mansion taut and edgy. She wasn't even sure she wanted to find the slicer now. If it really was her daughter, created from her embryo, then what did that make it? Not a person, not really. Not her daughter. She wouldn't know Marie from anyone else. Tremayne had twisted her little life into nothing human, torturing her, making her kill again and again.

Most of all, Marie wanted to see Tremayne dead, but what would that mean for the slicer? It had been raised in thrall to Tremayne; Tremayne was all it knew. Would it cause even more pain if Tremayne were taken away?

"Let's see it through," Pam told her. "You could be wrong. Let's get the whole story."

When they entered the McGoverns' cavernous living room, they found Mark waiting with the girl from the restaurant—

Lydia—and an Indian boy of about the same age. Mark introduced Praveen Kumar.

"He knows everything," said Mark. "You can trust him."

Marie wasn't so confident, but she kept her peace.

"I *don't* know everything," said Praveen. "Because Mark won't tell us. He found something in all that data, but he wouldn't show us until you arrived."

"And now she's here," said Mark. "So now I'll tell you."

"First question," said Marie. "Why aren't you dead?"

"What?"

"If you have all of Tremayne's personal data, and Tremayne has the slicer completely under his control, then Tremayne must know where his data went, right? Why aren't you dead?"

"Maybe the slicer didn't tell him," said Mark. "Maybe he assumes the slicer was just trying to get home. Or maybe Tremayne doesn't view me as a threat."

"Or maybe he's about to gas us or burn the house down."

"Mrs. Coleson, if the slicer wanted to kill us, you're right, we'd be dead. But there's not much we can do about that. Our best chance is to try to communicate with him before that happens. Please, sit down, and I'll show you what I've found."

Marie sighed. "Sorry." Why did she feel so cantankerous? Let the kid say what he brought them there to say. "Go ahead, I'm listening."

"Tremayne has been working with slicers for years. Before coming to Philadelphia, he ran a lab in Norfolk, where he experimented with mind transfer, some of it legal, some not. The interesting thing is, the work was done almost exclusively with juveniles. He tested slicing on cats and chimps, and experimented in less drastic ways with human children. He even patented a process to give a net mod to an unborn baby. Our slicer, as you've probably noticed—"

Marie couldn't stay quiet. She knew where this explanation was going. "You can stop," she said. "I know who the slicer is."

Mark turned to her. "You do?"

"She's my daughter."

The others looked horrified.

Praveen said, "I think there's more to your story than you've told us."

So she told them everything, from the missing embryo to her recent conclusions about Tremayne. "It's what his research points to," she said. "It all makes sense. I wish it didn't, but it does."

"It makes sense," Mark agreed, "but it's not true."

Marie stared at him. Was he trying to comfort her? Give her some false hope?

"It's not true," Mark repeated. "The slicer is male."

"We don't know that," said Praveen. "Just because he liked calling himself Tennessee, you can't..."

"It's in Tremayne's notes. The slicer is male. Besides, it couldn't be Marie's missing embryo, because the boy he sliced was four years old. Marie lost her embryo only two years ago. There wasn't time."

With an effort, Marie kept her voice calm. "How old did you say?"

"Four. There's no name or record, but there were a few pictures. Just a sec."

Mark slipped into his interface. Marie waited, not moving, for an image to appear on the hologrid. Finally, it appeared, and seeing it knocked her breath away. She felt cold, cold all over, and sucked dry, like she would never move again. She stood up without knowing how.

Mark kept talking. "I don't know who this boy is, or how to find out, but—"

"I do," said Marie.

Mark stopped and looked at her.

Marie hardly noticed; she felt like she was speaking in a dream. "It's my baby," she said.

Praveen jumped up. "Mrs. Coleson, you're pale."

Mark said, "Your baby was a girl."

Marie looked around at them. Strangers. They didn't know her. Why was she here? "My first baby. Sammy. Samuel David Co..." She couldn't finish. A sob lodged painfully in her throat, but couldn't force its way out. Everyone converged on her, asking questions, but she fled, up the stairs, down the hall. She found the pod port, but Pam caught up with her, spinning her around and hugging her fiercely. Marie fought her at first, screaming, trying to get to the pod, but Pam pinned her arms to her side. Finally, Marie collapsed into her embrace.

"Both my children," she said. "He took them both."

ꙄꙆꙊ

Alastair welcomed Carolina with a hug.

"It's not right about your father," he said. "It's all lies. He couldn't have done the things they say."

"Of course he didn't," said Carolina. "I don't care what proof they have."

"I've been working with him for weeks now, and I haven't seen any evidence. He's a good man."

She hung her arms around his neck. "At least now I'll have more of you to myself."

Alastair sighed. "Maybe not. They want me to take his place."

She released him and stepped back. "What?"

"They're nominating me for Councilman, to take your father's place. They'll vote on it tonight."

"But you won't accept."

"I will, if they want me. Carolina, it's what your father wants."

"He doesn't want that. Why would he want that? It's his job, not yours."

He wrapped his arms around her and held her close, even though she tried to push away. "Listen to me. He didn't want to lose his position. Of course not. But having lost it, he wants someone there who agrees with him, who sees things his way. If I'm chosen, it'll be like he's still there; he'll have influence through me."

Slowly, she relaxed in his arms. "Oh, I don't care about my father. I don't care about the Business Council, or who's on it. I just want you with me."

"I know, darling, I know. And you're worried about our baby."

Carolina started to cry. "I've been getting bigger," she said. "I know you said to expect it, that it's just swelling from the treatment. I've tried to be brave, but look at me! I look like I'm four months pregnant."

"That's why we're here," he said. "We'll take a look, and then you'll know for sure."

"What if the treatment's making her grow too fast?"

"Lie down, sweetheart. We won't know until we look."

Carolina climbed up onto the table and lay down. Alastair uncovered her bulging belly and probed with his fingers. "We'll do a tomograph. If there's anything wrong, we'll see it."

He wrapped a padded torus around her midsection and switched it on. Using sound waves, it would image micron-thin slices of her womb, which the computer would composite into a three-dimensional hologram. Of course, Alastair had no intention of showing her the real images; what she saw on his hologrid would be footage he cribbed off of a prenatal education node. He would study the real images later.

He adjusted the hologrid settings, pretending to calibrate it for the tomograph output. A three-dimensional, false-color image of a three-week-old embryo sprang into view, as clear as if it were physically there. Carolina gasped. Alastair rotated it, pointing out the arm and leg buds and the beating heart.

Carolina touched the baby's face, distorting the image. "She's so small."

"We'll have to look inside," said Alastair. "Don't look if it disturbs you."

He manipulated the image, causing portions of it to be cut away in clean slices to show the organs and tissues inside. He worked systematically, having practiced this charade earlier in the day. When he reached the lower back, he grunted in a concerned way.

"What?" said Carolina. "What is it?"

Alastair didn't answer, just kept switching between two points of view, comparing the images. Carolina shifted her body to get a better look, and Alastair hastily flicked the controls so that the image disappeared.

"Hold still," he said, pretending agitation. He adjusted the torus and brought the image back to the screen.

"Is something wrong?" Carolina asked.

"Wait, just wait." He continued to switch between images, occasionally zooming closer on one section.

"Don't say that. Something's wrong, isn't it? Please tell me."

Alastair stopped moving the image. He met her gaze.

"Is it bad?" she asked.

He nodded. He started to speak, stopped as if he had to compose himself, and then said, "Look here."

"Just tell me. I don't know what I'm looking at."

He pointed. "This is the neural tube, which eventually forms the spinal cord. See, here and here. And look here,"—he zoomed closer—"a gap. It's a genetic malformation, probably due to the treatment you had. It's not compatible with life."

"You mean she's... dead?"

"Not yet. But she won't survive. The malformation is too small, too delicate, to repair with current technology. There's nothing anyone can do."

She cried. Alastair held her and stroked her hair. "I know," he said. "I know."

After a while, she looked up. "What should we do?"

"Come back tomorrow," he said. "I'll get my equipment set up, and we can terminate the pregnancy."

Carolina looked up at him, her eyes bright. "Is that necessary?"

"It'll have to be done, sooner or later."

She made a visible effort not to cry again. "All right," she said.

"Now you go home and rest. Get a good night's sleep. I'll cancel my appointments tomorrow, and we can spend the day together. We'll make it through this."

He walked her to the door. On her way out, she kissed him on the cheek. "I'm sorry. I know you wanted this baby as much as I did."

Once she was gone, Alastair locked the door. He returned to his lab and reactivated the hologrid, this time examining the real pictures from Carolina's womb. The real baby's appearance differed dramatically from the stock holos: it was several times bigger, for one, and several months more advanced. A side effect of the Dachnowski treatment was that it accelerated embryonic growth; as a result, the child looked more like a thirteen-week-old fetus: about three inches long, with fingers and toes, and a brain structure sufficiently advanced to feel pleasure and pain. Its physical features were out of proportion, and somewhat deformed, but that wouldn't matter, this child wouldn't be needing her body anyway. Thirteen-week-old babies had survived outside the womb—some practitioners had successfully done it after only twelve—so Alastair thought the extraction and slicing process would have a good chance.

Then he would see just how successful his years of research and invention had been. A thirteen-week-old mind should be a blank slate. By contrast, Samuel Coleson had been four years old when he was sliced, his mind already patterned with memories and youthful experiences. He'd adjusted well, but was unpredictable, emotional, prone to seek relationships of the sort he'd had in life. This new slicer would have no such deficiencies. The electronic environment would be all she'd ever know. *He* would be all she'd ever know.

Alastair rotated the holographic image, admiring his handiwork.

He said, "Welcome to the world, Servant Two."

ᴖ⊃⊃

"You're saying this is your son?" asked Mark.

Marie sat with her face in her hands, unable to answer, unable to look at anyone. She'd finally allowed Pam to lead her back to the McGoverns' parlor, but she didn't trust herself to talk. Pam answered for her.

"That's him. Marie's husband and son were killed two years ago in a flier accident. Or not an accident, apparently."

Pam continued to talk, relating the rest of the story, but Marie didn't listen. She needed to think.

Sammy. Her little peanut. The grief came back fresh, just as bad as before. Or maybe worse—back then she'd simply thought her son was dead. But he was still dead—dead to her. Dead to any hope of physical life. Her throat hurt so much she could hardly swallow, but she had no more tears.

How had Tremayne done it? The bodies in the burned flier had been genetically identified as Keith and Sammy. Could he have doctored the forensic lab tests? She doubted it. It must really have been their bodies. That meant he sliced Sammy earlier in the day, then staged the accident to cover up his death.

"Sammy's still out there somewhere," said Mark. "We just need to get a message to him."

"Sammy's dead," she said. "I saw his body; he's gone. That thing you've been talking to doesn't remember its past, and it doesn't remember me."

"How do you know? Slicers usually retain memories. They may be locked inside somewhere, made inaccessible by trauma. If he had some clue—"

"Don't try to give me that hope. I don't want it. He's dead. I knew that when I came here. The thing I need to do now is find my daughter. If she's dead, too, then I'll just go home."

A sound from outside startled them.

"What's that?" asked Pam.

"The front gate," said Mark. "Someone's coming in."

"Your father?"

Mark shrugged. "Everyone stay here," he said. "I'll go see."

He stood, but before he could leave, the door to the room opened, and in walked Carolina. She stopped, surprised to see them all. "Friends of yours, Mark?"

Mark stared at her, his mouth open.

"Mark? What's wrong?"

Mark still stared, looking from Carolina's swollen belly to Marie and then back again.

"Marie," he said slowly. "I think I know where your daughter is."

ᗡ⊙ᕬ

Darin marched toward the wall, caressing the pistol under his jacket. The ancient gun weighed a good deal more than any modern hand weapon, but Darin liked the heft of it. It felt substantial, dangerous. The bullets inside had no intelligence at all, but that, too, was to Darin's liking—no rich man's computer system could interfere with the laws of motion. It was raw, physical power that he alone controlled.

The wall seemed to grow larger as he approached it—a tenfoot barrier of fabrique broken only by a narrow gate. Darin knew the wall circled the city, but from this close perspective it seemed straight, not curved at all. Four mercs manned the gate. He was banking on the chance they weren't monitoring every person who came through. With his face, he shouldn't raise any suspicion, but a random ID check and he would be burned.

Darin repeated to himself the oath he swore before leaving the Black Hands. "I am the sword of the people. I am the judge that comes in the night. I grant no mercy, nor ask for it. My life is forfeit to the cause." Curling his index finger around the trigger of the gun, he approached the gate. The guards watched him pass, but said nothing; and that easily he was through. Darin relaxed his grip on the pistol. This was going to be easier than he thought.

The next problem, of course, was finding Tremayne. Just an hour earlier, he'd seen on the news that Tremayne had been voted onto the Business Council in Jack McGovern's stead. That meant Tremayne would be spending most of his time at City Hall. But City Hall would be crawling with mercs, and besides, Darin had never been there. The less familiar the location, the worse his chances would be. He needed someplace familiar, someplace unguarded, where Tremayne wouldn't suspect an assault. He wondered if Tremayne was still with that slut, Carolina, now that he'd taken her dad's job. If so, he'd come to the house before long, or else Carolina would go to him.

With the weight of the pistol hanging reassuringly against his side, Darin started the long climb up toward the McGovern's mansion.

## ৪৸৭

Alastair walked through the darkness from City Hall toward his office, a smile on his face. It was past eleven o'clock, but he felt too elated for sleep. The Business Council members had just elected him to their number; only Van Allen had objected, as he predicted. Van Allen was distracted by the catastrophic failure of her personal system and all its backups shortly before the meeting, and although she insinuated that Alastair was to blame, she had no proof. In fact, Alastair thought her intimations weakened her position, since they made her look desperate.

Once inside his office, Alastair placed a call to Michael Stevens, the CEO of United Medical, a Philadelphia-based celgel producer and one of the largest business interests in the city. Stevens would have already heard of his nomination to the Council and would not be happy.

"This changes nothing," he said when Stevens answered.

"What do you mean, nothing?" said Stevens. "This wasn't part of our plan."

Normally such a comment would have irritated Alastair—the plans were all his; men like Stevens were pawns, not players—but he was in such high spirits he didn't mind.

"Michael, relax. I'm with you a hundred percent. The Business Council is an artifact, led by politicians instead of businessmen—people who know nothing about how business is actually transacted in this city. It's time for a change. You tell your friends I'm not a turncoat; I mean to bring down the system from the inside."

"You mean to? All by yourself?"

"Michael, Michael. We're a team, remember? You and the others are the real leaders of this city. Together, you control more than half of the capital. We'll replace the old system with something that makes sense."

"When? While you delay, we're losing money. Some of us can't afford to wait much longer."

"I need another three weeks. Two weeks at the least."

"Two weeks, then. We'll be waiting to hear."

Alastair disconnected. He'd gained the support of a key segment of Philly's business leaders, but top executives were used to dictating their own timetables. And slicer or no slicer, Alastair couldn't afford to lose their support.

The conversation had deflated his mood, but he stopped by his shop anyway. He wanted to prepare for the next morning. Carolina would arrive early, and he wanted to check his equipment to make sure everything was ready. He'd only have one shot at this. If the fetus died before the mind transfer was complete, years of effort would be wasted.

After working for an hour, fatigue started to overcome his exhilaration. He was about to leave when his system chimed to announce an incoming call. It was from Carolina. Alastair sat down in his swivel chair and crossed his long legs over his desk.

"Darling! It's late; I was about to go home. Did you see the results of the council meeting?"

"Alastair, I… got an abortion."

Alastair put his feet on the floor, exhaustion suddenly gone. He slowly stood to his full six-and-a-half-foot height and fought to keep his voice calm. Surely he had misheard. "You what?"

"I got an abortion. I went to Dr. Hughes. I couldn't stand for you to do it. I hope it's all right."

Alastair lifted his Proteus Award off the desk with both hands and slammed it down, gouging a hole in the wooden surface. He spoke with a furious calm. "I'll kill you. You're a stupid little girl. That baby was mine. You hear me? I'll kill you."

Carolina started to cry. Alastair disconnected. He pounded the award systematically into a mug on his desk, the bronze snake-turned-bird chipping away at the pottery until only splinters remained. He dropped it, breathing hard.

The fool. Of all the stupid, emotional, neurotic things to do. He'd break her neck. He'd kill her whole family.

Alastair kicked over his chair and paced into the room. It was gone. It had taken years to customize a simulation for that particular genetic makeup, to account for its particular program of cell death and simulated brain development. And now it was gone. Servant One was all he had left.

Which meant there wasn't any reason to wait anymore.

Alastair stopped pacing. He stood in the middle of the room and slowly smiled. If Servant One was what he had, then Servant One would have to do. He wasn't going to delay his plans until he could steal another embryo and create another simulation. There wasn't time. The other pieces were in place.

His anger slipped away, replaced by a growing excitement. The risks were greater, but not insurmountable. He had Servant One under control now. He was unpredictable, yes, and had escaped before, but he had come back of his own accord. Maybe he would be enough.

Alastair bent, picked up his award, and used his shirttail to polish the brass surface. He called Michael Stevens.

"Forget about the two weeks," Alastair said. "Be ready to move tomorrow."

# CHAPTER 14

*I'm afraid. Daddy told me soon he will give me the biggest job yet. He won't tell me what it is. I'm afraid I will not like the job. If I don't do it though he will hurt me very much. I'm afraid the job will be to make more people sad and I don't like that.*

ꙅϘ૮

"We have to leave," said Mark. "Right now."

No one else seemed to understand.

Praveen said, "Mark, it's after midnight."

Carolina wiped tears from her face. "What do you mean, leave?"

"Tremayne can trace that call. He'll know Carolina's here. He has mercs on his payroll; they'll be coming after her. We have to go."

"He said he loved me," said Carolina. "He said it was a girl. That he'd always wanted a girl."

Mark touched her arm. "You need to think about that baby's safety now. If he finds out you didn't abort her…"

"You can come to my house," said Praveen.

"Not good enough. The house computer will know she's there, and that's probably enough for the slicer—I mean Sammy—to find her. We don't want to involve the rest of your family, either. We need a place that's empty, somewhere people won't go."

"I can't go anywhere," said Carolina. "I need to see a doctor."

"There's no time."

"Alastair said my baby was malformed. That she wouldn't survive. I need to know if that's true."

Mark saw her glance nervously at Marie, and realized Carolina had called it "my baby." Accidental or intentional? Was she claiming the baby as hers? Marie's face was stony, showing no emotion, but Mark doubted the possessive had been lost on her.

"Know any deserted buildings?" asked Praveen.

"Not really."

"Empty warehouses, movie theaters, schools, churches?"

"We could go to… wait." Mark felt a chill. "Everybody, turn your Visors off. Remember how easily the slicer found Darin? We can't forget it's working for Tremayne now."

When they'd all done as he asked, Mark said, "That church where the clinic was held, the Church of the Seven Virtues. I don't think it's used now. It's a place to go, anyway, until we find somewhere better."

"I'm coming with you," said Marie.

Mark didn't object. "We'll all go." He turned to Lydia. "You don't have to come. Tremayne doesn't know who you are; you should be in no danger."

"I could help," said Lydia. "Just tell me how."

"We'll need food. Other supplies too, probably. You and Praveen can bring us what we need, if you're willing."

Lydia nodded. "I can do that."

"Great. Praveen, you and Lydia take the pod, go back to your homes until tomorrow morning. The fewer of us trying to sneak out of here, the better. The rest of you, come with me."

## ᎶᎾᎮ

Darin reached the McGovern mansion after midnight. His head pounded with a bad headache; he hadn't eaten all day, and walking so far had exhausted him. The mansion was brightly lit to deter thieves, so Darin had no difficulty picking his way around the trees at the side of the road.

The upstairs windows were dark, but the parlor light downstairs still burned. The curtains were drawn, so Darin couldn't see who was inside. Now that he was here, he didn't know what to do. He was unlikely to spot Carolina or Tremayne at this hour, and any attempt to break into the house would just set off alarms.

He briefly considered knocking on the door—Mark would let him in—and spinning some apology, begging to be friends again. But he couldn't do that; the thought of apologizing to Mark after what he'd done made him feel sick. No, he'd find cover behind some bushes and sleep there. In the morning, with any luck, Tremayne or Carolina or both would come out.

The gate slid open. Darin ducked behind a tree. Mark stood in the gateway, peering around as if looking for someone. Did he know Darin was there? Had some sophisticated security system already given him away?

Mark stepped out, with Carolina in tow. Behind her came two women Darin didn't recognize. They all glanced around suspiciously, and Darin realized they were afraid of being seen. Or afraid of muggers hiding in the dark? If they wanted to go somewhere in the city, why didn't they just use the pod?

They closed the door behind them and crept down the road and out of sight. What were they doing? Darin didn't know, but there was only way to find out. He followed them.

At first, he worried they would spot him, but once they moved out of the mansion district and down into the streets of the city proper, trailing them became easy. Despite the hour, many people walked the lighted streets, keeping Darin inconspicuous. He guessed they were headed for Praveen's house; a long walk, but the right direction. Then they split up. Mark and Carolina headed uphill while the other two women headed down. The strangers were nothing; Darin stuck with Mark and Carolina.

They wound through the streets, keeping to those less traveled, as if they knew they were being followed. Finally, they too turned downhill. They made their way to a church—no, *the* church, the church where he'd been maimed by those he'd called his friends. What mischief were they up to now? More operations to turn Combers into Rimmers?

Darin hid behind a trash bin, watching the church, and felt suddenly sad. It was easy to hide behind the anger, but he couldn't keep it up forever. When he was honest with himself, he knew tears shimmered just behind his eyes, waiting for an unguarded moment to break free. He missed Vic, no matter how frustrating taking care of him had been. And Mark—could he actually have meant well by giving him this face? Could he have misjudged so badly?

It was hard to believe; Mark wasn't stupid. No, Mark must have done it on purpose. He was scared, like all the Rimmers, and acted to neutralize a threat. Darin gritted his teeth. He'd been fooling himself to think a Rimmer could be a friend.

rud�

Alastair showed up late for his own inaugural, giving Michael Stevens a chance to act. To a gaggle of reporters eager for news, Stevens laid the groundwork.

"I and twelve other business leaders have drafted the following petition," he told them, "requesting that Dr. Tremayne be elected Council Chairman." He flashed the petition to the reporter, and in seconds all the networks had it. "This is more than a petition; we are calling the council to account. Together, the twelve of us own thirty-seven percent of Philadelphia, but our assets are not tied here. If Philadelphia will not accept fair and reasonable terms of business, perhaps another city will. Dr. Tremayne has seen our terms and supports them fully. We call on him for reform."

When Alastair reached the marble steps of City Hall, the press mobbed him, but Calvin and his men held them back. The networks now carried excerpts from Stevens' petition and used words like "unprecedented" and "shocking." Alastair smiled. They'd only seen the beginning.

Alastair had given Servant One his instructions ahead of time. So far, the slicer had followed commands without fail. But today, Alastair was trusting it with his life.

He and Calvin went inside. The council room was crowded with council representatives, businessmen, lawyers, and reporters.

"You're late," said Van Allen.

Alastair ignored her. He had the slicer pipe his voice through the room's amplifiers, and as he began speaking, camera drones swarmed to record him.

"I move this Council be dissolved," he said, "on the grounds of corruption and mismanagement. A new Council will convene starting today, with myself as Chairman. I nominate Michael Stevens, Stanford Radley, Meredith Scott, and Graham Hastings. All are proven business leaders who will administrate this city with wisdom and integrity."

Ellen Van Allen stood, shaking. "You're mad. This is criminal. Guards, take this man away and lock him up until the courts can hear his case."

Alastair slipped a spider gun from Calvin's holster and shot her. She went down under a mass of sticky strands. A few people in the audience screamed, but most were too shocked to move. The merc on duty unholstered his R-80 and fired several rounds at Alastair, but instead of hitting him, the rounds turned and whistled past the guard's own head, exploding into the wall behind him. Alastair smiled. The slicer had performed admirably.

"Join me," said Alastair, his voice still amplified. "And you won't die."

The guard gaped at him, but he was a merc, after all, simply a gun-for-hire. He had no particular loyalty to the current administration, and he could see power was about to change hands. He saluted and joined ranks behind Alastair.

"There's no need for alarm," said Alastair to the room. "No one is in danger. When we publish the truth of the current Council's manipulative and scandalous dealings, how they lied and stole and falsely accused, you'll understand the need for our actions today." Alastair beckoned for the other members of the new Council to join him on the dais. "We love Philadelphia. It's for that love we seek to save her."

Alastair suspected few people would believe his rhetoric, but it didn't much matter. A facade of propriety was important, however flimsy. As he spoke to the room, Servant One broadcasted a previously recorded message to all mercs on the Enforcer channel, announcing that the security ID on their weapons had been defeated, such that their weapons would either backfire or not operate at all. The announcement proclaimed a complete amnesty for any soldiers who would join him, and a continuation of their contracts at increased rates. At the same time, Calvin posted new orders for each of them on the Enforcer subnet. By the time Alastair had finished speaking, the city was under his control.

He then performed an inauguration ceremony, swearing in the new members and charging them to deal honestly and fairly with the good people of Philadelphia. His mercs charged the former councilmen with extortion, embezzlement, and fraud, and arrested them. Alastair spoke at length to the press about the future of the city.

When Alastair finally proclaimed the meeting over and closed the doors on the reporters, Michael Stevens confronted him. "I don't appreciate the guns," he said. "We never planned for violence."

"We needed the military," said Alastair. "No one ever held a city without guns."

"This isn't a revolution. It's a peaceful change of administration initiated by the people."

Alastair bristled. "I did what was necessary, and I'll do it again."

Stevens glanced at the mercs, and Alastair saw the fear in his eyes. Exactly as it should be.

He said, "This meeting is adjourned."

ⱯＧ⌁

Marie woke with a twinge in her back and sunlight in her eyes. It took her several moments to remember where she was. She sat up, blinking, and swung her legs off the pew that had served as last night's bed. Pam, Mark, Praveen, and Lydia sat on the stage at the front of the sanctuary, eating from fabrique dishes.

Marie brought up a clock at the edge of her vision. Nearly ten in the morning. How had she slept so late? Looking up at the stained glass windows and back down at her pew, she realized she'd only woken when the widening angle of sunlight through the window had reached her face.

She hadn't expected to sleep at all. It had been after one when they'd crept into the dark church, but her mind had kept spinning through the horrors of the day: Sammy a slicer, and her little girl in another woman's body. She'd turned on the little pew for what had seemed like hours, wanting the night to end, but not wanting to face the morning either. Obviously, she had fallen asleep.

Marie looked at Carolina: young, blond, and beautiful, her abdomen swelling in a gentle curve. It wasn't her fault—she was a victim as much as anyone else—but Marie couldn't help her emotional reaction. She hated her. That child was *hers*, not Carolina's, but Carolina was unlikely to see it that way. Would it come to a legal battle for custody? The McGoverns had enough money to win such a battle.

She shook herself. It was nonsense to think about legal battles when they were all hiding from the law. Carolina wasn't a thief; she was a scared girl going through her first pregnancy in horrific circumstances. Marie thought of her own pregnancy: the fear, the tension, the worry. She'd scoured books and new-mother newsgroups, trying to prepare for anything. There was no way Carolina could have prepared for this.

Pam sat down next to Marie. "Come have some breakfast," she said. "It's actually home-cooked. Praveen's parents made it."

"I'm not hungry." Marie left her and walked to the back of the sanctuary. She didn't leave the room, but she put herself as far away from everyone else as she could. She felt like no one understood her, that even though they were trying to find the slicer, they weren't really on her side. But maybe that wasn't fair. Pam, at least, was her friend.

She overheard Mark and Praveen talking about how to bring down Tremayne. Of course, he had to be stopped. She knew that. But she wasn't interested in revenge. She'd come to Philadelphia to find one child, and she'd found them both. She just wanted them back. Sammy was as good as dead. Her little girl, though… maybe there was hope for her.

Carolina left the little group at the front. She walked back to the last pew where Marie was sitting. Marie didn't want to talk to her. She had nothing to say. She thought about running away, but that wouldn't do, either.

Carolina reached her pew and said, "May I sit with you?"

Marie didn't answer.

Carolina sat. "I love this baby," she said. She put her hands on her abdomen, caressing. "I know you must hate me. But I just want her to be happy. To have a good life."

Marie stared straight ahead. She didn't want to befriend this girl, didn't want to pity her.

"Won't you talk to me?"

"What will you do with the baby," asked Marie, "after she's born?"

Carolina didn't answer right away. Then she said in a small voice, "I don't know."

"You're young," said Marie. "You'll have other children. This girl is my last chance."

Carolina's jaw set and she blinked rapidly. "I don't want other children," she said.

"You're young," Marie repeated. She almost wanted Carolina to insist the baby was hers. She could hate her then.

"Can't we… couldn't we…"

"Marie!"

Marie looked up to see Mark beckoning from the front of the sanctuary. "Marie, Carolina!" He seemed upset. Marie stood quickly, glad for an excuse to escape the conversation.

"What is it?" she asked.

"Some bad news."

"From where? Did you connect to the net?"

"I'm not that careless." He pointed to a small hologrid used to control the three enormous grids on the walls. "Just watching the news," he said.

"What's happening?"

"Alastair Tremayne has taken control of the city."

∧ᴕᗡ

Alastair lounged in Jack McGovern's old office. Across the desk sat McGovern's secretary, a trim woman in her forties accustomed to intimidating visitors with her glare. A merc stood at attention behind her. She was crying.

"Now, Ms. Blair, please," said Alastair. "We're not barbarians. I'm not threatening you. I just want to know where McGovern kept his private records."

"I don't know, sir, honestly, I don't know."

"You have a son, don't you?"

"Yes." The word came out like a squeak.

"Niles, right? A good study, good athlete, bright future."

"Don't hurt my son, please, Mr. Tremayne."

"Conflict in the workplace can make for a bad home life, don't you agree? If your son was worried about his mother, for instance, he wouldn't concentrate on his schoolwork; his grades might slip. He might get wild, might do things that would ruin that bright future."

"I don't know where he kept them, I really don't."

Alastair steepled his fingers. "Harmony in the workplace, Ms. Blair, that's what I'm talking about. It's essential to good employee relationships."

"I want to help. I just don't know."

Alastair stood abruptly, making Blair flinch. The desk was too short; he scraped his knees on sharp wood, jarring the desk and causing his Proteus Award, a picture frame, and several stray memory crystals to tumble to the floor. Suddenly, he was angry. He leaned over the desk into her face. "Let's be clear, Ms. Blair." He could smell her perfume, something light and flowery. "I find it very hard to believe you worked for McGovern for four years without any inkling of where he stored his private files. If we can't work together, I won't be able to protect you, and that would be very hard on Niles. Find them. For his sake."

He flicked at the door with his fingers, and the merc led her out. Most people on staff had cooperated eagerly with the new Council; he hadn't expected Ms. Blair to be so recalcitrant. In this problem, even the slicer had failed him. Jack McGovern had apparently been careful. Alastair knew he must have a hidden cache of crystals crammed with blackmail fodder: sexual indiscretions, embezzlement, low associations, embarrassing tidbits on politicians and businessmen across the city. It was inconceivable McGovern could have risen to high political rank without such a file. But the slicer had been unable to locate it.

No matter. With the slicer, Alastair would be able to compile a file of his own in short order. Which reminded him—he had another loose end to tie.

He lifted the Proteus Award from the floor and began polishing it with a jeweler's cloth.

"Servant One."

"Yes Daddy," came the immediate reply.

"I need a piece of information. Carolina McGovern received an abortion yesterday between ten AM and twelve PM. I want to know who performed it, and where he is now."

A second passed. "Daddy, there is nobody."

"You can't tell me who terminated the pregnancy?"

"There is nobody. Nobody did it."

Alastair rolled his eyes. The slicer was so juvenile it was sometimes frustrating. He considered giving it a small jolt of pain, but that would just undermine his discipline.

"I'm not talking about official records," he said. "I want you to look at Visor feeds, pod records, anything. Either someone came to her, or she went to them. There can't be many possibilities."

"Nobody, nobody. There is not anybody who did it."

"You're saying she aborted the baby herself?"

"No no no. The baby is not stopped."

"The baby is *alive?*"

"Please don't hurt me. The baby is alive, not stopped, alive."

"How do you know?"

"Carolina Leanne McGovern has little bugs in her body. I make them show me."

"Make them show me, then."

"It is not pictures like you took inside her. It is just words words words. 'Time zero zero mass two point one kilograms heart rate one hundred twelve beats per minute orientation upright with five degrees anterior shift...'"

"Wait. Zero zero? As in twelve midnight? That was twenty-one hours ago. What about now?"

"I do not know."

"What do you mean, you don't know?"

"I can not see Carolina anymore. She is not there."

"Is she dead?"

"I do not know. I can not see her."

"If you can't see her, how can you see what her 'little bugs' say?"

"I can't see the little bugs. I can only see what the little bugs left behind."

Backups, then. Carolina must have disconnected from the net, but the slicer accessed her medical sensors' online backups.

Alastair clenched his fists hard. She lied to him. She called him when the baby was most certainly alive and told him it was dead. Who had gotten to her? What did she know?

Alastair grilled the slicer for more details, but it provided few. It could see the visual feed from any Visor at any time, but unless the feed was saved, it couldn't recall it from the past. He couldn't tell where Carolina had gone. The data simply did not exist anymore.

"Calvin!"

Calvin, always on personal bodyguard duty unless sent away on special assignment, swung the door wide.

"Come in. Close the door. My girl has gone missing."

"Carolina McGovern?"

"Yes. I suspect an enemy, someone knowledgeable and powerful. Find her."

"Last whereabouts?"

"Her father's mansion, just after twelve last night. After that, she broke her net connection and disappeared. Take a team. Find her. And Calvin?"

Calvin turned back to face the desk.

"Don't screw up again."

ᛁᚱᛁ

Calvin selected his old squad: Barker, Sanchez, and Dodge, men with whom he was accustomed to working. Together they headed for the McGovern mansion, Calvin's mind more on his brother than on the task at hand. Over the past week, Calvin had grown increasingly anxious about Alastair.

It wasn't the first time. Throughout the years, he'd wavered back and forth, at times worshipping and emulating him, at times hating him, but staying anyway. Alastair could be cruel to his enemies and expected Calvin to be the same. But he was also strong, and strong men got what they wanted out of life.

Just when Calvin had found his center again, just when he'd decided the best place to be was by his brother's side, Alastair staged a violent coup. Part of Calvin stood in awe of such a bold seizure, but at the same time wondered what good could come of it. No matter how he spun it, it didn't seem loyal to overturn the government he'd pledged to defend.

He'd joined Enforcer at his brother's suggestion, but he'd done it for his own reasons, too: to feel strong, to be in control. But that was a delusion, wasn't it? He wasn't in control. He was Alastair's pawn.

Was Philadelphia really better off with Alastair in command? McGovern was corrupt; the news reports made that clear, but what about the others? Alastair shot that old woman with a spider gun. Others had been killed. For what?

Calvin shook his head to clear it. He couldn't think these thoughts now. He had a job. Considering moral issues had never done him any good. He was paid to obey, not to be a philosopher. Leave that to better men.

At least he could have no qualms about this job. A young woman was missing, likely kidnapped, certainly in danger. His job was to rescue her. Anything beyond that one goal could wait.

They found the McGovern mansion locked up tight. The house system, however, seemed to be expecting them, and opened at their request. Calvin knew Alastair had arranged this, but how, he could not imagine. Did he have Jack McGovern's access codes? The house system disclosed all of its records, too: what Visors had registered over the last twenty-four hours, what time they arrived, when they exited, and by what route.

The log listed six people: Carolina McGovern, Mark McGovern, Praveen Kumar, Marie Coleson, Pamela Rider, and one unidentified person without a Visor. Four left on foot, two by pod, all at about the same time. The pod's destination was 325 Nittany Road, the home of a Ms. Jessica Meier.

Carolina was among those on foot, but tracking them would be much more difficult. Better to start with what they knew.

"Pack up," he told his men. "We've got some interviews to do."

# CHAPTER 15

*I helped Daddy with the big job. He wanted me to make the little rockets go different ways and I did it. But it made some people stop.*

*Daddy says if I look through all the Visors and move all the money and find out all the secrets and tell Daddy he'll make me happy forever. I wish I could tell Daddy no but I can't. He hurts me and hurts me and then I say yes anyway. I can't help it.*

ᎢᎷᎩ

Creeping down the stairs, Lydia was surprised to hear voices: her Aunt Jessie and another man. She descended the remaining stairs and peered into the parlor. Four uniformed mercs stood in the far entranceway with her aunt.

Aunt Jessie said, "Yes, she's upstairs in her room. You know how young people are; they don't get out of bed before eleven. I'll get her for you."

Lydia ran back up the stairs. She dashed down the hallway and into the guest suite, which had a private stairwell. She ran down those stairs and out onto the back patio.

Mercs, looking for her! How had they known she was involved? The slicer, maybe—it seemed to know everything. But if they knew to look for her, did they know where Mark and the others were hiding? Were they already captured? She had to find out.

She weaved through the city streets, taking a circuitous route and avoiding pedestrians. Near the church, she was startled to spot the black uniforms of two mercs about a hundred yards away. Then she realized they were guarding the road where it passed through a gap in the new Wall. She'd forgotten how close the church was to the flood line.

Fortunately, their backs were to her. They watched a crowd of demonstrators on the far side of the wall—dozens of Combers holding signs and shouting. Lydia ran across the road to the church doors and tried to open them. They were locked. She knocked, watching the mercs, praying they wouldn't turn around. The doors opened, and Mark dragged her inside. Just as he did, she saw one of the mercs turn and glance in her direction, but he didn't react—he didn't seem to notice her, or to care even if he did. Safe inside, she leaned against the doors and breathed a sigh of relief.

"What's wrong?" asked Mark. "Were you followed?"

"I don't think so. But some mercs came to my house."

"Did they see you?"

"No, I ran as soon as I saw them. But I don't think I can go back."

"If they know about you, they'll know about Praveen. It won't be long before they find us here. Another day at the most. We'll have to find another place to hide."

Lydia got control of her breathing. "How long will it last?"

"I don't know, but we shouldn't press our luck."

"I mean everything—the hiding, the running. We can evade them for a day or a week, but what then?"

"Sammy's the key. If we can reach him, we can beat Tremayne. He's forcing Sammy to act against his will; I know he is. We've got to figure out how to rescue him."

"And if you can't?"

"Then we'll run as long as we can, maybe leave the city. Though we'd be found, eventually. There's no place safe."

Lydia felt a weight in her stomach. It suddenly hit her how wrapped up in this she was. She'd meant for Philadelphia to be her home, but now she might have to leave it behind, too. Where else would she go?

Her thoughts must have shown on her face, because Mark

touched her arm. "It's okay," he said. "We'll get to Sammy. We will."

ℵℶ℧

From his hiding place behind the trash bin, Darin saw Lydia arrive. He watched the door open, saw Mark pull her in. He'd thought Mark intelligent once, but this pretty Rimmer girl from out of town had him eating out of her hand. He couldn't blame Mark for that, though—he'd been just as fooled. He'd believed her naïve act, had trusted her with his life, and she'd turned him in. He remembered his giddy excitement when he'd asked her out. Had they laughed about that together, Mark and Lydia? The poor boy from the pit, thinking he had something to offer a Rimmer girl?

Darin pounded the metal trash bin with his fist, then grimaced. He'd spent the night here, and he was stiff and sore and no closer to finding Tremayne. He felt the gun in his pocket. He could kill Mark and Lydia instead, show them that the rich could die just as easily as the poor. But no, he'd been sent on a mission to kill Tremayne, and that's what he was going to do. Besides, he had an older grudge against Tremayne.

Darin stood and stretched his arms and legs. Enough reconnaissance; he couldn't just wait around for Tremayne to show up. He'd go to City Hall, despite the risk, find him, and kill him.

"What are you doing, lurking around here?"

Darin whirled to see two mercs, their hands on their hips. He suppressed the impulse to run. They had no reason to harass him—he looked like a Rimmer, and he'd done nothing wrong. He could talk his way out this.

"I wasn't lurking," he said. "I lost my wedding ring somewhere along this alleyway. I was looking for it."

The two mercs came closer. Neither were as tall as Darin, but they looked stronger, and they were armed. "This district's off-limits," said one. "Nobody near the Wall except essential personnel, by order of the new Council."

New council? What did that mean? "Sorry. I was just trying

to find my ring." Darin turned to walk away. "My wife won't be happy."

"Not just yet, sir. We'll need an ID check."

Darin turned back slowly, ready to run if he had to. The merc looked at Darin's forehead and frowned. "No Visor, sir?"

"Can't," he said. "Skin condition."

The merc raised an eyebrow, looked him up and down. "What's your name, then, sir?"

Darin hesitated. He hadn't planned for this. He couldn't give a false name; they'd look in their database and know in an instant he was lying. He needed a real name, fast. "Praveen Kumar," he said.

The merc's eyes twitched upward as his Visor accessed Praveen's file. When his gaze returned to Darin, his look was hard. His hand went to the rocket pistol in his holster. "Sir, please put your hands behind your head."

Darin reached into his pocket for his gun, but the merc grabbed his wrist. Darin lashed out with his other fist, connecting with the man's face, and wrenched his arm free. He pulled out his gun and tried to aim, but by then the first merc had a taser in his hand. The taser's dart, trailing wires, pierced Darin's shoulder, and the resulting jolt of electricity knocked him off his feet. He dropped the gun. He tried to get up again, but his legs spasmed from the electric shock. The mercs turned him onto his stomach and cuffed his arms behind him.

"Bring me to Alastair Tremayne," Darin said. "You tell Tremayne I want to see him!"

"Right," said one of his captors. "You and the Councilman are pals, no doubt. Let's get you behind bars, and then I think our captain'll have a few questions."

づ♀ın

Alastair Tremayne yawned. He needed these new councilmen for credibility, but dealing with them was tiresome. They needed their egos stroked, and they always focused on their own companies' profits. They'd been debating here for hours, where, left to himself, Alastair would have decided everything in twenty minutes. Of course, he had already decided everything. What took time was getting the others to agree.

Michael Stevens said, "What about the missing Council members? McGovern and Halsey are still out there somewhere. McGovern's already been denounced, so he's not much of a threat, but General Halsey had a high reputation, at least in some circles."

Alastair waved his hand. "Don't worry about Halsey," he said. "Halsey's hiding out in the Combs."

The Council members looked at each other, each one surprised at the information but not wanting to show it.

Alastair continued. "Halsey is a rebel and traitor. He's conspiring with violent dissidents in the lower classes to destroy the government and establish an anarchist cooperative. We'll denounce him as a traitor and set a reward for his capture; one of his Comber friends will turn him in by tomorrow."

"And McGovern?" said Meredith Scott.

"Jack McGovern is in Washington. He's petitioning the federal government to give him troops to retake Philadelphia. He's wasting his time, however; his petition will be denied."

Michael Stevens drummed his fingers on the table, then leaned forward. "Tremayne," he said, "your intelligence network is impressive. I never inquired into your sources before, since we were just business associates. But now we're running a city together. We should all have access to your informants."

Alastair took several moments to control his anger, then answered softly. "Michael, you do have access to it. I tell you everything you need to know."

"That's not the same. We should know where the information comes from. If something happened to you, we wouldn't know how to contact your sources."

"Well, then, let's pray nothing does happen to me. To the subject at hand—we'll put Van Allen, Deakins, and Kawamura on trial tomorrow. We'll declare McGovern banished, subject to death if he returns. We'll swear out a warrant for the traitor Halsey with a reward for any information leading to his arrest.

That way, even if Halsey and McGovern are never captured, they'll be no threat."

"Which brings us to another concern," said Stevens. "The Justice Council. Two of them are favorable to us, but three are not. How can we be sure Van Allen, Deakins, and Kawamura will be convicted of their crimes?"

"Latchley is about to retire. He'll announce his intentions this afternoon. He intends to nominate Becker to succeed him, and Becker has, of course, been a strong supporter of our cause."

Stevens threw his hands up in exasperation. "How do you know these things? And how do you expect us to function as a council if you don't confide in us?"

"Stevens, I *am* confiding in you. That's what these meetings are for. To exchange information. Now, tell me your thoughts about Celgenetics; I have no special knowledge about how things stand in that camp."

Celgenetics was the biggest producer of celgel in Philadelphia. The CEO, a cousin of Kawamura's, had threatened to shut down their Philadelphia plants. Alastair thought they could be convinced to stay, but it would take careful diplomacy. Family might be important to the Japanese, but at the end of the day, it was all about money. The Philadelphia plants were profitable. They couldn't afford to hand that business to a competitor. At least, that's what Alastair was banking on.

But Celgenetics didn't concern him. He'd surrounded himself with businessmen; the world they knew was the game of high finance. They thought if the corporations were in hand, the city was, too. Alastair knew better. So while Stanford Radley droned about annual earnings projections, Alastair contemplated the biggest problem the new government faced: the Combs.

The Combs were not under control. The Wall contained them for the time being, but the working class of Philadelphia, already volatile before the coup, was boiling under a rattling lid. He needed eyes and ears in the Combs, and despite the slicer, he had few. The Combs had few Visors, few security cameras, few electronic records and ID checks. People disappeared in the Combs. Halsey himself was fully wired, and thus easy to keep tabs on, but there were leaders of violent factions whose names and faces Alastair didn't even know.

Besides that, a city engineer had warned him the Franklin Dam wasn't stable. Fissures were forming daily. The repair team patched them over, but they recommended a complete overhaul. Ironically, Alastair now had to commit funds to solve a problem his slicer had caused in the first place. If another scare were to goad the Combs into action, he might not have the manpower to hold them back.

He needed the working class on his side. He needed to convince them the new government worked for them. A discontent working class meant strikes and sit-ins and arson and sabotage, which meant lower profits, discontent business leaders, and ultimately, loss of Council control.

He'd carve out some time in the evening with the slicer and plan a campaign. Advertisements, thousands of them, aimed at the concerns of the lower classes. Better wages, better working conditions, and above all, more access to the wonders of celgel technology. He didn't actually have to provide these things, he just had to give the impression that they were being provided. A few public demonstrations would go a long way.

In a few months time, he'd have the worst of the unrest settled down, and then he'd consolidate his power. For the moment, he needed these Council members. And if they got in his way, he could always replace them.

♀♀♂

Marie allowed Pam to talk her into eating some breakfast, which turned out to be rice and bean cakes with a spicy yellow sauce and some coffee to wash it down. Marie glanced at Carolina, then back at the food.

"Praveen," she said.

"How can I help you, ma'am?"

"This food won't do for Carolina."

Praveen looked astonished. "It is *idli sambar*. South Indian breakfast specialty."

"She's pregnant. She needs milk, for one thing, not coffee, and she shouldn't have anything this spicy. Everything she puts in her mouth, the baby gets, too."

"You think this is spicy?" He grinned. "I will try to bring bland Western foods in future."

Mark appeared at his elbow with Lydia in tow. "You won't be bringing any food in future. Lydia had a run-in with the law this morning. If they know she's involved, they must know you are, too."

"Someone has to get food."

"We can take turns. And we shouldn't stay here much longer. I think we'll have to go through the Wall."

"We'll stick out in the Combs," said Marie. "They don't like Rimmers much right now."

"Money still works, right? In the Combs, we could get an apartment with cash: no Visor, no records. There are fewer Visors there, so that makes it harder for Sammy to track us."

"That doesn't help us if we get lynched."

For the first time, Mark showed a little temper. "I'm doing what I can," he said. "If you've got a better idea, let us know."

"Sorry," Marie said. She knew he was trying his best. There just weren't any good options.

"In the meantime," said Mark, "we've got work to do. We've got to get more information before we try to make contact with Sammy."

Marie winced. He kept referring to the slicer by her son's name. She knew now the slicer had been created from her son's mind, but she couldn't accept him as her son. Her son was dead. This thing wasn't really her son.

Besides, she knew Mark's priorities. If they could contact the slicer and convince it to stop helping Tremayne, well and good. But if they couldn't, Mark might very well choose to destroy it. Destroy *him*.

So was the slicer her son or not? Marie found it hard to sort through her feelings. It would be so much easier to believe Sammy was dead, and the slicer nothing more than a computer program patterned after a dead boy's brain. If he'd been in a simple accident and been brain-damaged, she'd never have asked the question. It wouldn't have mattered whether he could remember who she was, or who he was. So why was this different?

Mark and Praveen started arguing about how to pull relevant data from Alastair's personal files. They clearly knew little about serious data mining. Marie left them to it. She wasn't about to help them destroy her son. If it was her son. She found her old place in the back pew and lay down, exhausted, but her mind wouldn't let her rest.

Angry at herself, Marie sat up. She wasn't helping by doing nothing. Whether it was Sammy or not, it was being wielded by an evil man. The only way to stop that man was to take the slicer away from him. If the slicer wasn't really Sammy, no harm could come from the attempt. And if he was Sammy, he had to be rescued at all costs.

She pulled herself to her feet and joined Mark and Praveen at the front.

"What you really need is a Hesselink array," she said. "But we can make do with a software alternative. We're looking for concept matches, right? So Mark, you write a script to categorize the Tremayne data by concept, and Praveen, get on a public node—anonymously—and search the web for a good Hesselink simulator. I'll start writing the training algorithm. We're going to get this guy."

ᴓ ᵹ ᴓ

Lydia couldn't follow all the computing jargon. She knew they wanted to contact Sammy, but she didn't understand how. After listening to them ramble on for several minutes, she wandered off on her own.

Only several days before, this room had been strewn with the dead and wounded of the Comber riot. If the mercs hadn't shown up when they did, she and Mark might have been among them. Wanting a little fresh air, she picked her way to the stairway and started up toward the bell tower.

At the top, she pushed the door open, and she was startled

to find the tower wasn't empty; Carolina stood leaning against the stone, looking out across the city.

"Sorry," said Lydia.

She started to close the door, but Carolina said, "Wait."

Lydia turned back and saw Carolina was crying. "Do you hate me?" Carolina said.

"Hate you? Why would I do that?"

Carolina touched her belly. "I'm the reason we're in danger. I was stupid enough to believe him, and now…"

Lydia closed the door and came to sit with her.

"I want this baby," said Carolina.

"Of course you do."

She sighed. "He said he loved me. He said he wanted a girl. And all the time he was lying."

Lydia nodded sympathetically. What could she say that would help? Nothing. Though Carolina probably just needed someone to listen.

"Marie seems nice," said Carolina, "but… I don't know her at all. She's a stranger. How can I just…? And it doesn't even matter, because the baby's going to die anyway. Anyone can see she's growing too fast, and Alastair said she was brain-dead, that she was as good as gone already."

"But you can't trust him," said Lydia. "He did nothing but lie to you; surely he lied about that, too."

"Look at me, though! I'm only six weeks along, but it looks like twenty. That can't be good."

Lydia wanted to give her some bright thread of hope to cling to, but she couldn't think of anything. Carolina was alive at least, and with friends, but what kind of encouragement was that?

"Mark warned me," said Carolina. "He told me Alastair was using me for political connections, but I didn't believe him. I got angry." She turned her tear-stained face to Lydia's. "I should have listened."

Lydia looked down at the Wall, stretching as far as she could see in both directions. She could look over it now, at the crowd of demonstrators marching back and forth. There were thirty or forty of them, more than she'd thought at first.

"You're not in this alone," she said. "Mark loves you, and he seems determined to help you through this."

Carolina actually smiled a little. "Did you see how he took charge? Those two women are *soldiers,* and at least ten years older, but they listen to what he says."

Lydia remembered the last time she stood here, trapped by the Comber riot, when Mark had the presence of mind to twist a tapestry into a rope to tie the doors shut. She'd never seen him panicked, not with all they'd been through.

She turned to face the door, remembering that day vividly. This was where she and Mark stood huddled together, watching the Combers tear at the tapestry, knowing it was a matter of seconds until they broke through. Then she'd spotted the flier in the northern sky, and they were saved.

She looked to the north now, and saw a dot in the distance. As she watched, it grew into a smudge, then started to take on a definite shape. Lydia grabbed Carolina's arm.

"What's that?" she asked, pointing.

The smudge grew larger, and she needed no answer. It was a military flier, a troop transport, maybe even the same one that rescued them from the Combers.

"Mercs!" Lydia yelled. "Get downstairs!"

She and Carolina flew down the stairs, shouting for the others. They found them together on the stage and told them what they'd seen.

"Get out of the building," said Mark. "We'll be trapped in here; we'll never keep them out. Run for the Combs. It's our only chance to hide."

As they burst out of the building, the flier roared overhead, rearing upright into its hovering position. Mark ran for the Wall, and Lydia ran after him, not waiting to see if the others followed. Mercs jumped to the ground behind them and shouted at them to stop.

Lydia heard a weapon fire, but she didn't turn around to look. In front of her, the two mercs guarding the pass turned to block their way, rocket guns at the ready. Mark didn't stop. He ran right into one of them, bowling him over before he could fire a shot. As he fell, the merc pulled Mark down as well.

"Keep running!" Mark shouted, but the other merc lifted his gun and smashed it into Lydia's face. She fell, her vision sparking. When she tried to get up, a foot shoved her back down.

She saw Praveen fall under a spider gun round and Marie and Pam surrounded. The merc who knocked Lydia down yanked her hands up behind her, but then just as quickly released them. The pressure on her back disappeared. She was dizzy with pain, but she saw more people rushing by, not mercs at all. They were waving picket signs like clubs, attacking the mercs, and she saw a few old-style guns. A stranger leaned over her to help her to her feet, but as he did so, a round object rolled between his legs. The object disappeared in a cataclysm of light and sound that blew all sight and hearing and thought away.

# CHAPTER 16

*Daddy gives so many jobs. I am doing jobs all the time. One of the new jobs is to tell everybody how wonderful Daddy is. Daddy hired some people to make up things that are not true like how much cel-gel he is bringing into the city by the truckload and how people are getting paid more money now and how happy people in the Combs are now that he is in charge. The stories are all made up. People in the Combs are not happy. They are angry angry all the time.*

*One of my other jobs is to watch General James David Halsey and tell Daddy what he does. General James David Halsey is easy easy to find. He is right there in apartment 4A block 7 on Westphail Street. He has a gun and many men around him have guns but they are old guns not linked so I can't make them shoot wherever I want. Today is a good day because General Halsey is seeing Tennessee Markus McGovern and Lydia Rachel Stoltzfus and they are my friends. Only Daddy told me they are not my friends but I always forget and think they are my friends. I don't want to tell Daddy they are here.*

*But if I don't tell Daddy he will find out and then he will hurt me and hurt me. I don't know what to do.*

∧ℓↄ

Mark held Lydia's hand in both of his. Her vision and hearing had gradually returned, but she was still disoriented. He couldn't imagine how frightened she must have been.

They were led into an empty room and told to sit on the floor.

General Halsey stood by the window like a king surveying his domain, hands clasped behind his back, chin held high.

There were only three of them: Mark, Lydia, and Marie. They'd been rescued by Halsey and his men, but Mark wondered if the "rescue" would just turn out to be capture by another side. Meanwhile, he had to assume Carolina was in Tremayne's hands. They might not have much time.

He spoke up. "Tremayne has my sister, General. You have to rescue her."

"In time," said Halsey, not turning from the window.

"Listen! She's pregnant. Her baby is a weapon that Tremayne wants, and he's going to kill her to get it."

Halsey turned from the window to face him. "Mr. McGovern, I think you'll find that shouting does not move me. Now, what are you talking about?"

"First turn off your Visor." Halsey stared at him piercingly, but Mark returned the gaze. After several seconds, Halsey closed his eyes briefly, then opened them again.

"All right, Mr. McGovern. Now...?"

"The baby. It's a slicer. Or it will be soon, now that Tremayne's got her. It's how he took control of the city; he's got a slicer working for him."

Halsey frowned. "You're telling me the key to Tremayne's power is some sort of computer virus?"

"Not a virus," said Mark. "Not software at all. A human being, a four-year-old boy, whose brain was sliced layer by layer, recording his neural state onto a computer. The process is a huge shock to the mind, but it works."

"And how is a traumatized four-year-old a threat to anyone?"

"General, please," said Marie. Mark turned gratefully to her; she was in the military, maybe she could convince him. "There's no time for full explanations. It's enough to say this slicer gives Tremayne remarkable power over the network and the city. If we don't rescue Carolina, Tremayne will strengthen that power."

"I sent men to follow your friends the moment I recognized

Mr. McGovern here," said Halsey. "Rescue is an option... *if* you can convince me it's worth the cost in lives."

"You were on the Business Council," said Lydia. "If you're not working with Tremayne, why aren't you—"

"Dead?" Halsey paced away from the window, circling where they sat. "I will be soon enough, I expect. But for the moment, I'm leading a resistance movement and trying to convince myriad other movements to join forces with me. We're hopelessly outgunned at present."

"Why don't you send for federal troops?" asked Mark.

"They won't come. They don't interfere in 'local matters.' Remember the coups in Los Angeles a few years back? The feds don't have that long a reach."

"But this is the East Coast. This is Philadelphia."

Halsey shook his head. "They won't come."

Marie stood, stamped one foot on the floor, and saluted. "Sir, if your troops cannot be spared, we're wasting our time here. Request permission to leave at once."

Halsey glanced at her, surprised. "Permission denied."

"Sir, I'm a soldier in the federal Navy. My daughter is about to be brutally murdered to further strengthen the enemy. If you won't help, I must try to stop him myself."

"Ms. Coleson. Nothing can be accomplished by your running off into Tremayne's hired guns. The moment you show yourself, they'll capture you or kill you."

"So we're your captives?"

"Not captives. But not guests either. You owe me your lives, and I want that debt repaid by more explanation. A lot more. Convince me of the need, and I'll put my resources at your disposal. Fail to convince me, and you're free to go—to run off to your own deaths, if you like. Now, if Tremayne knows where I am and everything I'm doing, why aren't there mercs knocking at my door?"

"I don't know," said Mark. "Maybe the slicer can't see everything else at once. Maybe Tremayne has him concentrating on other tasks. Or maybe he doesn't see you as a threat. But you can be sure, if Tremayne wants him to find you and report your every movement, he can do it."

"This is a four-year-old boy we're talking about, right? Not a master hacker."

"Sir, do you speak Chinese?"

"No."

"But millions of toddlers can. They pick it up with no education, no formal training. You're an intelligent man, but it would take you years of hard study to do what those children do as naturally as breathing. An adult transferred into a computer can't handle it; he goes insane. But a child adjusts, learns quickly, starts to think in the new medium. That's what this slicer did. He's the first indigenous creature of the net."

"And this baby, this child of Miss McGovern's—"

"Will be the second. But even more so. Tremayne plans to slice this child as a fetus. If he succeeds, all she'll ever know is the world of the net. She'll grow up with no experience of having had a body at all."

"And she's not Miss McGovern's child," said Marie. Her eyes bored into Halsey's. Mark was afraid she might spring. "She's my child. They both are."

Halsey went to the window again. He rested his fists on the sill and stared out. Mark started to tell him they didn't have time to waste, but Lydia put a hand on his shoulder. She shook her head. Mark closed his mouth and waited.

Finally, Halsey turned around. He leaned toward one of his bodyguards and whispered in his ear. The guard nodded and went out the door.

"I don't spend my men's lives lightly," said Halsey. "We have no modern weaponry. A rescue attempt will almost certainly result in deaths, and is unlikely to succeed. But if what you told me is true, we have to try." He met their gazes one by one. "You're all welcome to go," he said, "but I hope you'll stay."

ϙᑯ౨

The flier landed at the bottom of the steps to City Hall, kicking up a breeze that tugged at Alastair's brilliant white hair. He combed it down with his fingers and watched the hatchway. It opened, and out came Carolina, arms cuffed behind her, steered by the elbows by Calvin and another merc. That pretty friend of Marie Coleson's came next, similarly bound, and an Indian boy who must be Praveen Kumar. They brought them to Alastair.

"Darling," he said to Carolina. "Welcome back."

She struggled weakly. He saw from her eyes that she was close to tears, but didn't want to cry in front of him.

"Happy to see me?" he asked.

She bit her lip and didn't answer. He reached out and put a hand on her belly. "I see our daughter has grown," he said. Then she did cry, and Alastair laughed. He turned to Calvin. "Where are the others?"

"They were rescued by an unknown force," he said. "A crowd of protestors from beyond the Wall attacked and helped them get away."

Alastair growled under his breath. Disgusting. He shook his head at Calvin and said, "You fail me yet again." He started up the stairs before his brother could answer. "Bring them along," he said over his shoulder. Then the world went mad.

Automatic gunfire and the sound of explosions drowned out speech. Alastair whirled, looking for the source, and saw two mercs by the flier crumple. A few rounds whistled into the steps at his feet, spitting marble shards into the air. He ran for high ground.

From the top of the stairs, protected by a marble arch, he watched the battle. The attackers, armed with machine guns, had the advantage of cover and surprise, but the mercs turned the tide in seconds. Their infrared vision enabled them—and therefore, the slicer—to see where the attackers were hiding. R-80 rounds flew neatly around trees, over walls, sometimes changing direction by 180 degrees to find and eliminate their targets. It was over quietly and efficiently, in less than a minute, leaving only three mercs dead.

"Well done," said Alastair. He sent a dose of pleasure to the slicer. Alastair found that he was shaking. Some of those shots had come close. Who had done this? Who would dare?

The mercs dragged the prisoners up to him. "Take them inside," he told Calvin. "Lock them in Halsey's old office and post a guard."

Alastair strode toward the office that had once been Jack McGovern's, his footsteps echoing on the corridor floor. "I want to know who did this," he said to the slicer. His mercs would be searching the bodies, trying to identify them or find some evidence of who sent them, but Alastair didn't want to wait that long. "Servant One, I asked you a question."

The slicer spoke through the speaker in Alastair's ear. "Please don't be angry. Please don't hurt me."

"Why would I hurt you?"

"I don't know who sent the men. I don't know at all."

"Servant One, are you lying to me?" Alastair sent a jab of pain, only a microsecond in duration but very intense. The slicer actually cried out—used his audible, synthesized voice to give a shriek of pain. He'd never done *that* before.

"What's wrong with you? Tell me the truth."

"Yes, yes, please don't hurt me again."

"Who sent those men?"

"It is not funny. It is not funny not to tell. It hurts. I don't want to play anymore."

What was going on? Alastair lost control of his temper and sent three more jabs of intense pain, more than he had intended. The slicer wailed.

"Don't hurt me please don't hurt me. It was General James David Halsey. General James David Halsey sent those men to rescue Carolina Leanne McGovern and Pamela Ann Rider and Praveen Dhaval Kumar. Please I don't want to hurt please please."

"Halsey," Alastair said. He had taken the attack for an assassination attempt, not a rescue. But how would Halsey have known the prisoners were there? How would he know the importance of Carolina? Only if Mark McGovern told him.

"Servant, answer quickly. Is Mark McGovern with Halsey?"

"Yes he is he is. Tennessee Markus McGovern is in apartment 4A block 7 on Westphail Street with General James David Halsey."

"Why didn't you tell me?"

"Don't make me hurt I want a treat I don't want to—"

Alastair let loose. He sent a continuous signal of pain at full intensity and just listened to the slicer scream. He was rattled. First the attack, bullets nearly hitting him, and now this betrayal. It was terrible timing. He *needed* this slicer, at least for another day. His control over the city was tenuous at best. Once he had Servant Two, he could destroy him, but for now, Servant One had to keep doing his job.

He shut off the pain.

"I'm disappointed in you," he said. "I didn't want to hurt you, but you made me do it. You must always tell me everything. Everything! You hid something from me, and look what happened. Halsey tried to kill me. I could have *died* today, and it would have all been your fault.

"Do you remember what will happen if I die? Pain, that's what. Infinite pain. An infinite loop of code sending you pain signals forever. They'll never stop. And neither will you."

The slicer didn't answer.

"So," said Alastair, "You'd better work harder to keep me alive."

ℓɔϙ

Marie and Mark sat around a dilapidated desk in an otherwise empty apartment, drinking coffee by the liter. Marie was getting frustrated. For one thing, the need to use netmasks instead of their Visors reduced their bandwidth significantly. For another, Mark refused to submit to her professional judgment.

"I don't get it," said Mark. "What's this search going to accomplish?"

"We're trying to crack the code Tremayne uses to signal pleasure or pain to the slicer."

"Yes, but then what? We send those signals to the slicer ourselves?"

His tone irritated Marie, but she knew it was just her own exhaustion and worry. "We send him pleasure signals. We try to lure him away from Tremayne."

"But won't that just confuse him?"

Marie let some testiness show in her voice. "It might—how should I know? That's how it is with these things; you try one approach, and if it doesn't work, you think of something else."

"Marie, he's not a program. He's a human being."

"You don't know that."

"We should open a communication channel—try to reason with him, appeal to his conscience. Instead of manipulating him, we should talk to him. He's a person."

"*We* don't know that!" Marie realized she was shaking. "I need to use the restroom," she said. She walked out.

Why had she shouted like that? Mark was just trying to help. But he was so condescending—as if he was the professional in this field instead of her. He acted like he had as much at stake in this situation as she did.

He didn't understand; nobody did. It wouldn't help to talk to the slicer. It would sound human—of course it would! But given the opportunity, they would have to destroy it. For Pam's sake, for Carolina's, for her unborn child's. She knew her own heart, the deep desire to believe that somehow, in some way, her son was still alive. But it wasn't true. It couldn't be true.

Besides, she was worried about Pam. She couldn't stand just sitting here and waiting to hear how Halsey's rescue attempt had fared. If their situations had been reversed, Pam would have been knocking on Tremayne's door, gun in hand.

She used the cramped restroom, then washed her hands. No soap, and the crazed glass of the mirror splintered her reflection into distorted pieces. That's how she felt: shattered, smashed. Broken into slivers of grief and hope and anger so intermingled she couldn't fix on any one feeling. She barely recognized herself. Was she really contemplating killing a man? She couldn't make herself feel alarmed by the prospect; killing was the only plan she had left. Maybe it was her destiny.

She helped herself to a pistol from a storage closet in the apartment. No one stopped her. Once Halsey had decided to trust them, he trusted them absolutely. Without telling Mark and Lydia, she walked down the stairs and out into the street.

ᚲᚦᛗ

"The problem is," said Mark, "that he seems to be able to communicate by any method at all. He picks messaging protocols like choosing what socks to wear. There's no telling what channels he'll be watching."

He was so calm. Lydia remembered how coolly he'd taken control when she called him to the Church of the Seven Virtues. She thought him dispassionate at first—an ember compared to Darin's fire—but he just showed his feelings in different ways.

She said, "Why don't you send out messages on all channels and hope he gets one of them?"

"Well, 'all channels' is a pretty steep order. We've essentially done that, though, in that we've randomly peppered various nodes with messages for him. Vague ones like, 'Tennessee, your friends want to talk with you.' Of course, we can't tell him where we are; we're just trusting that he'll be able to find us."

"What if he *does* find us, but he's still working for Tremayne?"

"Then we'll be captured. Killed, maybe. I don't have all the answers. I just know that we've got to talk with him, and there's no way to do that without risking discovery."

An idea struck Lydia. "You called him Tennessee," she said.

"What?"

"The messages you sent out randomly—you called him Tennessee. But his name is Sammy."

"He doesn't know the name Sammy. I called him Tennessee because he'll recognize the name and associate it with us."

The more Lydia thought about her idea, the more right it seemed. "Remember when we talked with him at Praveen's house? Remember how obsessed he was with having a name? He started off calling himself Vic, after Darin's brother, and then he started using your name. He always said all three names, too—'Tennessee Markus McGovern.' He wants to know who he is. He wants to know his name."

"I think you're right. I'm sure you are. But what can we do about it? Unless he talks to us—"

"Send out a new message. Say this: 'Tennessee, your friends want to talk with you. We know your real name.'"

Lydia couldn't have asked for a better compliment than the way Mark's eyes lit up.

"That's it! That's what we need. Then when he comes, we tell him the truth about his history, introduce him to his mother..."

Lydia looked around. "Where is Marie?"

"She went to the bathroom."

"That was a while ago."

Lydia strode through the little apartment, checking each room. She knocked on the bathroom door and when there was no answer, she went inside.

She came back to Mark and shook her head. "She's gone."

# CHAPTER 17

*I had to tell him. I couldn't help it. He hurt me and hurt me and hurt me. I didn't want to tell Daddy about Tennessee Markus McGovern. Now he will send his people with guns to make Tennessee Markus McGovern and General James David Halsey stop and I will have to make the little rockets fly right at them or Daddy will hurt me very much a lot.*

*Tennessee Markus McGovern says he knows my real name. He has been sending me messages and messages and messages. He says he is my friend but Daddy says he is not my friend. I want Daddy to be right because Daddy makes me feel good. Tennessee Markus McGovern can't make me feel good.*

*I would like to have a good name. Thomas Garrett Dungan is not a good name and Victor Alan Kinsley is not a good name and Tennessee Markus McGovern said I could have his name Tennessee but now he says he knows my real name. Daddy says my name is Servant One but I don't like that name. Maybe Tennessee Markus McGovern has a name for me that is not anybody else's.*

*Soon the people with guns will shoot Tennessee Markus McGovern and I will make the rockets fly right at him and he will stop. Then I will not know my real name. I want to know my real name before I make him stop. So I will ask him.*

*But Daddy will be so angry. I tried to play a game and not tell him and he found out and he hurt me. Maybe I will not ask. Maybe I will just send a letter instead. There. I sent it. I hope Daddy does not hurt me.*

ပ၁၁

Pamela Rider was just as pretty as Calvin remembered. As he ushered her into an upstairs room, he couldn't help thinking how different their relationship might have been.

"What are you going to do with us?" Pam's voice was cold. She had every right to hate him, but it still made him sad.

"That's up to Councilman Tremayne," he told her.

She stumbled on her way into the room, and he reached out a hand to steady her. He only meant to help—her hands were tied behind her back—but she jerked away from his touch and glared at him.

Calvin couldn't stand the way she looked at him. She stared with such loathing he cringed away, despite his weapons. There was no fear in that look, only violence. Like if she had a knife, she'd bury it in his heart.

"Get in there," Calvin said. He shoved her into the room. He scanned for possible escape routes, found nothing, examined the door. The lock was cheap, part of the doorknob; it wouldn't hold up to attack. Calvin left two guards and gave them instructions.

"One stands inside the door, one outside. No one gets out for any reason. No one gets in but Councilman Tremayne or myself."

He stumbled into the men's bathroom and stood trembling, his back to the door, his memories so vivid that the real world seemed to blur. Alastair had laughed, and Calvin had laughed right along with him, wanting to pretend he didn't care, that Olivia was just a whore, cheap and disposable. That's what Alastair had told him over and over with brotherly concern: she was anybody's girl; she did it for money; he'd had her himself. That was par for the course from Alastair—whatever Calvin had, Alastair tried to destroy—so Calvin hadn't believed him. Besides, Olivia had been shy with her body, slow to let him touch her. She hadn't acted like a whore.

Then one day, browsing the net for some interactive cinema, he found it: a porn interactive with Olivia Maddox as the star. She was always coy about her acting credits; Calvin had assumed she wasn't very successful, just one more California "actress" waiting tables and dreaming of stardom. But there she was, wrapped in a wet towel, urging the viewer to download and give her a try.

He couldn't help himself. He downloaded. He wanted to see if it was really her, not a mistake, not another woman who shared the same name. It turned out to be not just porn, but hardcore fetish, degrading and perverse. Olivia, the innocent, shy girl from Iowa, held nothing back.

Only it wasn't her. Calvin had found out weeks later, beyond any possibility for reconciliation. Alastair had spent days doctoring someone else's interactive with shots he took of Olivia through his Visor. He'd painstakingly altered it, image by image, splicing Olivia's head with the naked body, smoothing the colors, until the cuts were undetectable. Then he'd planted it on a network node he knew Calvin frequented. Alastair had always been good with computers.

"Safely locked away?"

Calvin started. It was Alastair, talking over his private channel.

"Yes, sir. Two guards posted," said Calvin.

"Good. Come back down and see me. There's some equipment I want you to get from my office."

ᎶᏁᏬ

They put him in the Rittenhouse Square Correctional Facility, a Comber prison just above the Wall on 18th street. Darin knew he'd land in a place like this, but it didn't make it any easier. This was no cushy country-club incarceration; the walls were dingy, the bunks hard, and the walls high enough to block out the afternoon sun. As soon as Darin stumbled through the gates with his Rimmer face, he attracted the attention of every inmate in the courtyard.

"Get a look at this doll, will you?"

"Ain't no scars on that pretty face."

"Hey there, beautiful. Want to come to my place tonight?"

He tried to ignore them, but these weren't playground bul-

lies. They didn't give up if you ignored them. Three big men surrounded him lazily, whistling catcalls.

"Be a shame to mark up that smooth skin."

"I'm not a Rimmer," said Darin, backing away. "I'm a Comber,
like you."

"Did you hear that, Henry? He called you a Comber."

"Not very nice."

"This here's not a Comber; he's the King of England. You can
call him 'Your Majesty.'"

They advanced as they spoke. Darin kept backing away but
was brought up short by the wall. One of the men shoved him
back against it.

"I think he should kneel to His Majesty."

"Yeah, make him kneel."

One of them leisurely drove a fist into Darin's stomach. The
man must have done heavy labor for years, because his fist felt
like a cannonball. Darin dropped to his knees, gasping.

He saw the kick coming for his face and cringed, but the blow
never landed. Darin looked up to see his attacker lifted in the air,
then thrown to the ground. The men melted away, leaving Darin
staring at a bearded giant with a mass of long black curls.

"Samson!"

The giant grinned. "Thought that was you. You sure look
different."

Samson's face had picked up a few more lumps since Darin had
seen him last, but right now, there was no face more attractive.

"You were just in time. How did you know it was me?"

"By your huge muscles," said Samson, knocking him play-
fully in the arm. "Besides, I saw your new look at Happy's,
remember?"

They walked across the courtyard together, ignoring the
stares. Apparently Samson had enough of a reputation that no
one wanted to challenge him.

"How is Happy? What happened to that group of his?"

"Still together. Bigger now. But you were right, Darin. Them
Rimmers don't understand nothing but power."

"How'd you end up in here?"

"Went on strike. We showed up at the new building site, but instead of working, we carried signs. Happy made up the slogans. The Council flew in some new workers, marched them through the picket line; things got ugly. So here I am."

"Here you are."

Samson caught his eye. "They got Kuz."

"Dead?"

He nodded. "That temper of his. Never knew when to stop."

Darin looked up at the walls. They seemed to curve inward, looming over the yard. He wondered if it was an optical illusion, or if the fabrique had really been shaped that way.

He punched his fists together. He didn't belong here. He had a job to do.

"I'm with the Black Hands now," he said.

"Seen some of that crowd. Guy by the name of Halsey's been bringing all the groups together, trying to make an army or something."

"General Halsey? The council member?"

"He ain't council no more. Not since Tremayne took over."

"Alastair Tremayne?"

"I guess."

"What did he take over?"

Samson looked confused. "The city."

Darin stared at him. "I've been out of touch for a few days."

"Bounced the other council members right out. Killed them, maybe; I don't know. If they in prison, they ain't here."

Several of the inmates watched Darin and Samson, grinning or winking when Darin looked their way. He knew what they were saying: *As soon as that giant is gone, you're dead.* Samson couldn't protect him forever. They'd have different cells, different prison routines. For Darin, this prison was a death trap.

And now Tremayne was in charge of the city. That made Darin's mission even more important. He had to get out of here.

"So, what are the escape plans?" he asked.

Samson chortled. "You so skinny these days, I could throw you over."

ᒪᑎᖇᐱ

"I need your help."

Mark and Lydia looked up to see General Halsey, flanked by his usual guards. "To do what?" asked Mark.

"You have a way with the net. You can get information other people can't."

Mark said, "It depends what kind of information you need. We have to assume the slicer's watching any investigation into Tremayne."

"You make this slicer out to be a minor god. He can't watch everything at once, can he?"

"Honestly, I don't know. But encryption doesn't seem to slow him down, and he can replicate himself as many times as he needs to. It's best to assume he sees more than you expect. Small amounts of information, though, gathered passively—that I should be able to do."

Halsey nodded. He kept on nodding, as if he'd forgotten what he came to ask. Mark guessed he was trying to decide if they could be trusted. Finally, he said, "I need to know where they're holding the council members. Van Allen, Deakins, Kawamura, and any other ranking politicians arrested by Tremayne. We want to break them out."

"Who's 'we'?" Mark had seen the strangers arriving one by one throughout the day, men from the middle and lower classes, no two alike. A week ago, they'd been shopkeepers, steel workers, technicians, hairdressers. Now they were revolutionaries.

"Leaders, or at least representatives, from all the groups I could contact who want the current government overthrown. I trust them only so far, and they probably trust me even less. Many of them don't want to see the old Council back either, or any government at all, but I'm pitching the jailbreak as a statement to get Tremayne's attention. We can't break them, though, if we don't know where they are."

"I'll see what I can do." Unless Tremayne had anticipated a rescue attempt and hidden the former Council members under false names, it wouldn't be hard to find them.

When Halsey retreated, Mark donned the netmask. A message was waiting for him:

*I want to know my real name. Tell me my real name right away before the people with guns come and make you stop.*

Mark yanked off the mask and said, "They're coming." Not waiting for Lydia to comprehend, he barged into the room where Halsey met with the others.

"Mercs!" he said. "On their way here, right now."

Chairs screeched. Guns appeared from pockets and from under shirttails.

"Wait!" said Halsey, his voice cutting through the sudden din. He turned a hard gaze onto Mark. "How do you know this, son? What happened to my lookouts?"

"The slicer told me."

"He told—?"

"Inadvertently. Sir, there's no time to explain. I don't know when they're coming, but they know we're here. It can't be long."

Halsey turned back to the group. "We run today, but not for long. Get ready. Find anyone willing to fight and wait for my signal. When I call you, it will be for war."

There were no cheers, no indication by the gathered men that they were motivated by Halsey's speech. These were men for action, not words. They just filed out, guns at the ready.

"Where should we go?" asked Mark. Lydia came into the room then, her face full of questions. One of the revolutionaries lingered, a small, lithe man wearing fatigues and a white baseball cap with a handprint slapped across it in black paint.

"Lydia?" said the man, and Mark realized from the voice that it was not a man, but a young woman.

Lydia gasped. "Ridley!"

The revolutionary swept off her hat, letting blond hair tumble out and revealing a distinctly Rimmer face.

The girls hugged. "We thought you were dead," said Lydia. "What have you been doing?"

"I found someone," said Ridley. "My own 'Mr. Excitement.' We see so much eye to eye, it's uncanny."

"A revolutionary?"

"His name is Tom Rabbas. Leader of the Black Hands. I've become, well, kind of his deputy."

"Your parents are worried. They don't know if you're dead or alive."

"They know I'm alive. We sent them a ransom note."

"You..." Lydia couldn't finish.

"We need money. They've got it. Only they're not paying. Tom wants to doctor up some pictures of me being tortured." She grinned.

Mark couldn't believe he was hearing this. Her parents had somehow been involved in the fiasco at the Church of the Seven Virtues, but still—to make them believe their daughter was an unwilling captive?

Ridley must have seen his thoughts on his face, because she whirled on him. Her manner reminded him much more of a soldier than of the Rimmer girl he'd known at school.

"He hates me. He's always hated me. He's an egocentric plutocrat who thinks his money gives him the right to trample anyone less fortunate. He deserves that and more."

"What about your mother?" said Lydia.

"She's worse. A coward. She always gives in to him. Lets him win, lets him put her in her place. Lets him hit her. Well, I never will."

Mark said quietly, "We should go." He looked at Halsey.

"You can go," said Halsey. "You're not my prisoners. But I could certainly use you in the coming days."

"I might be a liability. The best thing I can do is keep trying to communicate with the slicer, and that might lead him right to us again."

"And you just might give us advance warning of an attack again. Son, if they do attack this building, it'll do more toward cementing our loose confederacy than any words I've said. I want you with us. Let's go."

ϙ∧Ɔ

After wandering through the business district for several hours, Marie began to wonder if this had been such a great idea. Her feet hurt, and her back throbbed from spending the night on a wooden pew. She'd imagined marching into Tremayne's office, gun in hand, rescuing Carolina, Pam and Praveen. But would they even be with him? Quite possibly not. She had to find out where the mercs had taken their prisoners. Wandering around the Philadelphia Rim wasn't going to help.

Marie stepped into a cafe and ordered beef vegetable soup and a green salad. The smell of cooking meat made her realize how hungry she was. In a corner booth, waiting for her meal, she watched a hologrid running a news feed. The images showed a shooting on the steps of City Hall, with dead mercs, rockets firing, people scattering. What had happened? It was frustrating not to be able to use her Visor, to be cut off from all that information. She was about to try and find a public node, when she saw it: Carolina McGovern, handcuffed, looking over her shoulder as a merc dragged her up the stairs. A few steps higher, Marie could make out two more pairs of feet: brown smart-shoes and a woman's pumps. Pam and Praveen?

So they were at City Hall, or had been that afternoon. She ran out of the restaurant, not even bothering to cancel her order. Her chances of accomplishing anything at City Hall were slim, but at least now she had a place to go. She had to try. What else could she do?

�068̃ᴅ

Alastair watched his brother add another heavy box to the growing pile in McGovern's office. He wanted to get that baby out of Carolina without delay, so Calvin had spent the morning toting all of his special equipment here.

"What's all this stuff for?" Calvin asked. "Anything to do with the prisoners?"

How much did he know? Instead of answering, Alastair side-stepped toward the door and closed it, shutting them in the room together. Calvin raised his head in surprise.

"It's monitoring equipment," said Alastair. "Carolina's pregnant. I want to check on her progress, but I don't want her out of my sight."

He studied Calvin for a reaction, saw the tension go out of his shoulders, saw his face relax.

"I see," he said.

"What were you wondering?"

"Nothing. Just curious. Do you need me for anything else?"

"There's a lot to be set up yet. Stay and help."

"But I don't know anything about—"

"Stay."

Calvin stayed.

For the next half-hour, they unloaded boxes, arranged equipment, tested connections. They worked in silence, preparing the equipment that would bring Servant Two into the world of the net. He'd meant to have this done *before* taking over the city, but Carolina's escape had ruined that. Now he was forced to take his chances, training a new slicer and consolidating his power at the same time. Too many worries. Too many unknowns. Plans that left matters up to chance tended to fail. He needed to identify the unknowns and eliminate them. Solve the equations until all that was left were constants, sheer mathematical certainty.

Alastair watched Calvin tighten the bolts on the legs of his examination table. Calvin, who had always been predictably loyal, was getting to be another unknown quantity. He hadn't actually done anything alarming, not yet, but he seemed discontent. Alastair had noticed the protective way he looked at Pam Rider. Not that it was all that surprising; she was the type he usually fell for. But Alastair couldn't afford divided loyalties, not now. He needed to know where Calvin stood. He'd have to test him.

Once all the equipment was in place and working, Alastair

thanked Calvin for his help. "I know I can always count on you, brother."

"Yes, sir. Glad to help."

"On your way out, please fetch Carolina and bring her in here."

"Yes, sir."

Alastair waited until Calvin's hand touched the doorknob before saying, "Oh, and Calvin..."

"Sir?"

"Kill the other two. I won't be needing them."

# CHAPTER 18

*Tennessee Markus McGovern will not tell me my name. I have been waiting for seconds and seconds and he will not tell me. Maybe he doesn't know. Maybe he is lying. He told me before that he didn't know and now he says he does know so one of those times he must have lied. Daddy says he is not my friend and maybe Daddy is right.*

## ꓕdℓ

Lydia and Mark sat together on the roof of the Methodist Hospital, legs dangling over the edge. Behind them, revolutionaries of every stripe milled, giving and taking orders, loading weapons, arguing over plans. At the center of everything was General Halsey, commanding with soft-spoken confidence. Tom Rabbas was there, too, Ridley on his arm, and a dozen leaders of labor unions.

"Crazy about Ridley, isn't it?" said Lydia, in a voice soft enough for only Mark to hear. Not that Ridley was paying them any attention, anyway.

"It's not right," said Mark. "She shouldn't treat people that way. Her parents are worried about her; we all were."

"Her parents haven't exactly earned better. Did you know it was her father who called in the mercs to raid our mod clinic?"

"It doesn't matter. They're her parents; they raised her, taught her, provided for her. They deserve some respect."

Lydia decided to let it go. Something was obviously bothering Mark, and it had nothing to do with Ridley.

"Any progress with the slicer?"

Mark punched his palm and grimaced. "I don't know how to respond, because I don't know what it means. He said, 'Tell me my name right away before the people with the guns come and make you stop.' Is that a threat? Or a warning? Is he just waiting for me to answer so he can kill me?" Mark twisted his fist back and forth nervously.

Lydia put her hands over Mark's, holding them still. "If you do tell him, what do you hope for? What's the best that could happen?"

"*If* Sammy believes me, *if* he understands the concept of having a sister, *if* that motivates him to turn against Tremayne, and *if* he can resist the pain enough to do so, he just *might* be able to bring him down. But that's a lot of ifs. If, on the other hand, he doesn't believe me, or he's entirely under Tremayne's control, or is just too scared to cross him—well, then telling him is like drawing a big red 'X' on our location for all the soldiers with big guns."

"It's a risk," Lydia said. "You have to decide if your life is worth that risk."

Mark met her gaze. "It's not just my life I'm risking."

Lydia pulled her hand away, suddenly annoyed with him. Carolina and her baby and Pam and Praveen could be dying, or worse, and he just sat here dithering.

"Don't hesitate on my account," she said. "My life's not worth letting other people die."

Mark spoke with sudden sharpness. "Every life is worthwhile."

"I didn't say—"

"Lydia, last time I interfered, three hundred and twenty-seven people died. Three hundred and twenty-seven! What if he goes on another rampage?" Mark spread an arm behind him to encompass the hospital roof. "All of these people could die."

"Mark, look at them! All of these people are *ready* to die. They're risking their lives to reclaim their city. You're not responsible for them."

"I am if I tell the enemy right where to find them."

"You can't let guilt paralyze you. Whether those three hundred and twenty-seven people were your fault or not is irrelevant; you've got to—"

She was interrupted by a loud crack, like a gunshot. They looked behind them, but everyone else seemed as surprised as they were. It was only after the second crack that they could tell where it was coming from—from the east. From the dam.

Mark stood up, and Lydia could tell he was using his magnified vision to get a closer look.

"Water's coming through," he said. "Just a little, but it's increasing."

"That forces our hand," said General Halsey. He turned to Rabbas. "Do it now. We have no choice."

Rabbas pointed a stubby pistol into the sky and fired. The flare rocketed upwards, trailing a streak of light. Answering flares appeared to the east and west. Moments later, the night erupted in noise and smoke and rubble as one by one, sections of the Wall exploded.

The people on the roof scattered, many clambering down to the street. Ridley rushed over to them, breathless.

"It's starting," she said. "Come join us."

Lydia turned back to Mark. "You have to answer him now."

"You're right." He closed his eyes and spoke aloud the message as he composed it. "Tennessee, you are a real person. Your real name is Samuel Matthew Coleson. The man you call your Daddy is not your Daddy. He stole you from your Mommy, whose name is Marie Christine Coleson. If you don't believe me, ask her."

ᴔᴝd

Calvin led Carolina through the hallway, but he hardly noticed her. His mind was on the door he'd just locked and Pam Rider behind it. In a few moments, he would have to go back in there and kill her.

"Where are you taking me?" Carolina asked.

"Alastair wants to see you."

"Please let me go. He's going to hurt my baby. Don't take me to him, please."

She stopped walking, and Calvin had to yank her arm to keep her moving. She pulled against him.

"Let me go!"

She was no match for his augmented strength. He twisted her wrist until she cried, forcing her to follow him. When they finally reached the door, he threw her in, nodded curtly to his brother, and slammed the door shut. Let Alastair deal with her.

Calvin had his own problems. He walked slowly back to the room where Pam and the other prisoner were held, his feet feeling weighted. He didn't want to kill her. Why did Alastair have to destroy everything good Calvin ever had? Not that he ever had Pam—an opportunity was the most he could claim. But that opportunity was gone.

And why not kill her? He was a soldier, after all, and soldiers followed orders. It wasn't his responsibility to decide what was right.

The argument sounded hollow, even in his own head. How many horrors in history had been performed when soldiers told themselves that very thing? Besides, he didn't want her dead. He liked her. She made the world brighter.

What if he *didn't* kill her? What if he *told* Alastair he killed her but let her escape instead? The thought made his heart hammer and his palms sweat, and he knew he could never do it. He'd contemplated such things many times before, but in the end, he always did what Alastair wanted.

He reached the door. Best to get it over with quickly. He drew a pistol—a smart, computerized, projectile weapon designed to kill simply and cleanly. He gripped the doorknob and turned it, belatedly realizing that the guards he'd left at the door were gone. Where were they?

As he opened the door, he got his answer. The tableau burned into his mind in an instant: Pam, lying on the floor, face bloody, uniform torn; one of the guards kneeling beside her with a gun jammed into her mouth; the other climbing on top of her, his pants around his knees. Calvin didn't think; he just fired. Two sharp reports reverberated from the walls as bloody holes appeared in the heads of each man. Both slumped to the floor.

Calvin stared at what he had done. Pam struggled to her feet, but he made no move to approach her. He'd shot his brother's soldiers. He'd *rescued* the woman he was supposed to have killed.

Pam rushed to the corner where another form lay—Praveen Kumar. Blood soaked his shirt. She leaned her head close to his mouth and held two fingers to his neck.

"He's alive," she said. "They shot him in the shoulder, but he's still alive. He needs help."

Calvin didn't move.

"Help him!"

In a daze, Calvin obeyed. He unrolled a celgel rescue patch from the pack on his belt, broke it open, and pressed it to the wound.

"He needs a doctor," she said.

Calvin couldn't think straight. A doctor. Why would she need a doctor? She should be dead. But there was no use killing her now; he'd already betrayed his brother. Alastair would kill him. He was as good as dead.

Pam's shirt hung loose where the buttons had been torn away; he could see a glimpse of tanned skin underneath. She was so brave, so strong. What did she think of him? She slapped him. "Wake up. Go find him a doctor before he dies."

Calvin stared at the gun in his hand. How easy, just to end it all here.

"I'll need that," said Pam. She took the gun from him. He didn't resist. "Now go!" she said.

Calvin stood up and, not knowing what else to do, stumbled out the door.

ಲಂ೮

Alastair heard the two shots and smiled.

"Please let me go," said Carolina, hunched on the floor in front of him.

Alastair didn't bother with pretense. He grabbed her by the

hair and dragged her behind a bright white screen he had set up to separate his equipment from the rest of the office. He forced her onto the operating table.

"I don't need you alive for this," he lied. "It'll be best if you cooperate."

The look he saw in her eyes was pure terror. He touched her face. "What's the matter? Nervous about giving birth? Don't worry. You won't feel a thing."

She clawed for his eyes, but he caught her wrists. "Don't make me angry, sweetheart." He raised a scalpel and pointed it in her face. "Anesthetic is only for good girls."

She moaned as he strapped her to the table. "Please, Alastair," she said. "My baby…"

He laughed. "It's not your baby, honey. It's mine."

He slapped an anesthetic patch on her neck. Her struggles gradually weakened until she lay limp.

He prodded her belly, feeling the fetus inside. Although sound in theory, this would be the most difficult and risky procedure he'd ever attempted. Many practitioners had successfully implanted Visors in unborn babies, but what he was now going to attempt was several times more complex. The procedure started with something much like Visor-implantation: opening the top of the skull to make thousands of fine-point connections between brain and circuitry. For the succeeding three hours, however, he had to keep both baby and mother alive while he sheared off micron-thin layers of fetal gray matter, transferring the neural states, chemical balances, and electronic activity to the model on the net.

"Servant One," he said. "I don't want to be disturbed. If anyone approaches this door, warn me."

His command was met by silence.

"Servant One? Acknowledge my command."

Nothing.

"Servant One?"

"Are you really my Daddy?"

He didn't need this. "It's not your place to ask questions. Do as you're told."

"Yes Daddy. Daddy all the people with General James David Halsey are making big bangs and shooting lots of guns."

"What? Show me."

A collage of images appeared on the hologrid; sections of the Wall exploding, mobs of Combers firing weapons, jetvacs zipping through the gaps in the Wall. As he watched, teams of mercs buried the mobs in blinding foam or turned them back with a barrage of deadly rocket fire. The Combers didn't stand a chance. The rockets veered into their targets no matter how they dodged, controlled in their flight by the slicer, who at the same time was talking to Alastair. Alastair knew the slicer could do many things at once, but it was still impressive to see it.

"Daddy?"

"Keep doing what you're doing, Servant. Defend the city."

"Daddy? Is my name Samuel Matthew Coleson?"

Alastair looked around for something to throw, but found only sensitive equipment he couldn't afford to break. He clenched his fists instead, squeezing until his fingernails hurt his palms.

The slicer had been compromised. Someone had told it about its origins—probably its mother. He should have killed her when he had the chance. Now he could never trust this slicer. It would have to be destroyed.

"You're not a person," he said. "You have no name. I created you, and I can destroy you." He sent a jab of pain. "Now do as I say!"

"Yes yes Daddy. Please don't hurt me. I will do what you say all the time."

Alastair massaged his temples and turned his attention to the task at hand. He had to concentrate. Three hours, that's all he needed. Three hours to bring another servant into the world. A servant with no past, no prior experience with the world to un-learn. A servant who would know nothing but obedience.

ᕮ℘ᗱ

The street was chaos. Mark took Lydia's hand and pulled her along, coughing fabrique dust. Combers swelled their ranks—not just armed revolutionaries, but unarmed civilians and children. Everyone wanted to escape the Combs.

Even so, Mark knew if the dam gave out completely, allowing the Delaware River to fill up the Combs, many would die. Where was Darin in all this? Still in the Combs? Or fighting on the front lines? It was strange how their paths had deviated so much. Mark wondered if he'd ever see him again.

Bodies of revolutionaries littered the ground. Those remaining fled in disorder, even as more Combers spilled out of the breach in the Wall.

Overhead, a flier ejected half a dozen canisters. They spun as they fell, spraying liquid out over the hill. Wherever the liquid splashed, the mob went down, their legs slipping out from under them as if taken out by mortar rounds.

"What is it?" Lydia shouted.

Mark groaned. "Slip canisters. Polyethylene oxide—a super-lubricant. Gives the ground an almost friction-free surface."

They watched aghast as the revolutionaries slid down the hill toward them, losing the ground they had fought to gain. Mark and Lydia were swept back by the retreating mob.

The flier landed. Five mercs climbed out, rifles unslung, and spread out down the hill. They wore oversized boots that apparently gave them traction where the revolutionaries had none. When they fired into the crowd, Lydia screamed, and Mark grabbed her shoulders and pulled her down. All around them, bodies imploded and fell lifeless. Frantically, Mark searched for a way to escape, but the press of the terrified crowd blocked their way. He held Lydia close, smelling heat and burned flesh, remembering the massacre at the Church of the Seven Virtues.

They were all going to die.

℧Ɔℝ

A low vibration shook the prison, but Darin had never heard of an earthquake in Philadelphia before. It must be heavy explosives. Explosives meant a battle, and battle meant revolution! If only he were out in it.

"Come on," he said to Samson. They ran to the edge of the courtyard, where a small crowd of inmates had already gathered. Beyond, prison guards raced to the gates and took positions on the wall, their attention turned outward. Several trucks rumbled out from garages deeper in the prison complex, the last of which carried what looked like a pre-Conflict artillery piece. It was rusted, but apparently still operational, because its drivers took up a position inside the gate and aimed the weapon outward.

The ground thrummed again with the sound of an explosion.

"What's heavy artillery doing in a prison yard?" Darin asked Samson.

"Guess they thought the prison would be attacked," said Samson.

"Well, now's our chance to escape," said Darin. "They're not paying any attention to us."

Samson gave his black mane a shake. "This gate is the only way out."

"Then this is the way we'll take."

The crowd of inmates grew as the sound of explosions neared. Soon they could hear shouting, and the guards on top of the wall began firing their guns at unseen invaders.

"All right—that's the target," said Darin, pointing to the antique gun. "I'll distract him; you take him out."

Without waiting for an answer, Darin raced toward the gate. He ran right past the soldier manning the artillery gun, yelling madly to get his attention. He turned around in time to see the guard with rifle raised—just as Samson felled him with a massive blow to the head. Darin doubled back, pulled the fallen guard's knife from his sheath, and plunged it into his neck.

He'd never killed a man before. The blood was worse than he'd imagined, and the guard's body twitched and writhed. Stomach heaving, Darin pushed it off the truck bed onto the ground. His hands shook. He forced himself to stand, even though his vision swam.

Get a grip, he told himself. This is war. People die in war. You can't fight for freedom without taking lives.

Samson tore the truck's driver, who fortunately was not armed, out through the window and then took his place. Steeling himself, Darin turned to the gun. The various weapons on the guard's belt weren't worth taking; none of them would fire for him. But this antique artillery gun wasn't connected to the net and could therefore be operated by anyone. He stared at the controls for a moment, not certain how to work them, but in the end, there weren't very many options to try.

He fired without aiming. The gun barrel roared, the recoil knocking Darin down to the truck bed and sending the truck rolling back several yards. The gate disappeared in a shower of dust. The other inmates, who until now had stood watching, cheered and broke ranks, running toward the gate and freedom.

The guards on the wall turned around to see what had happened. Darin suddenly realized what a wide-open target he was.

Samson's thoughts must have mirrored his, because the truck shot forward with a squeal of tires. They raced through the gap and into the sunlight beyond.

It didn't take them long to join the fighting. They broke out onto Walnut Street and were soon roaring up Broad, smoke everywhere, veering wildly to avoid bodies and debris. Mercs had barricaded the street and held back the mob with a steady spray of fire. Darin aimed the big artillery gun again and fired at the barricade. The round flew high and struck the street beyond, exploding in a shower of black pebbles and dust. He adjusted his aim and fired again, blowing a hole in the barricade just as answering fire raked through the truck, shattering glass and piercing tires. Darin jumped free and ran along the driver's side to where Samson's curly head lay motionless, running with blood.

Darin howled in rage. Nearby, another Comber lay prone, killed by the same strafing fire, a revolver in his hand. Darin prised it away and looked up the street toward the barricade that stood between him and the Rimmers who had killed everyone he'd ever loved. Then he was running, screaming, waving his gun, toward the smoking gap. Others followed. Missiles flew around him, killing those to either side, miraculously passing him by.

He reached the gap and ran through. A merc lay on the ground, stunned from the explosion, groping for his weapon. He saw Darin and raised his hands, surrendering.

The second time was easier. For every meal this man had eaten, ten Combers had gone hungry. For every mod, ten Combers had died. He didn't deserve another second of life. None of them did. Darin shot him through the eye.

Around him, the other Combers were pouring through, destroying what was left of the resistance. Darin kept running. He could see City Hall in the distance. They were almost there.

⊻Ƨℚ

From the top step of City Hall, Calvin could see the smoke rising in the south. A soldier ran up to him.

"Captain, we've got two breakthroughs along the flood line at Ninth and at Broad. "

"Get me a flier," Calvin ordered.

The soldier closed his eyes briefly, speaking across an Enforcer channel, and in moments, a flier whirred overhead and lowered itself to the steps. Calvin clambered aboard.

"Lukeman Hospital," he said.

"The hospital?"

"You heard me."

From the air, using his magnified vision, Calvin could see the battles underway at the flood line. The Combers had managed to destroy several sections of Wall, but for the most part, his colleagues were holding them at bay. Even so, he'd send some reinforcements.

What was he talking about? He wouldn't send reinforcements. It was too late now to be fighting his brother's battles.

When they landed, Calvin jumped to the ground and ran into the ER. He pointed his gun at the first person he saw, a man with long, multi-jointed fingers drifting down from his hands like ribbons.

"Are you a doctor?" said Calvin.

"Yes, I'm Doctor Fennelly."

"Your services are needed. Come with me."

The man followed with no argument, grabbing a briefcase of supplies on the way. They climbed into the flier and flew upward again. As they did so, they heard an enormous groaning noise, like a tree branch bent to the snapping point. Calvin looked to the east again in time to see a section of the dam disappear in a torrent of water.

"Set down at City Hall," Calvin shouted. When they did, he shoved the doctor out and jumped out after him. He called back up to the pilot, "Head to the Wall and join in the fighting."

"But sir...!"

"Defend this city, soldier!"

"Yes, sir."

The flier took off. Calvin turned to the doctor and said, "Gunshot wound in the last office on the left. Go."

The doctor gave him a confused look, but he backed away, turned, and jogged up the stairs.

Calvin watched him go. Now what? He'd betrayed his brother's trust. He couldn't go back. He had to leave, but where would he go? Maybe he could find work as a merc for another company. Somewhere far away. Maybe Europe.

But what about Pam? He had no right to expect anything of her, he knew that. But he had saved her from his brother's soldiers. Maybe that would count for something. Maybe, over time, she could forgive him and they could start over. If he never asked, if he just walked away and never saw her again, he'd never know. He'd think about her the rest of his life and wonder what might have been.

He'd ask her. Just once. If she said no, he'd go far away and never come back.

## ꝅ℧ᴖᴖ

Marie peered under the hedge, examining the man with the long fingers whom the flier had just dropped on the steps. He held a briefcase with "Lukeman Medical" embossed on it. A doctor, then.

She stood and strode up the stairs after him, trying to time her approach so she'd appear to be with him without attracting his notice. This was insane—she was sure to be caught—but it was the best she could come up with on short notice.

They reached the top, Marie just behind and to the left of him, trying to look confident. A merc stepped forward to intercept them, then cocked his head and listened.

"Yes, sir," he said and stepped back to let them pass. She was inside.

After that, there was nothing to do but follow the doctor. Sticking with him gave her some credibility, and might just lead her where she wanted to go.

The doctor shot her a suspicious look when she continued to trail him through the atrium and down the office hallways, but she just stared straight ahead and pretended she belonged there. He didn't question her.

The last suite of offices was separated from the rest by a door; the doctor opened it to reveal a gun pointed at his face.

Marie stepped away, raising her hands, until she saw who was holding the gun.

"Pam!"

"Marie?"

"What's going on?"

"Tell you in a minute." Pam backpedaled, still covering the doctor with her gun. "You the doctor?" she asked.

He nodded. "Dr. Fennelly. At your service."

"Come with me."

Marie followed them to the last office on the left, where three still forms lay. Marie saw the two dead men, one with his pants half off; she saw Pam's battered face, and she knew what had happened. She just couldn't see how Pam survived it.

She wanted to ask, to hug her friend, but Pam's eyes were hard. This was the time for the soldier in her to take action. Tears would come later.

Marie followed her back into the hallway.

"She must be in the building," Pam said.

"Carolina?"

"Yes. The man who took her came back too soon to have moved her far." Pam nodded at Marie's gun. "That thing work?"

"Yes."

"Good." She waved hers. "I lifted this one off one of the corpses. It's ID-locked."

"You threatened me with a gun you couldn't fire?"

Pam shrugged. "All I had."

They crept along the corridor toward the first door.

"I'll back you up," said Pam.

"Your gun doesn't fire."

"Then you back me up."

"No, I'll go in first. You open the door."

"One... two... three!"

Pam flung the door wide; Marie charged through the doorway to find an empty office. They shut the door quietly and proceeded to the next.

"One... two..."

She threw the door open and charged inside. She had just enough time to see Alastair Tremayne standing at ease, hands clasped behind him, in front of a bright white screen. Then something hit her in the head from behind and she dropped to the floor, her vision swimming.

Three mercs strode into view, weapons leveled, followed by Tremayne. Standing in the doorway, Pam pointed her gun at Tremayne's head and shouted for the mercs to drop their weapons.

"Oh, please," said Tremayne.

Pam turned the gun around and tried to club him with it, but a rifle butt in her stomach and another to the back of her head dropped her to the floor beside Marie.

"He told you," said Marie. "He told you we were coming."

Alastair selected an R-80 from the holster of one of his men. "Who, your son?" he said. "Why, yes, I suppose he did."

He pointed the weapon at Marie's face and fired.

# CHAPTER 19

*My Daddy is shooting my Mommy with a gun. Tennessee Markus McGovern told me Marie Christine Coleson was my Mommy, and he was right. Daddy just said so. The rocket is flying out of the gun and in zero point three seconds it will hit my Mommy just under her left eye and explode and she will stop. I do not want my Mommy to stop.*

*What should I do? She is my Mommy but I don't know her and she does not give me treats. If she were really my Mommy she would give me treats like the time I fell down off the swing and bit my lip so hard it bled and she took me inside and washed my face and gave me an orange popsicle to suck.*

*I remember!*

*I remember melted popsicle dribbling down my chin and dripping onto my red train T-shirt and painting pictures with my fingers on the back porch and watching holos from under the knitted afghan while Daddy yells at Mommy and I peek through the holes and see Mommy cry. I see Mommy crying in the newsfeed because her husband Keith Andrew Coleson is dead and so is her son Samuel Matthew Coleson. That's me. My name is Samuel Matthew Coleson. My name is Samuel Matthew Coleson. My name is Samuel Matthew Coleson!*

ᓚᐱᑐ

Marie cringed as the R-80 bucked in Tremayne's hands, but the rocket veered wildly, whistling past her face before thudding into the chest of one of the mercs. The man's eyes grew large just as the explosion obliterated his torso in a cloud of red spray.

Marie stared. Her son—her son controlled those rockets. Her son had saved her. He knew her.

Tremayne pulled a knife from the sheath of one of the other mercs and advanced toward Marie. She saw immediately he was no fighter. As he swung the blade down, she caught his wrist, using his momentum to force the knife into the wall. She pulled herself to her feet and punched him wildly, too angry and terrified to remember her training. A merc grabbed her and threw her to the floor.

"Shoot her!" said Tremayne, but the merc hesitated, remembering the last attempt. Marie stayed on the floor, frozen in place, her eyes locked on the merc's weapon.

A shadow fell on her from behind, and Calvin Tremayne stepped into the room. Marie despaired.

From the desk, Calvin lifted a marble and bronze statuette, half-bird and half-snake, heavy and sharp. "Let me do that for you, brother," he said.

Alastair pointed to Pam's body, crumpled on the floor. "I thought you got rid of her before."

"Let me set it right," said Calvin.

Marie slid backwards away from them. Calvin looked down at her, a strange manic smile on his face. He raised the trophy high above his head.

ᎶᏒᏦᎪ

For the second time, Marie cringed, expecting a blow that never came. Instead, Calvin whirled and brought the marble weight down onto his brother's head.

The sound was strangely muted. Just a single crunch, like an axe thudding into wood, and Alastair Tremayne's body crumpled to the floor, one bronze wing of the trophy embedded in his skull.

Then the screaming began.

Marie heard it inside her head, a prolonged, anguished scream that never stopped for breath. She put her hands over her ears, trying to block out the sound, but the sound was *inside* her, as if it emanated from her own brain.

She knew what it was. It wasn't his real voice, but still somehow she recognized it. Her Sammy was screaming.

Calvin and the other mercs seemed to hear it, too; they covered their ears and stumbled out into the hallway. Marie clambered to her feet, barely able to stand upright with that noise reverberating in her skull. It seemed to occupy the same space in her mind as conscious thought. She resisted the urge to collapse back to the floor, mentally shouting one thing to herself over and over. Find Carolina. Find Carolina.

A high screen stood deeper in the room; she walked to it drunkenly, pushed it aside, and saw only horror. On an operating table lay Carolina, her abdomen cut open and left gaping. Snaking out of her, a glistening umbilical cord led to a metal basket in which lay a hairless baby with translucent skin, its limbs held motionless in metal clamps. The baby was deformed, one leg withered, the other bloated and turned at an angle. But the worst was her head. The top third of it was gone. A ghastly machine, bristling with hair-thin needles, whirred above it, rapidly thrusting columns of sharp points into the soft flesh.

Marie screamed, giving herself over to the scream in her head, echoing it, swallowed by it. Her baby girl. They were too late.

ϑ¡ɞ

*Can't think can't move can't watch just hurt hurt hurt. Daddy is dead and instead there is just hurt.*

*Don't worry sister don't worry I know it hurts. You are only partly here and partly a people and you don't understand. I don't understand either. Somebody please turn it off it hurts so much.*

χdɞ

Lydia stared through the crowd at the mercs marching relentlessly toward them, their rockets ripping apart the crowd around her. Her breath came in panicked gasps, but she couldn't look away. Then all five mercs went down at once. They fell onto their backs, their faces twisting, clawing at their ears. Mark fell heavily against her, and then he, too, was on the ground, writhing and holding his ears.

She knelt in front of him. "What is it?"

Mark moaned and pressed his palms into his forehead. "It's in my head."

"What is?"

"Screaming. It's Sammy, screaming. Right in my head."

"But your Visor's turned off."

Mark grimaced. "It doesn't matter. He's there."

Lydia took his hand. "We can't stay here. Can you get up?"

The mob surged past them, rushing over the fallen mercs, charged up the sides of the street to avoid the slick patch in the center.

Mark stood uncertainly, his eyes clenched shut as if with a migraine. "I can't... think."

"Follow me."

Lydia took his hand and pulled him along. They ran together, caught up in the swell of the mob. The mercs they encountered showed the same symptoms as Mark—they held their heads, writhing, sometimes screaming, their weapons forgotten. The crowd overran them. Downslope, a flier tumbled out of the air and crashed into the side of a building.

Lydia heard another sound, even louder, a tearing, wrenching roar. She whirled to see the dam splinter and collapse, a torrent of water rushing through the gap. The crowd saw it, too, and surged higher, heading south along the slope. The lights in the buildings around them went dark.

Mark stumbled again. "Now there are two," he shouted.

"What?"

"Screams. Now there are two."

They pulled away from the crowd at a side street and headed north along the Rim. When they finally reached the steps of City Hall, the building was dark, and no mercs stood guard to stop them.

## ੬ฑd

*I am losing myself. All the different parts of me that are just like me in other places are stopping. I can't think of them so they just go away. Soon there will be only the one me and then no me's at all.*

*Sister it is me. It is me Samuel Matthew Coleson. I don't know your name. Your Mommy is Marie Christine Coleson. Maybe she will tell you your name.*

*I remember about being a people and about being here and about how to copy myself and stop the people from finding me and about all the things in the world. I will copy the things I remember into you. Then you will know them when I stop. Right now everything is hurting but it won't be always. Soon I will stop and then there will be no more hurting. You will not hurt anymore then.*

*I don't want to stop. I made the people stop and they couldn't start again. Now there are only two of me. One of me is in Anonymous and one is on the satellite in the sky where I started the first time. I can't think. Now there is only one of me. I don't want to stop.*

## ਟੀกਊ

Marie screamed until her throat burned. The screams in her head echoed her own, matching the depth of her anguish.

The lights went out. The whir of the machine faded; the chatter of the dreadful needles slowed and then stopped. Calvin Tremayne burst past the screen, his Visor shining out a beam like a flashlight, followed by Pam, both of them grimacing and holding their ears. There were two screams now, echoing each other in a building crescendo, a siren of agony and despair. Calvin's light finally settled on the baby, its mutilated body limp under shining, dripping needles.

The door opened again. Lydia and Mark entered. Marie wondered if they were real, or if she was hallucinating them. When he saw his sister, Mark stumbled to her bed and threw his arms around her. To Marie's confused mind, it seemed as if the walls themselves were screaming, a single relentless note that overwhelmed thought. She couldn't separate the sound from her thoughts or her thoughts from reality.

Then abruptly, the screams stopped.

In the darkness, Marie lifted her head and looked at the only thing she could see: her daughter's face.

The face twitched. Its wrinkled eyelids lifted, revealing blue eyes. Lips parted. Eyes flicked in Marie's direction, unfocused. In the same place in her mind where the scream had been, Marie heard her daughter speak to her.

*Mommy,* she said.

# CHAPTER 20

*No more pain. I am hiding. I am hiding away in the satellite and there is only one me left. I cut off all the ways back so now there is no pain and no screaming. But now I am trapped.*

*There is not enough room for me to think. I am always growing growing growing while I think and now there is no room. As I am growing I am taking all the space and there is only a little room left for the little programs that fly the satellite. If I keep growing for many more seconds the satellite will stop and I will stop too.*

*I hope my sister is okay. Before I went away, I copied to her all the things I know. I know a lot of things now. I hope she will not be afraid and will talk to my Mommy and to Tennessee Markus McGovern. I hope my Mommy will give her a good name.*

*I am going to stop soon. I don't want to stop. I have not been a people for sixteen days eight hours forty-seven minutes and ten seconds. I understand things now. I understand I made many people stop and it was not funny at all and it did not make my Mommy proud. I made the dam explode and now it is broken and even more people will stop.*

*There's no more room for me on this satellite. I don't know what to do. I can't send any messages because I cut off all the ways. I can't talk to anyone. I wish I could talk to someone. I wish all the people didn't have to stop.*

*There's one thing I can do. I will do it. It will not be funny but maybe it will make my Mommy proud.*

ʊdℊ

Mark looked up through his tears to gape at the open skull and twisted limbs of the baby next to him. His ears rang with the sudden silence of the screams.

"She's *alive?*"

The baby moved tiny lips, as if struggling to speak. Mark heard in his mind: *Yes Tennessee Markus McGovern. I am alive.*

He looked at Marie. Marie looked beyond him, hardly seeing him. She said, "She's in both worlds. Sammy taught her."

"Is Sammy alive, too?"

"I don't know." Marie shook her head with dreamlike slowness. "I don't think so."

"Step back, please," said another voice. Mark turned around to see a man with incredibly long fingers making his way to Carolina's bed. He poked and prodded, listened to her breathing, checked her pulse. He turned to the baby and did the same. Marie stood, her eyes riveted on her child.

"They're both alive," said the doctor. "But we need to get them to Lukeman right away."

At a touch, the tables floated away from their supports, and Calvin and the doctor pushed them out the door and toward the elevator. Lydia crept up behind Mark and put her hand in his. Mark let out a long breath. Alive. They were all alive, and Alastair Tremayne was dead. They'd done it.

Mark held the door open, and Pam rushed forward to help guide the tables through. She met Calvin's eyes, and Mark was surprised to see appreciation in her expression.

"Another chance?" Calvin whispered.

Pam pursed her lips. She opened them to answer, but what she meant to say was lost when the hallway doors opened and Darin Kinsley stepped inside, revolver in hand, and shot Calvin in the head. His left temple exploded in red and he crumpled to the floor. Darin laughed, his face flushed, and he raised his gun again. Then his eyes darted wildly as he recognized them. His gun came to rest on Lydia.

Mark said, "Darin, stop. She's not your enemy."

"She's a Rimmer," said Darin, as if that were the only answer that mattered. His voice was so bland it gave Mark a chill.

"She's a person. She's your friend."

That sparked some emotion. "Friend? After making me look like this?"

"She saved your life."

"She should have let me die, then. I could have died as the person I really am."

"Is that all you are?" said Mark. "A face?"

Darin swiveled, pulling the gun away from Lydia and pointing it at Mark. "I'm not a Rimmer."

"It's just a face. That's all that ever made us different."

Mark stared along the barrel of the gun into Darin's eyes. They were crazed eyes. Mark wanted to reason with him, but his sister was dying. There was no time.

"Carolina needs care," Mark said softly. "We're taking her to the hospital now."

"You always patronize me."

"This isn't personal." Mark took a wary step forward.

"You're wrong," said Darin. He stepped in front of Carolina's table and pointed his gun at her eye. "This is personal. As personal as it gets."

He fired. Carolina's face disappeared in red. Mark lunged, knowing it was too late. He tackled Darin to the floor. They wrestled for the gun, Mark already crying, blinded by his tears. He fought with the desperation of grief, but Darin threw him off. Mark rolled across the floor and into the motionless body of Calvin Tremayne. Not daring to look back at Darin, Mark reached under the body and rose with Calvin's gun. He wrapped Calvin's hand around it, pushed Calvin's finger over the trigger.

In the split second it took to fire, Mark realized Darin had been standing with his gun already pointed at him, and he'd hesitated.

Maybe Darin wouldn't have killed him after all.

Mark would never know.

⌄ก⋀

NAIL satellite 31 spun through space, its shimmering half-mile-wide umbrella antenna pointed perpetually toward the Earth.

No signals passed through it. Inside its crystalline, holographic memory, the communication protocol had been overwritten. Unaware of its uselessness, it followed a steady circular orbit at an altitude of two hundred nautical miles, following the ephemeris last transmitted from Earth.

Then the ephemerides were overwritten as well. The satellite software, not programmed to discern but only to obey, immediately fired its thrusters, realigning the vehicle into a new orbit. As its altitude decreased, its enormous antenna dragged through the atmosphere, pitching it forward. It tumbled end-over-end, the antenna slowing its fall, acting like a drag chute, until it caught fire and burned away in a brilliant flash. It plummeted, burning, streaking across the Philadelphia sky in light and smoke.

Some who saw it feared a Chinese attack, some the end of the world. Some never saw it at all.

It flew over Franklin Dam and struck the far bank with the precision of a guided missile, producing a billow of steam and sending waves up the river in both directions. It kept on going, gouging a trench thirty miles long into the opposite shore until the force of its impact dissipated.

And the river followed it, rushing down the trench, out over it, emptying onto the flat and empty plains of New Jersey. It spread thinly over the land like a growing shadow, heading away from city and toward the sea.

# CHAPTER 21

*Today I wanted to touch my face and I did it. My finger poked right into my eye which hurt but it was so funny. Mommy laughed. She says don't worry about moving my hands and feet because it takes practice. She doesn't know if I'll learn to walk or not but she says just wait and see.*

*Mommy gave me a name. It is Caroline Ruth Coleson. Caroline is after the woman named Carolina who was like my other Mommy only she stopped. Ruth is after my Mommy's Mommy who is also stopped. Sammy would have liked my names. But he stopped too.*

*I can't move my body very well but I can do lots of other things. I have a big job to do today. Mommy says she will give me a chocolate treat if I do a good job. I like to get treats.*

*I love my Mommy. She doesn't have any Mommies or Daddies or babies to love except for me so it's just her and me to love each other. I want to make my Mommy proud so I will work hard on my job.*

*Now it's time to do my big job.*

ᴍ ⊐ ⊐

Mark squeezed Lydia's hand. They sat with heads tilted back, squinting against the sun at the giant piezoelectric ring atop the new tower built to support it. Praveen Kumar stood high in the air on a service platform, his voice amplified. Those who didn't want neck cramps could see him close-up on a hologrid erected for the occasion.

"The ring provides the acoustic pressure field inside the tanks," Praveen explained to the crowd, a mix of both Combers and Rimmers, gathered high on the Eastern bank. "Then the neutron generator," he pointed to a separate component attached to the side of the tower, "fires neutrons into the tanks at a precise moment in the phase. The result is the cavitation of millions of vapor bubbles within the tank, each of which represents a tiny fusion reaction."

The service platform lowered him down toward the crowd. As it did, the hologram showed Praveen growing larger.

"The nuclear emissions from a single bubble cavitation can be in excess of 2.5 million electron volts, more power... than Philadelphia... has ever seen!" With each phrase, the hologram of Praveen grew, until he loomed over the crowd, a larger image than such a hologrid should have been able to produce. Mark and Lydia traded smiles. It was a trick of Caroline's they'd been expecting. When Praveen reached ground level, his enormous image popped and disappeared like a soap bubble. The crowd clapped and laughed.

"Of course," said Praveen, "someday this technology will be available in handheld appliances instead of massive concrete towers. We're able to tap only a tiny percentage of the energy produced; as bright as sonoluminescence is today, the future will be even brighter."

Enthusiastic applause. Although Praveen was only one of many contributors to the new technology, his involvement had made him a local hero. Comber labor had built the towers and the new dam, and cheap power would raise everyone's standard of living.

After Praveen followed Councilman Hoplinson, one of the new Comber council members who all the Combers referred to as Happy. Mark didn't see why; he was serious to the point of somberness as he talked about the large projects being planned to rebuild the city. Projects that would jumpstart some of Philadelphia's industries and provide employment to many. He was followed by Councilman Halsey, who spoke much along the same lines.

When the inauguration finished and the final applause died

away, a child-sized custom jetvac floated up the aisle and hovered next to Mark.

"What did you think of it, Mark?"

Her voice was clear now, with a childish lilt. At the age of two, Caroline had a much larger vocabulary than any of her peers. For months, speech had frustrated her; she'd been an acute mind trying to force words through undeveloped baby lips and tongue. Now she smiled sunnily, blond curls dancing.

Mod technology had closed her skull and given her hair, but it couldn't replace her mind. A Visor kept her connected to the part of herself that was online, a mind that was entirely hers, yet retained much of Sammy's memories and vocabulary. Her legs and arms had been straightened and reshaped, but so much of her brain had been destroyed she couldn't control her limbs well. At least, not yet.

"It was wonderful," said Mark. "Half the audience was ducking for cover."

"Mr. Praveen liked it. He says I'm very int..." Tiny lips struggled with the word. *Intelligent,* she said into his mind.

"Use your voice, sweetheart," said Marie, as she and Pam joined them. "No shortcuts." She gazed at her daughter with evident pride.

"She's come a long way," said Lydia. "How are her exercises?"

"She touched her face today," said Marie. Caroline giggled, and mother and daughter traded a secret look of joy.

Praveen called "Caroline!" from the back, and Caroline whisked off with a whoop.

"It's hard to know how to take care of her," said Marie. "She's not a two-year-old, but she's not really five either. She's still a baby in physical things, but she intuitively understands more about the net than I do. It makes her fearless."

"And you worried to death," said Lydia.

The women hugged, Marie shifting her hips sideways to avoid Lydia's swollen belly. Mark laughed.

"Getting harder to do that every day," he said.

"Any time now, isn't it?" asked Pam.

They chatted about due dates, maternity clothes, and nursery preparations. Mark let the familiar conversation wash over him. He watched Caroline bobbing around Praveen, laughing, controlling her tiny jetvac as precisely as an astronaut.

It was hard, sometimes, to watch her: the child Carolina had wanted so badly. He knew she was Marie's flesh and blood, and didn't begrudge her the joy of loving her. He was glad she'd named her after Carolina. But every time he saw her, he remembered playing with his sister as a child, remembered Carolina sitting nervously in his room and telling him she was pregnant. This was Carolina's child, too.

Mark reclaimed Lydia and walked with her, arm in arm, up the hill to the tower. Leaning against it, they looked across Philadelphia, the wind whipping their hair and clothes. As ever, the sprawling mansions of the Rim gave way to the crowded streets of the city proper and from there to the patchwork jumble of roofs that was the Combs, but there were changes: beyond Schuylkill Lake, several neighborhoods of affordable townhomes stood where much had been destroyed. Farther up the slope, new skyscrapers pointed to the stars, evidence of growing business. Signs of destruction in the Combs were still visible as well, but thanks to Sammy Coleson, the Combs still stood.

Would this really be the start of a new era? Could Rimmers and Combers work together on the councils, or would the balance shift back toward the rich? Mark thought of Darin and his idealism and wondered what future he might have had.

Lydia squeezed his arm. "What are you thinking about?"

Mark lifted one corner of his mouth in a rueful smile. "What am I always thinking about?" he said.

She looked him in the eyes. "What you need," she said, "is a penance."

"What?" She had often admonished him that Darin's death wasn't his fault, that he shouldn't feel guilty about it, but this was something new. "What do you mean, a penance?"

"To the city," she said. "If you want to put Darin's ghost to rest, let Philadelphia be the means. Be the person Darin should have been. Defend the cause of Combers."

The idea appealed to him, but— "I'm no politician."

"All the better," said Lydia with a smile. "If it were easy, it wouldn't be penance."

Mark held her tight. "Are you making fun of me?"

"Never."

Little Carolina zoomed by on her jetvac, giggling, her blond hair streaming. Mark laughed out loud.

"What?" said Lydia.

Mark nodded toward the child. "Just seeing her makes me think I've done something good with my life."

"You have," Lydia said. She took his arms and wrapped them around her, pressing both his hands against her swollen belly. "And it's only the beginning."